Every Common Sight

A novel

Tim Madigan

Every Common Sight

Ubuntu Books

Copyright © 2015 by Tim Madigan

Front cover design by Mark Hoffer

Author photograph by Kay Pritle

Praise for Tim Madigan

I'm Proud of You: My Friendship with Fred Rogers

"A loving testament to the power of friendship and to a most remarkable man. Goodbye, Fred, we'll miss you. And thank you for this book."—*The Boston Sunday Globe*

"*I'm Proud of You* is a beautiful book...for fans of Mister Rogers or those seeking a quiet, uplifting read, *I'm Proud of You* is an absolute treasure."—*Bookpage*

"Deeply Moving."—*Library Journal*

"Fred comes to life in *I'm Proud of You*, with his simple goodness etched on every page, and his complicated greatness etched in the heart of every reader who finishes this book and decides to become a better person."—Tom Junod, writer at large for *Esquire*.

"I just finished reading it and find myself sobbing and laughing all at the same time as I remember all that Mister Rogers meant to me. You have touched me with your words in ways that you will never know. It is almost as if those letters you have hidden away are partly mine, that somehow Fred wrote them not just to you, but to me, to all of us.— Karla Neese, Edmond, Oklahoma.

The Burning: Massacre, Destruction and the Tulsa Race Riot of 1921

"Truly an eye-opening book, this is essential reading for anyone struggling to understand race relations in America."—Robert Flatley, Frostburg State University

"This cultural and sociological dissection of a twentieth-century tragedy makes difficult but compelling reading."—Margaret Flanagan, American Library Association.

"Madigan somehow manages to tell the story of what happened with grace, purity and haunting starkness."—Buzz Bissinger, Pulitzer Prize-winner and best-selling author of *Friday Night Lights*.

"A powerful book, a harrowing case study made all the more so by Madigan's skillful, clear-eyed telling of it."—Adam Nossiter, *The New York Times Book Review*

For LaVerne

Chapter 1

She conceived her desperate mission the moment she saw the crude sign by the country road, but Claire doubted from the first that she actually had the nerve to see it through. She doubted, in fact, right up to the moment she approached her boss at the information desk of the Arlington Public Library. Even then, Claire changed her mind three or four times waiting for Lucille to hang up the phone.

"Yes, dear?" Lucille asked finally.

Claire did it. She told her lie.

"I'm sorry, but I just came down with the worst stomach cramps," Claire said.

"Child," Lucille said. "No need to apologize. Take a break. I can cover the desk."

"I was wondering. Do you think I could have the afternoon off instead?" Claire asked. "I'm sure a few hours off my feet at home are all I would need."

"Of course, dear," Lucille said. "Are you OK to drive? I could take you. Have you called Larry?"

Another jolt of panic.

"No need," she said. "I'll be fine. I'll see you tomorrow."

She turned and was halfway to the door before she remembered her purse behind the desk. She scurried back to grab it, feeling Lucille's concerned eyes on her until Claire disappeared through the sliding glass doors. It scarcely registered that the inside of the Impala was a furnace. She turned from the library parking lot, speeding past the Jiffy Lubes and Whataburgers and faceless subdivisions of brown brick homes, until finally the homes gave way to the rolling hills of the Texas countryside where cows competed for shade beneath spotty oaks. She chain-smoked, her window cracked to vent the fog, while trying to remember the route of the country drive with her family a few days before.

Larry would be furious—no, just deeply wounded—if he found out. Lucille, kind as she was, would no doubt fire her. Claire did the math again—roughly an hour to get there; an hour, max, to make her inquiry; an hour back. That brought her to three in the afternoon, well before she was due to pick up little Mike at day care. Who would be the wiser?

Thank God the little town was where she remembered it. At the lone stoplight she turned onto the busy two-lane road that led toward Dallas. In a few hundred yards the sign appeared on the side of the road and she sighed again with relief. She flicked on her turn signal and let a cement truck roar past in the other direction. She turned into dense trees and slowed to a stop so her eyes could adjust from the glare. That's when the tears pooled, as she sat concealed from the rest of the world, alone with her folly. Larry was oblivious at the plant. Little Mike was napping on his rug after lunch. And Claire was...where exactly? God only knew what kind of murderous pervert lived back in these woods. She sniffled, brushed away her tears, and began to laugh at her insanity.

"Shit, mother," she said out loud.

Just then she saw the large white truck rumbling slowly toward her through the trees, filling the road, leaving Claire no way to escape but the way she had come. She looked over her shoulder and jammed the Impala into reverse, but sat paralyzed as the truck slowed to a stop ten yards in front of her car.

She heard gears grinding. Two big men sat next to each other in the cab. The truck's passenger door finally opened and the man on that side stepped down, walking slowly toward Claire's car with his hands in his pockets and a pronounced limp.

He was very tall and husky, but older, with thick white hair matted at the temples by sweat. The knees of his green trousers were damp and grass stained. Perspiration darkened the armpits of a denim shirt, sleeves rolled up to the elbows. Claire rolled down her window halfway and looked up at him like she would a traffic cop. The old man bent over, squinting through the window. He had huge gray eyes and a square jaw. The man straightened before speaking, then took a few steps away from the car. He took a hand from his pocket and scratched his head, a hand that shook like he had a fever or was really upset. She thought about running from her car, figuring she would be fast enough to beat a guy that age back to the main road. He turned and walked back to her window. His voice was scratchy, as if rusty from lack of use.

"What brings you here, young lady?" he asked.

"I came about the sign," she said.

"The sign?"

"By the road," she said "The piano sign."

"Sweet Jesus," he said. "I only hope you haven't come far."

"From Arlington," she said.

"That's forty miles."

"I saw it last Saturday," she said. "My husband and I were on a long drive."

"That's a long drive, all right."

"He wants to build in the country," Claire said. "Larry even mentioned getting a few goats."

"Larry is…"

"My husband."

"They do keep the grass down," the man said.

"They?"

"Goats."

"Shit," Claire whispered.

"Though I prefer an old-fashioned mower."

He looked into the trees and cleared his throat.

"You must want a piano pretty damn bad to drive all this way."

"It would seem so," Claire said.

3

"But I'm afraid I can't help you."

"Why am I not surprised?" Claire said.

She now felt more embarrassed than afraid. The guy didn't seem like the murderer-rapist type.

"We haven't sold pianos for years," the man said. "Just never gotten around to taking down that old sign."

She looked up at him.

"You must think I'm a complete idiot."

"Don't know you well enough to say," he said. His face softened and he smiled. "But I'm awfully sorry for your trouble. The sign's going to come down tomorrow."

"I'll just back out the way I came," Claire said. "Sorry to bother you."

She took her foot from the brake and checked over her shoulder. The car inched back.

"You've come a long way," the man said. "Wait one second."

For some reason Claire did as she was told, shifting the car into park. The old man pivoted and hobbled back toward the truck. He climbed into the cab and talked to his companion, who looked straight ahead, shook his head a few times, but seemed to say little. Then the man from the passenger side hobbled back to Claire's car.

"Come back to the house for a cold drink," he said.

"Oh, gee," she said. "I can't."

"It's just a little farther through these trees."

"You and your friend look busy."

"Young lady, I haven't been busy in years and that old fart in the truck will make do," he said.

"That's very kind of you, but I need to be going," Claire said.

"My name is Wendell Smith," the old man said. "The other fellow goes by Francis. I didn't catch yours."

Claire was suddenly exhausted from the hours of adrenaline. She rolled down her window the rest of the way.

"It's Claire," she said. "Claire Cavanaugh."

He returned to the truck and the other man backed it through the trees. The truck retreated, stopped, and backed up some more as Claire inched along in front of it. After fifty yards, they passed through a white gate into paradise.

The trees thinned. Lush grass filled in around the oaks. Vivid clusters of red and pink roses, red geraniums, red and white tropical hibiscus, impatiens and begonias dotted the sprawling property. Crepe myrtles lined the road.

Wendell stepped down from the cab when the truck stopped by the old white house, gesturing for her to pull in beside him. The truck was loaded with boards and bags of cement, and it said Smith and Sons Lumber Co. on the door. Wendell hurried to offer Claire a hand out and she stood with him by her car, looking around at the property.

What looked like a guest cottage stood near the bigger house. A large red barn sat off by itself. There was a horseshoe pit near the barn and a large garden where the slender green leaves of cornstalks rustled in the occasional puff of breeze.

"Beautiful," she said. "It must take a tremendous amount of work."

"My wife's doing," he said. "I just try to keep the weeds down."

He looked down at her, his hands still in his pockets. For the first time she noticed a pale scar that circled his right eye. He smelled of sweat and aftershave.

"Could I tell you something?" Wendell asked.

"I guess so," Claire said.

"You look a lot like her," he said.

"I beg your pardon?" Claire asked.

5

"Like my wife, when she was closer to your age."

She looked toward the truck where Francis remained behind the wheel, then the flower gardens. Jesus.

"I don't know what to say," Claire said.

"I've embarrassed you," he said.

"I…ah…I'm sure your wife was much prettier than me."

"Thought for a second back there that Selma had come back from the grave to march me around for a day or two more. That's hard on an old man's heart."

His face reddened and he grimaced.

"I'm so sorry," Claire said. "Your wife has passed."

"Six months ago," he said.

"I'm very sorry, Mr. Smith," she said again.

He rubbed his eyes.

"Please call me Wendell."

He led her back to the truck.

"This is Claire," Wendell said when the other man rolled down the truck window. "Claire, meet my old friend, Francis."

Francis looked at her briefly.

"Howdy," he said.

"Pleased to meet you," Claire said.

"Like I said, we're going in for some tea," Wendell said. "You gonna come?"

"Some folks still have to work for a living," Francis said.

"Suit yourself," Wendell said.

Francis rolled up his window and ground the truck into low gear before it rumbled off through the trees.

"I've known that man for nearly fifty years," Wendell said. "He gets more pigheaded by the day. After you."

"Maybe this isn't such a good idea," Claire said.

"I've frightened you with my strange talk," he said.

She smiled.

"Maybe just a little," she said.

"I'll get you a glass to take with you then," he said. "But it's awfully hot. You're welcome to wait inside."

"I suppose I could sit for a minute," Claire said.

He held the front door.

His house was dark and shadowed with the pleasantly musty scent of families who had come and gone. Only the steady purr of central air conditioning and a ticking clock disrupted the silence. Wendell led her down a hallway where family photographs filled the walls on each side. They also crowded onto end tables in the large living room at the end of the hall and the fireplace mantel and bookshelves and the top of an old spinet piano in front of a picture window.

"The last one left around here, I'm afraid," Wendell said. "It belonged to my wife, though she could hardly play a note. She tried to get our boy interested, but he didn't get far either. Make yourself at home. I'll just be a minute."

He limped through a swinging door, leaving her with the pictures. Most were of the person Claire assumed was Wendell's dead wife. She had black hair and dark skin, a striking woman with huge, dark eyes. In one she stood by a large pond, playfully holding a fishing rod. In another she was on her knees in a flower bed, smiling over her shoulder. Then her arms fell lightly around the shoulder of a little boy who was also grinning broadly as he sat next to her on the front porch. Always the same radiant smile. You favor her, Wendell had told Claire. There was no resemblance that Claire could see.

The wife's long hair was streaked with gray in some of the photos, but her face remained ageless until Claire came to one picture so different from the others that she lifted it from the piano for a closer look. Wendell's wife leaned over the railing of a cruise ship or ferry, looking out across dark green water at sunrise or sunset, a brilliant sun fading over the horizon, her face lit in a dreamy smile. But the long hair was gone. Selma wore a baseball cap. She was pale; her eyes sunken and weary-looking.

There were no pictures of Wendell and this beautiful woman together, as if that would be too painful for him to see. Among the dozens of photographs Claire saw only one of Wendell. The larger color portrait of a smiling young man was probably a graduation picture because blue and gold tassels dangled from the frame. Next to it on the living room wall was a solemn-faced soldier in black and white, with the familiar gray eyes.

Wendell pushed through the swinging door, balancing a tray with two glasses of iced tea, paper napkins and two sugar cookies.

"That's you," Claire said. "The soldier."

"A long, long time ago," Wendell said, setting the tray on a coffee table next to a neat stack of *Field and Stream* magazines.

A newspaper crossword puzzle was nearly finished, done in pen. Black-rimmed reading glasses sat on top of the puzzle.

"Have a seat on the sofa," he said.

He handed Claire a glass and took one himself, sitting in a wicker chair across from her. He raised his glass halfway to his mouth, but lowered it because of the trembling that caused tea to spill onto a hardwood floor. He blushed and returned the glass to the tray.

"I forgot to ask if you took sugar," Wendell said.

"This is fine."

She took a small bite of the cookie, slightly stale, and placed it on a napkin. She sipped tea, sinking deeply into a sofa upholstered in dark purple fabric. Artificial cool raised bumps on her arms. Ferns and philodendrons were placed around the room in terra-cotta pots, all of them thriving. The wife again, Claire thought.

"I was right," Claire said. "Your wife, Selma, is that her name? She was much prettier than me."

"Let me apologize again," he said. "That was silly, even for an old fool like me. And thank you. Selma was beautiful."

Wendell bit into a cookie.

"She taught around here, and all the schoolboys were in love with her," he said. "Me included."

"Your wife was your teacher?"

"We got together a few years after high school," Wendell said. "But for one year she taught me English."

He leaned forward, looking at the spilled tea, then up at Claire. Wendell's elbows rested on his knees, his hands clasped in front of him. Claire considered asking about his wife's illness but thought better of it. The air conditioning clicked off. A grandfather clock ticked in the adjoining room.

"You really keep this place up alone?" Claire asked.

"Like I said, I just keep the weeds down," Wendell said.

"You're being too modest, Mr. Smith," Claire said.

"Wendell, please. And I've got nothing but time," he said.

She nibbled on her cookie, realizing she had skipped lunch and was suddenly famished.

"From the sound of your accent, I'd say you're not from around here," he said.

"We moved down from Minnesota last November," Claire said. "My husband was transferred from St. Paul to the auto plant in Arlington. I work at the public library there and look after our boy."

"Tell me about him."

"Mike. He was three in February."

"A lively age, if my memory serves."

"Is that your son on the wall?"

"My wife named him William, after Shakespeare," Wendell said. "Funny to see him up there so young. He'll be fifty before long, but sometimes you wouldn't know it."

Claire waited for him to explain but he didn't. He just reached for his tea, lifting the glass tentatively to his mouth. This time he managed to sip without spilling.

"Don't they have pianos for sale in Arlington?" he asked.

Claire's heart skipped. She shuddered from a sudden chill and the swirling that had resumed in her head.

"Not on my budget," she said.

"They are damned expensive," Wendell said. "I guess you want one for the boy."

"No. It's for my mother," Claire said. "She is the one in the family who plays, or she used to."

"She's down here, too?" Wendell asked.

She set her glass on the table. Now *her* hand trembled.

"What is it, young lady?"

She rubbed her eyes before tears had a chance to escape.

"I should be going," she said. "I've taken enough of your time. You've been very kind."

"You're welcome," Wendell said, his voice now just above a whisper. "But like I told you before, time is one thing I have plenty of these days."

The next tears ran down her face, and Claire settled deeper into the sofa. Wendell stood and limped from the room, returning seconds later with a box of Kleenex. He pulled out two, laid them next to her half-eaten cookie, and returned to the wicker chair.

"My wife taught me something besides how to keep up a garden," Wendell said. "Selma used to say: 'Anything mentionable is manageable.'"

He still leaned forward. His gaze never left her.

10

"My mom's in prison up north," Claire said. "She has been for fourteen years. I'm the one who put her there."

The air kicked back on. Wendell looked down at the floor, then back up at Claire, waiting for her to continue.

"She might be getting out soon and has no place else to go," Claire said. "A piano is the least I could do. Jesus, why am I telling you this? You're a perfect stranger."

"Maybe it's easier that way," he said.

"Did your wife tell you that, too?"

"Maybe I've figured a few things out on my own."

"I need to go."

"No," he said. "You don't."

"Anything mentionable is not manageable," Claire said. "There are things better left unsaid. With all due respect, what your wife said was crap."

She stood and scurried by his chair, starting down the hall. She heard his weight shift in the wicker chair and his creaking footsteps behind her. Wendell remained on the porch as Claire hurried down the steps toward the Impala, rummaging desperately in her purse for the keys before remembering that she had left them in the ignition. She turned toward him.

"I'm very sorry to have bothered you," Claire said.

"You've done nothing of the sort," Wendell said.

She glanced up at him once more, got in the car and put it in reverse. He stood with his hands in his pockets, looking like he desperately wanted to say something, without knowing just what.

Chapter 2

They buried her on a brilliant afternoon in autumn but the weather turned nasty just after the mourners scattered, the first gray huff of winter blowing down across the Plains from Canada. The north wind battered his old doublewide while Francis took off his funeral clothes that night and was still at it when he got up at seven the next morning. He stood at his bedroom window in his boxers, looking out at a sky the color of cold ashes. He dressed for work and combed what was left of his hair. He putzed around in his small kitchen but left most of his oatmeal uneaten. He dug out his jacket and gloves for the first time that season. His old pickup groaned from the cold when he started it for the drive to work.

In the office, he took the first delivery ticket from behind the desk and headed out without a word to the others. The wind raised funnels of dirt in the back lot where he loaded heavy planks onto the truck bed, grunting with each board as much from anger and heartbreak as exertion. He was between planks, cleaning foggy glasses on a protruding shirt tail, when he saw William walking toward him from the office. William's graying ponytail flapped behind him in the wind. Francis turned away and muttered.

"Morning, Franny," William said. "Christ, it feels like January."

Francis pulled another plank.

"One of the young guys should be out here in this weather," William said.

"I'll manage," Francis said, hefting the board onto the truck.

"You always have," William said.

Francis turned toward the younger man.

"Can't you see I'm busy?" he said.

"I came to say goodbye," William said.

"Damn hurry if you ask me," Francis said.

"I told you yesterday," William said. "My students' exams won't wait."

"More like your latest piece of college tail won't wait."

William's eyes widened as he tugged the zipper of his black leather jacket closer to his throat.

"Jesus," he said. "I'll pretend I didn't hear that."

"Pretend all you want," Francis said.

"I know how much you loved her," William said. "This is a hard time for all of us."

"Especially your dad," Francis said.

"Yeah, especially him," William said.

William took a few steps toward the office. Francis' voice stopped him.

"You've got more college degrees than I've got fingers," he said. "All I've ever known to do was drive a truck for your dad and his dad before him. My first day was in '46 and this is '91. Help me with the math. But it doesn't take a genius to be a good son, and I was that before my parents passed. And it doesn't take an hour's worth of college to be a friend."

More dust swirled, and William rubbed his eyes.

"Frankly, I was counting on that," he said.

"You've got some damn nerve," Francis said.

"I'll be back at Thanksgiving," William said. "I'll call."

"Not that he'll talk when you do."

"Exactly," William said, turning toward the office.

"Your mother asked me to look after him," Francis shouted. "With your Uncle Tommy dead, I'm the only one left. She knew she couldn't count on you."

William stopped. Francis saw his shoulders tense beneath the leather jacket. Then the son kept on into the dismal day.

The sun had fought through thinning layers of cloud by the time Francis finished his second delivery. He wiped his nose on his jacket sleeve and checked his Timex as he headed toward his pickup. He turned onto the highway and in a few hundred yards drove past the handmade sign that advertised pianos for sale, which caused another hard spasm of grief because the pianos had been her crazy idea, too. At the sign, he turned off the main road onto a paved path that led into the oaks.

The leaves were all reds and browns, vivid colors that she had remarked on just a few days before she died. Francis drove through the trees, then an open gate. The trees thinned and lush grass spread out over an acre. He parked in front of the old white house, next to Wendell's pickup, which had been washed and shined for his wife's funeral. He climbed the four porch steps and didn't knock.

A grandfather clock ticked in the living room down the hall but there was no other sound, no television or radio, so Francis headed up the stairs, huffing by the time he reached the top, cursing his age. Wendell's bedroom was thick with the scent of flowers from funeral bouquets someone had thought to place on the dresser and at various spots on the floor. The bed was unmade. Wendell sat in an old chair by the bathroom door, slumped in a pair of boxers and a T-shirt, as if he had gotten up to pee but only had the energy to make it halfway to the commode or halfway back to bed. He didn't look up.

"We should light the furnace," Francis said.

Wendell finally lifted his head, but his eyes seemed uncomprehending.

"I'll fix you something to eat," Francis said. "Put on some clothes and meet me in the kitchen. I'm not your damn butler."

"It's turned cold," Wendell said finally.

"The kind of day you always looked forward to during the summer."

"She's in the ground out there," Wendell said. "Isn't that something?"

Francis fumbled for words.

"That's where we're all headed in the end," he said, regretting it the moment the words left his mouth.

Wendell didn't seem to hear.

"Did we dress her warm enough in that casket?" Wendell asked. "And it must be damn hard to breathe beneath all that dirt."

Francis thought of William, halfway back to Lubbock.

"Wendell, your wife has passed," Francis said. "She's with Jesus now."

He felt frozen there, standing in the door, nearly choking from the pollen and his own feelings.

"So they say," Wendell said.

Francis had an idea on the Sunday after the funeral. The sun was shining and the autumn morning had turned summer hot as he drove through the trees in his church clothes. He went straight to the barn and rolled up the big door. Francis sat down on the riding mower, fired it up, and motored loudly out into the day, heading to the lawn in back nearest Wendell's bedroom window. When he finished there, Francis drove to the front, to the expanse of grass and flowers that Wendell and Selma had tended together for nearly five decades.

Out came Wendell, standing on the front porch in his grimy underwear. He began limping slowly out across the lawn in stocking feet. Francis circled the thick trunk of an old oak. He killed the engine.

16

"The hell you doing?" Wendell asked.

"You should put on some clothes if you're going to be out here," Francis said. "You could get arrested."

"You should stay off my damn mower."

"This warm weather has the grass growing again," Francis said. "You'd be in no position to notice, I guess."

"What business is it of yours?"

"I had this crazy notion of Selma coming home to the place in a ruin," Francis said. "How would that be?"

"Selma's passed," Wendell said. "You reminded me the other day."

"If you don't mind . . ."

Francis started the engine and roared off, leaving Wendell standing in his underwear, mouth agape in the shade of a hot October morning. Francis saw him shuffle back to the house. A few minutes later, Wendell reappeared on the front porch in his green work pants and a faded blue T-shirt. He walked to the shed and came out wearing gloves, carrying a pair of pruning shears in one hand and a spade in the other.

In an hour, Wendell had cut away dead branches on the rose bushes. He dug out beds of fading impatiens and begonias, making piles of the dead flowers as Francis continued to buzz around on the mower. Wendell paused to drink from the garden hose, and Francis drove over to get a drink himself. It was nearly three when Francis drove back into the barn and Wendell put up his spade and shears.

"I'm parched," Francis said.

"It is damn warm," Wendell said.

"Hop in," Francis said.

Francis was surprised when Wendell slid into his passenger seat and buckled the belt.

"You smell like shit," Francis said.

"Don't know how you can smell anything over that piss you call cologne," Wendell said.

Francis turned to back up his truck.

"I think I like you best when you're not talking," he said.

They sat in a corner table of Lilly's Diner. The owner hurried over with two glasses of iced tea.

"It's so good to see you, Wendell," she said, sneaking a concerned glance at Francis. "Have you been eating?"

Wendell raised his tea but his hand trembled so badly that big drops spilled on the table. He returned the glass to the table without taking a sip, dabbing at the spilled tea with a napkin. Lilly looked back and forth between the two men.

"That's why we're here," Francis said. "The boss has some catching up to do. Bring us the usual."

"Coming right up," she said, touching Wendell on the shoulder. "Francis, you got your good shirt all dirty. I've always said you needed a wife."

Wendell picked up his tea, spilling some more, but managed to get his glass to his mouth, taking several thirsty swallows. Francis stirred sugar into his and drank.

"A wife, she says," Francis said.

Wendell spilled more tea and drank again. A young couple at the next table stole glances in his direction.

"What business is it of hers that my shirt gets dirty?"

"She's had an eye on you since her husband passed. God only knows why," Wendell said.

Lilly returned with heaping plates of meatloaf and mashed potatoes for Francis, liver and onions for Wendell. Wendell bowed his head and waited while Francis crossed himself and whispered the Catholic blessing. Wendell ate ravenously, setting his fork down on an empty plate before Francis was half done.

"How are things at the lumberyard?" Wendell asked, his eyes suddenly twinkling, a wry smile on his face.

"That damn kid you sold the place to can't tell the difference between a square of shingles and a six-pack of beer," Francis said.

"Neither could you, in the beginning."

William rolled up in his sports car the Tuesday before Thanksgiving. It was a crisp mid-afternoon and Francis and Wendell were headed out on the last delivery of the day. Francis was behind the wheel. He stopped the truck when William pulled in off the highway. Wendell and Francis stepped down from the cab, leaving the truck idling behind them.

William got out of his car and shook his father's hand.

"When you weren't home I figured you might be over here," he said.

"Son," Wendell said.

"You've gained weight," William said.

"Damned Lilly," Wendell said.

"And you've got some sun," William said.

"I try to help out here," Wendell said.

William looked at Francis for the first time and extended his hand. Francis shook it limply.

"I guess you're the boss now," William said.

"With your mother gone he needed one," Francis said.

William looked quickly at his father, then into the sunny afternoon.

"I suppose you're right," he said.

Chapter 3

Francis owed his life's work to a rotting tooth so painful that even he could not ignore it. That August afternoon in 1946 was his first and last visit to the dentist. Tommy Smith was there for a checkup.

"I'll be damned. It's Big Devos," Tommy said, getting up from his chair in the lobby. He offered his hand. "Guess I don't need to ask why you're here. Your jaw looks like someone smacked you."

"Feels like it," Francis said.

"Where you been keeping yourself?"

"Here and there, odd jobs mostly."

"I'm getting ready for Baylor," Tommy said. "To play football."

"I heard."

"I never would have got the chance if it wasn't for your blocking last year. A running back never had a finer guard."

"I was big is all," Francis said.

"I just had an idea. You know, Francis, you'd make a damn good lumberman," Tommy said. "With me gone, dad will be one man down. Let me put in a good word."

A week later, Francis rolled up to Smith and Sons lumberyard on his bicycle, nervous about the job and rubbing elbows with the brother who still worked for his dad. Wendell Smith, three years older than Tommy and Francis, was said to be the finest football player Bisbee had ever seen. After high school, he single-handedly captured a bunch of German soldiers, or so said stories in all the newspapers. He came back from the war and was nearly killed in a car accident in Fort Worth, but two girls in the car with him had not been so lucky. That made the papers, too.

Sure enough, Wendell was the first person Francis saw when he stepped into the office. He was standing behind the counter drinking coffee, a bear of a guy with longish brown hair. A scar circled one eye and Francis wondered if it was from the accident or the war. Before either of them could speak, Wendell's father came charging through the door to the lumber shed, holding a clipboard. Jim Smith was the same size as his son, but his gray hair was cut to a burr. He wore glasses like Harry Truman's.

"See you've met Francis," Jim Smith said. "You probably know him from Tommy's team."

"Can't say I've had the pleasure," Wendell said.

"Take him out and show him around," Jim Smith said.

Wendell drained his coffee and headed into the shed, walking with a pronounced limp. Francis followed, wondering again about the source of the injury. Despite the morning heat the shed was dark and cool and the air was thick with the smell of resin, a scent Francis loved from that day forward. Wendell dug in his pants pocket.

"Forgot the damn keys," he said.

Wendell turned back toward the office and Francis looked up at boards of every description stacked two stories high on both sides of a concrete floor. A menacing electric saw with a blade a foot in diameter stood in a corner with mounds of yellow sawdust beneath it. Wendell reappeared and walked past Francis out of the shed into the sunshine. A truck was fully loaded with two-by-fours and four-by-sixes, and a pile of Sheetrock six feet tall.

"Might as well get in," Wendell said.

The job site was a farm about three miles away.

"You couldn't find anything better than hauling wood?" Wendell yelled at him over the wind and the truck engine.

"A good job is hard to come by," Francis said. "All the vets need work, too."

"This isn't a good job," Wendell said. "That what you're saying?"

"Your brother said it was good, honest labor for a fair wage. I'm happy to have it."

"See how happy you are when you're picking slivers out of your skin."

Sure enough, Francis caught big slivers on both hands when they unloaded the boards, piling them near a fresh concrete slab. He pulled them out with his teeth. Together they tackled the Sheetrock, pulling the four-by-six-foot pieces off the truck one at a time. Each piece weighed a hundred pounds or more and tended to buckle in the middle, making it particularly unwieldy. But Wendell and Francis found a wordless rhythm because they were of nearly equal strength. The truck was empty in less than an hour. Francis was thirsty but he wasn't about to say so.

"Tommy said that you were a damned good blocker," Wendell said on the trip back. "Unless I'm getting you confused with one of the other guys."

"That's likely," Francis said.

"It was you," Wendell said. "He used to call you Big Devos."

"Yeah."

"He said if it wasn't for Big Devos, he wouldn't be going to Baylor," Wendell said.

"He told me that, too," Francis said.

"My old man doesn't think much of the idea," Wendell said. "Going to Baylor. Can't say I do, either. Too many damned Baptists."

"I wouldn't know," Francis said.

"You're not a Baptist are you?" Wendell asked.

"Catholic," Francis said.

"A mackerel snapper. Should have figured."

"What's that supposed to mean?"

"You fish?" Wendell asked. "Mackerel snappers must fish."

They met at dawn in the lumberyard parking lot. Francis put his fly rod in the bed of Wendell's pickup and they sped east out of town as the sun flickered over the hills. Twenty wordless minutes out, Wendell turned off the blacktop. The gravel road became a dirt path through rolling country and stubby cedar. They were jostled by ruts in the road. Long grass brushed against the pickup. Grazing cattle turned and looked, chewing. Wendell slammed the truck into low gear to climb a steep hill. At the top, they looked down on a still pond, mirror-like water reflecting wisps of cloud that tumbled across the sky.

"This land belongs to a farmer we know," Wendell said. "The pond's a secret and I'd prefer to keep it that way."

"Why'd you bring me then?" Francis asked.

Wendell looked over at him.

"Damned if I know," he said.

Wendell pushed his door open, grabbed his rod and tacklebox, a lunch basket from the back of the truck and headed down the hill. Francis followed with his own gear through knee-deep brush the color of straw. Wooded hills circled the water. A beaver had been busy by the pond; trunks of small cedars were lying near freshly gnawed stumps. Three green-headed mallards made their way across the water, small ripples in their wake. A hawk circled overhead, calling. Meadowlarks chattered. A jackrabbit dashed away through the brush. The hooves of cows and deer had dimpled the mud along the bank.

Wendell stopped beneath a massive cypress whose gnarled branches were also painted in the water. He knelt beneath the tree and opened his tackle box, poking around inside until he found a red and white daredevil that he tied onto his line. Francis assembled his rod, threaded yellow filament through the loops on the pole, and tied a small hook and piece of feather onto the end. Insects pitted the surface of the water and fish came up for breakfast, roiling the pond.

"Fly rod?" Wendell said.

24

"Well it ain't a yardstick," Francis said.

"Good for streams, I heard, but this isn't a stream," Wendell said.

"We'll see," Francis said.

Wendell walked to a sandy spot by the water and with a flick of his rod sent his daredevil drifting through the air. The lure plunked down a few feet past a tree limb sticking up from the water. Wendell reeled it past the limb three times with no luck.

"Not biting," Wendell said.

"Let me have a try," Francis said.

"Suit yourself," Wendell said.

Francis took Wendell's place on the sand and flicked his rod back and forth, creating a growing arc of filament that whipped through the air. He finally let the line unfurl and the fly settled onto the water a few yards from the limb. Francis drew it slowly back toward him across the water until a big bass rose to the surface and swallowed the fly. His reel whined as the fish fled into the cool depths. Francis let him go. When the bass was exhausted Francis slowly reeled it in, lifted it from the water, admired his catch for a few seconds, and pried the hook from the mouth of the big fish. He bent and set it back in the water and watched it swim away.

"Something for you to try and catch," Francis said.

He moved a few yards down the shore, put his fly back out onto the water and landed another bass on his next cast.

"These fish want insects for breakfast, not that scarecrow you've been casting around," he said.

He extended the rod to Wendell.

"See for yourself," Francis said.

Wendell dropped his own rod by the cypress.

"Looks easy enough," Wendell said.

He whipped the rod back and forth as Francis had, but the line caught in some brush behind him.

"Goddamnit," Wendell said.

Francis freed the line, smiling.

"Work the rod ten o'clock to two," he said. "Use your wrist. Let the line out a little at a time as you go."

Wendell cursed again but followed instructions.

"Your wrist, not your whole stinking arm," Francis said. "And just let out a little line at a time until you get the hang of it. Better.... Now let it settle."

The fly landed softly just beyond the log. He retrieved it slowly by hand as Francis had done. A bass rose up to take it.

"Goddamn," Wendell said.

Wendell caught one bass after another as the sun rose. Francis was content to watch. When the fish stopped feeding for the morning, the men sat in the shade of the cypress eating fried egg sandwiches made by Wendell's mother. Wendell finished eating and rolled up his left pant leg. He untied the laces of his boot and winced as he pulled it off. He peeled away a heavy woolen sock. Francis saw three reddened stumps where the smallest toes had been. He looked at Wendell and back at the mangled foot.

"Two toes gone on the other foot, too," Wendell said, massaging his foot just above the stumps. "This foot always hurts the worst for some reason."

Francis could not look away.

"The war?" he asked finally.

"They called it trench foot," Wendell said, untying his other boot. "Our first night in the damn foxhole was just before Christmas, but instead of snow the rain came down in buckets and we were standing in six inches of muddy water. Then it got cold, godforsaken cold for a boy from Texas, and the water froze around our feet. They sent a bunch of us back to France and chopped off our toes to save the rest of our feet. At least that's what they told us. Every night they tossed buckets of blackened toes into the fire because they didn't know what else to do with them."

"Goddamn," Francis said.

"God damned us all right."

"That's why you limp," Francis said.

"I didn't think it was so bad at the time. That hospital tent was a lot warmer than the foxhole. More than that, I figured my war was over. But one day this young lieutenant comes up and says I am due back at the front in five days. He makes a note on his clipboard and moves on to the next guy. Sure enough, a few days later I was on my way back with a new pair of boots and two fresh pairs of wool socks. Just in time for what they're calling The Battle of the Bulge."

"How many Germans did you kill?" Francis asked.

Wendell's face reddened, the muscles in his jaw tightened and his eyes turned to ice. Francis didn't ask that question again.

Chapter 4

On a Saturday a few weeks later Francis pedaled through the dawn to the lumberyard. Wendell's pickup was waiting. Francis dropped his kickstand and was about to put his fishing gear in the back when he noticed Wendell was not alone inside the cab. Francis looked once, then twice. He could not have been more surprised if Eleanor Roosevelt had been sitting in the truck next to Wendell. Miss Sanchez had taught high school English to Wendell and Francis both.

"She promised not to bring up poetry," Wendell said.

"Good morning, Francis," Miss Sanchez said, smiling like she always did. "Nice to see you again."

"Ma'am," Francis said, glancing at her, then at Wendell, then the dirt.

"I begged him to let me tag along," Miss Sanchez said. "Do you mind?"

"No, ma'am."

He climbed in next to her, remembering how all the high school boys had tugged on her braided ponytail or threw spitballs at the blackboard when she wrote out poetry. Francis never carried on that way. But there was no stopping the sinful thoughts. He could not help wondering about what was beneath the floor-length wool skirts and long-sleeved blouses that she always wore buttoned to the neck. He wondered how she would look if her hair fell out of the ponytail.

Miss Sanchez also seemed to appreciate, in a way no one else did, that words on a page were an impossible jumble for him. The first time she called on him in class he tried to sound out a passage of Poe but gave up, and the other students hooted with laughter. Miss Sanchez never called on him again. Instead, once or twice a week, he went to her classroom after school and she read passages of novels or poetry to him, then asked him what he thought the words meant. It was after those private sessions that Francis struggled most to tame his imagination where the beautiful young teacher was concerned.

And now, three months after graduation, she was sitting in Wendell's pickup. Strings from her red dress were tied over her shoulders, but otherwise they were bare. Francis could see the tops of her breasts and a shadow between them. The dress rode halfway up her muscular legs. Francis felt stiffening in his pants. He silently started to pray a Hail Mary.

A slender hand with red-painted nails came to rest on Wendell's thigh. Even the Blessed Virgin couldn't help Francis with his feelings then—disappointment, a curious kind of heartbreak. Francis searched for peace in the passing landscape. The engine was loud and wind blew in through the open windows, causing her scented hair to fly in Francis' face. Miss Sanchez smiled and apologized, but he was glad they otherwise rode to the pond in silence.

Wendell nearly ran to the water with his new rod, leaving the two of them to walk down the hill. Francis carried his fishing gear, she a picnic basket.

"Have you ever seen Wendell so excited?" Miss Sanchez asked.

"No, ma'am," Francis said.

"Like a little boy with that new rod of his. He said you were the one who opened his eyes, though I don't understand what could be so different about this new way of fishing."

"It's not all that different," he said.

"You wouldn't know it by him," she said.

Wendell snuck glances toward her as he settled his fly onto the pond. A bass hit his third cast. She applauded from the shade of the cypress, where she had laid out a blanket. He and Francis fished their way around the pond in opposite directions. Francis landed several bass himself, which helped take his mind from the morning's bewildering turn of events.

She had kicked off her sandals and was reading a book of poetry on the blanket when they rejoined her.

"As good as advertised, I take it," she said.

"Can't wait to get Tommy out here and show him," Wendell said. "But I don't expect that will be anytime soon now that he's a football star."

"That means you're stuck with us," Miss Sanchez said. "Francis and me."

"Maybe that's up to Francis," Wendell said, smiling. "Do we need a cheering section? This ain't football."

"That's all I am?" she asked. "Taste these tamales. Maybe I've earned my keep."

"We'll see," Wendell said.

She produced a tin-foil package from her basket and handed Wendell and Francis two tamales each. Francis had never eaten one, so he watched Wendell peel away the yellow husks and pop the brown meat into his mouth. Francis did the same.

"Am I right?" she asked. "Francis?"

"They are tasty," Francis said.

"One for the cheering section," she said.

They ate and took drinks of water from a jug. She brushed sweaty locks of Wendell's long hair out of his eyes with her index finger. She kissed his cheek. Francis looked toward the pond.

"I came to see this new fishing rod," she said. "But there is another reason, Francis. Wendell and I figured it was time to let the cat out of the bag."

She tucked hair behind her ears.

"I've fallen in love with your friend here," she said. "And he's willing to put up with me, too. We need to let the world in on our little secret, and Wendell thought you would be a good place to start."

Francis looked back and forth between them.

"Me?"

"Wendell said you were his best friend," she said. "Someone he trusts."

"Huh?"

"I've always been so fond of you, too, Francis," Miss Sanchez said. "The very salt of the earth. So, what do you think?"

"About what?" Francis said.

"Do we have your blessing?" she asked.

"You're pulling my leg," Francis said.

"Maybe just a little," she said. "But I was ready to burst. I feel better already. Wendell?"

Wendell had been squinting at the water.

"It's the damndest thing," Wendell said, finally looking at Francis.

"You'll get no argument from me," Francis said.

"But is it wrong?" Wendell asked.

Wendell waited, like he actually wanted an answer.

"It's not my place to say," Francis said.

"But you have an opinion," Wendell said.

"My opinion is, however this happened," Francis said, "you are a damned lucky man."

Miss Sanchez crawled across the blanket and kissed Francis on the cheek. She put her arms around his sweaty shoulders and hugged him. She made her way back across the blanket, took one of Wendell's hands in hers and kissed it. Tears spilled down her cheeks. Francis thought he saw Wendell's eyes pool, too.

"I know it will seem improper to some," she said. "But hearts tend to have their own way. That's what I've always believed."

The fishing was done. Miss Sanchez placed everything back in her basket. They headed up the hill and drove back without talking. Selma held Wendell's hand when he didn't need it to shift gears. She hugged Francis again at the lumberyard.

"There's something else," she said. "Something I haven't even told Wendell. I'm pretty sure I'm pregnant."

On a Saturday morning a month later, the three of them took another drive, this time in her Packard. Wendell wore a white shirt and black bow tie, Miss Sanchez an ankle-length blue dress and white carnation in her hair. Francis had put on his best shirt and church pants.

Tommy Smith and a pretty, blonde-haired girl were waiting for them in the dormitory parking lot. They slipped into the back seat next to Francis.

"This is Fay," Tommy said.

Miss Sanchez smiled at her.

"You're very kind to join us," she said.

Wendell followed his brother's directions through the quiet streets of Waco and they pulled into a park where an old man was waiting. He shook hands with Wendell and Tommy, nodded to Francis and the women, and led them all to the top of a levee.

The old man stood with his back to the river, Wendell and Miss Sanchez facing him. Tommy stood next to his brother, Fay beside the bride. Francis was a few yards down the levee. Wendell and Miss Sanchez exchanged vows, and he slipped a ring over her finger. They kissed.

"This will take some getting used to," Tommy said after the old man drove away.

The five of them were sitting at a picnic table in the park. He turned to Fay.

"Miss Sanchez had all three of us in English," Tommy said.

"Don't you think it's time you called me Selma?" she asked.

A gust roiled the branches above them.

"What do mom and dad have to say about this?" Tommy asked.

Wendell looked at the branches, then at his brother.

"I haven't told them," he said.

"Holy crap," Tommy said.

"I will today when we get back," Wendell said.

"They'll be damn surprised," Tommy said.

"I expect they will," Wendell said.

Chapter 5

Wendell was at work the following Monday morning, wedding or no wedding, and Jim Smith dispatched them on their deliveries, as usual.

"You're probably wondering," Wendell said when they climbed into the cab for the first trip out.

"I'm surprised you're still in one piece," Francis said.

"My dad said, 'Jesus Lord.' My mom said, 'Oh, my, Wendell.'"

Wendell chuckled and started the truck.

"Until Saturday night, the only time they had met her was at school," Wendell said. "Then in I come, with this Mexican who was my teacher, and now all of a sudden she is my wife, with a baby on the way. I'm thankful neither one fell over from a heart attack."

"I thought your dad might cut himself a switch, war hero or not," Francis said.

"If it had been any other woman, I probably would have deserved whipping."

"Did Miss Sanchez say anything?" Francis asked.

"Call her Selma."

"Not sure I'm able," Francis said.

"She apologized for the shock and the secrecy, but she said that under the circumstances maybe my mom and dad could understand. She promised a church wedding if my folks wanted. She said she was going to resign at the high school, because tongues would wag, and she wanted to be home with the baby, anyway. Otherwise she sat there, holding my hand like she owned it, smiled that smile of hers and looked so damn happy. Next thing you know, she was mashing potatoes next to my mom. By the end of supper, you would have thought we'd been married a decade."

"Wonders never cease," Francis said.

"Care to guess where we slept?"

Francis blushed.

"In our old room, Tommy's and mine," Wendell said. "Selma wanted the top bunk."

"Your wedding night," Francis said.

"Mom said I seemed to have quit the bottle in the last little while, and didn't seem as surly as before. She figured Selma had something to do with that. I guess she's right," Wendell said.

"I think you're still pretty surly," Francis said.

Wendell and Selma shared the bunks for the next three months, though she took the bottom when her growing belly made it hard to climb on top. Wendell, his father, and Francis built a small cottage for the new family next to the big house. The newlyweds moved in just before Thanksgiving. Francis was the first non-relative to hold the baby boy and was terrified he would drop him. Selma insisted on naming the baby William, after Shakespeare. William James Smith, nine pounds seven ounces, another husky Smith male from the start.

Selma tried to fix up Francis with various women, and he went on a few awkward dates to placate her. But Selma eventually became reconciled to the fact that Francis was perfectly content as he was. He had his own mother and father, to whom he was devoted, and his sisters. Francis also took evening meals with the couple and their growing son a couple times a week. Francis was along on one of their many trips to the pond when the three-year-old boy caught his first fish. Selma went back to teaching when William was old enough for school.

The happy time ended on a scorching summer evening, July 17, 1954. Thunderclouds loomed closer and closer in the west and a boxcar of cement needed unloading before the weather hit. Normally, Jim

Smith left the heavy lifting to Wendell and Francis, but the approaching storm caused the older man to roll up his sleeves. The last bag was put into a bin as the first big drops pelted the dust. The three men were hurrying to the office when Jim said, "Oh," and collapsed before Wendell or Francis could catch him.

"What the hell," Francis said.

"Dad, goddamnit," Wendell said, kneeling next to his father.

Jim's eyes stared into angry clouds, raindrops sliding down his face like fat tears. His glasses lay muddied on the ground next to him.

"He's gone," Wendell said.

"What do you mean, gone?" Francis asked.

"Dead," Wendell said.

"How would you know?" Francis asked.

"I know," Wendell said.

Francis was eight years old the last time he had cried. That day his mother met him at the door after school and his father was home from his job behind the counter at the local hardware store. She was the one who broke the news about the mongrel, Lester. The dog was the same age as Francis and had followed him everywhere, but would no longer, because Francis' dad had found Lester that morning behind their house, killed by another dog or a wolf.

Francis raced out the back door to the new mound of dirt near the vegetable garden where Lester had already been buried. He fell to his knees and pawed at the soil, trying to dig his way back to his best friend. His mother took him by the shoulders and pulled him away. That's when Francis started to cry, huge sobs and thick tears that came from a place deep inside of him.

"Stop that nonsense," his dad said. "You'd think you were a little girl."

"But…" Francis said.

"Or I'll give you something to cry about," his dad said.

On a scorching afternoon eighteen years later, Francis took a handle at the front of Jim Smith's casket, joining five burly carpenters. They struggled out of the crowded country church and up a hill. The minister led, followed by the casket and its perspiring bearers, the mourners after that. Francis heard the sniffles behind him and the occasional sob, and he swallowed hard against his own profound sadness. He was pretty sure that pallbearers, like little boys, were not allowed to cry.

They set the casket next to a newly dug grave. Francis glanced at the faces as they filled in around the coffin. Wendell's mother dabbed her eyes beneath a black shroud, holding Wendell's hand. Tommy had tears running down his cheeks and snot dribbling from his nose, which he couldn't do much about because his wife, Fay, had one hand and Selma the other. Selma was a mess, but she cried at sunsets. Young William held his mother's other hand and cried because everyone else was. Everyone but Wendell. His face had been set in stone since the moment his dad hit the dirt and it pretty much stayed that way as he went about his father's arrangements.

Back at the house after Jim had been laid to rest, a mourner dropped a full plate of casserole in the Smith family living room, making a loud crash. Francis saw Wendell jump two inches in the air and raise his arms into a fighting posture as he turned toward the sound. Selma moved in to clean up the mess. Later that night, Wendell tried to raise a glass of water to his lips, but trembling hands caused a lot of it to spill on the kitchen floor. Francis had just stepped in to say goodnight and saw the trembling for the first time.

"I guess I'll see you tomorrow at the yards," Francis said.

Wendell didn't reply. Selma hugged Francis on his way out.

"Jim loved you like a son," she said.

Francis had to pull over on his way home. Alone in the dark, hidden on the side of a Texas country road, Francis wept for the first time since the death of Lester. There was no one there to tell him he couldn't.

Chapter 6

Selma came by the lumberyard two weeks after the funeral and invited Francis for supper. She made sure Wendell heard her. Wendell was still at his desk when Francis drove home to clean up. Selma answered the front door when Francis knocked. The house was filled with the smell of cooking meat. She handed him a glass of lemonade and he stood with her in the kitchen while she tended to broiling steaks.

"Where is he?" she asked.

"I'm sure he'll just be a minute," Francis said.

"He hasn't been home for supper since…"

She turned away from Francis but he could see that she dabbed at her eyes with a dish towel.

"I'll go see what's keeping him," Francis said.

Back at the lumberyard he heard the big saw whining out back. In the shed, Francis saw Wendell bend to pick up a wood scrap, lift it with trembling hands to the saw, and cut it into several little pieces for no good reason that Francis could see. Francis moved slowly toward Wendell, trying not to startle him. Wendell looked up and shut off the saw.

"Supper is waiting," Francis said when the noise died down.

"I'm busy here," Wendell said.

"Doing what, exactly?" Francis asked.

"Tell Selma I'll eat later."

"You know, Wendell, life goes on," Francis said.

Back at the house, Selma had wrapped his steak and a baked potato in tin foil. The table had been cleared.

"I knew somehow," Selma said.

"I'm sorry," Francis said.

"We have to be patient," she said.

"I guess," Francis said.

At home, Francis took a few bites of the food but didn't have much appetite. He rocked in his chair with his cat in his lap and thought about his friend. Since his father's death, Wendell did the work of three men, and if there wasn't work to do he made some up, arriving with the sun on most mornings, then staying at the lumberyard until late at night, loading trucks or going over figures, then going over them again.

As time went on, the bags beneath Wendell's eyes seemed to become permanent. His pants sagged in the rear and his work shirts drooped. Selma brought Wendell's supper over to him at the lumberyard. William helped to carry the food. There was little conversation among them. More life seemed to drain from Selma's eyes with every passing month. It was for her sake that, about a year after Jim Smith's death, Francis sought out Wendell, who was working the adding machine at his desk.

"I heard it said once that I was your best friend," Francis said.

Wendell looked up from a balance sheet.

"So I thought I'd ask: What the hell you think you're doing, treating your family like this?" Francis said.

Wendell ignored a pencil that rolled off his desk.

"Treating my family like what?" Wendell asked.

"Selma's a widow."

"I keep a roof over their heads."

"That's about all," Francis said.

"This is none of your goddamn business," Wendell said, his anger rising.

"Name the last time you had an evening meal at home," Francis said. "Tell me when you took that boy fishing."

"You work for me, remember," Wendell said. "Keep this up and that might not be the case."

"What's wrong with you, Wendell?"

"It's time you got on," Wendell said. "I'm busy here."

On his drive home Francis thought about trying to find another job but knew he never would. There was too much water under the bridge where Wendell and Selma were concerned, too many memories, most of them good. But Francis figured that Selma's patience would eventually reach its end.

He was right about that. One morning in November 1956, Francis arrived at the lumberyard and found the front door unlocked but Wendell nowhere to be found. What looked like a full plate of roast beef and mashed potatoes was spread across the floor and onto the walls around his desk. The plate itself was in three pieces on the floor. Tin foil was crumpled nearby. Francis smiled, imagining the scene. He cleaned up. Selma's mother from San Antonio was the one who answered the telephone. She said Wendell would not be at work that day but wouldn't say why. Francis could close the lumberyard and take the day off, too, if he wished. In the decade that Francis had been around it was the first day Wendell had missed.

Wendell was back the next day. He never said a word about the mess in the office, other than to thank Francis for cleaning it up. From that day on, Wendell locked the doors no later than six in the evening and headed home.

Wendell put on some weight, but every time he held a pencil or a cup, every time he lifted a forkful of food to his mouth, his hand still shook like he had a raging fever. Francis was again occasionally invited to the Smith family table. Wendell and Francis didn't say much during the meals, listening as Selma lavished attention on the growing boy. Wendell generally left his food half-eaten and otherwise spent hours in front of their new television, as if hypnotized by Jackie Gleason or Jack Benny. He turned away from the tube whenever there were news reports of the Vietnam War. Any fishing was done at Selma's insistence.

Otherwise, from the morning when Francis found the mess in the office, Wendell's life was lived by her dictates. It was Selma's idea that William, despite no apparent interest in the family business, begin to help out around the lumberyard in the summers. The boy was lazier than an old cat, which exasperated Wendell and Francis both, but there was not much they could say or do because William was the proverbial apple of his mother's eye and he knew it.

Selma had them move into the big house after Wendell's mother died from a stroke in 1959. It was her suggestion that Wendell and Francis saw down a lot of the trees closer to the house and rip out the stumps so they could seed Bermuda grass and plant all those flowers. When William went away to college in Lubbock—a secret relief to both Wendell and Francis—Selma insisted that she and her husband begin to travel. They visited a small town in Mexico where Selma's grandfather still lived, and Ireland, then Niagara Falls and Victoria Island in Canada. Each destination had been Selma's idea, too.

Her strangest whim came in the late summer of 1986. Selma had recently retired from teaching and apparently found herself at loose ends. Wendell and Francis were loitering behind the counter at the lumberyard when Selma showed up and announced her "wonderful idea." The high school music teacher had recently complained that too many children couldn't play the piano because of the cost.

"I've checked the classifieds in the Fort Worth paper," Selma said as Francis and Wendell exchanged glances.

"I'm afraid to ask why," Wendell said.

"For used pianos, darling," Selma said. "People are almost giving them away."

"How does this concern us?" Wendell asked.

"You boys could go buy them, bring them back here on a truck, and I'll find a rightful owner, a young family who couldn't afford one otherwise," Selma said, beaming.

Wendell looked again at Francis, pleadingly.

"Damn things are expensive, I heard," Francis said, smiling.

"Shit," Wendell said. "You think we have time to be driving to El Paso and back for old pianos?"

"Just every so often," Selma said. "And think of the good we'd do."

Wendell finally smiled, too.

"I'll try it once or twice," he said. "Don't get your hopes up beyond that."

Francis counted seven trips in the truck, thirteen pianos that changed hands. Selma was so pleased that she insisted on what she called "a little local advertising." Hence the sign along the highway that Wendell and Francis built one weekend in 1988. It attracted few inquiries.

Chapter 7

Wendell and Francis drove Selma home from the hospital for the last time, traveling slowly from Fort Worth because she winced with every bump. Wendell had hired a paving crew the week before for just that reason, so the road from the highway to the house was smooth. When they turned onto the tree-lined stretch, the air smelled like tar.

Selma took it all in, the thinning leaves of brown and red and the fragments of sunlight that fought through to the ground. Her arms were pale twigs. Her thin legs were lifeless in gray sweat pants. Her hair had been reduced to thatches of white fuzz beneath her ball cap. She held Francis' hand.

"It feels like I've been gone a year," she said.

Wendell parked by the porch, lifted his wife from the cab and carried her inside. Francis held the door. Bouquets of fresh flowers from her garden sat on either side of the bed upstairs. Curtains rustled in the gentle breeze.

"My goodness, Wendell," Selma said when he laid her down. "The flowers."

"Francis had a hand in them, too," Wendell said.

"William will be home tomorrow?" she asked.

"So he said," Wendell said.

"The four of us," she said. "Just like old times."

She smiled at Francis.

"Yes, ma'am," Francis said.

The nurse came by every afternoon, but Wendell was his wife's caregiver. He rubbed lotion into her skin every morning. He slipped the straw between her lips and the slivers of ice into her mouth. He doled out the morphine from the plastic bottles lined up on the table next to her bed, moving his lips while he read the labels. He bathed her. He read poetry to her. He rarely left her side, delegating grocery shopping and errands to William and Francis.

She slept more and more as the days passed, long, drug-induced naps in both the morning and afternoon. She woke one afternoon to the autumn sun slanting in across her face through partially closed blinds. Wendell closed his book. Francis dozed in a chair.

"It looks like a marvelous day," she said, her voice dusky from sleep but stronger than usual.

"Pretty as they come, I suppose," Wendell said.

"Take me out," she said.

"If you're strong enough," Wendell said.

"Like a mule."

Francis had stirred and he hurried down the stairs to prop open the front door. Wendell wrapped his wife in a blanket and hoisted her from the bed, carrying her down the stairs and onto the porch. He settled her into a rocking chair and pulled its twin to within a few inches. Francis took the porch swing. The sun fell full and warm on Selma's face as she gently rocked an inch or two. Through the branches the sky was a brilliant, cloudless blue.

"Where's William?" she asked.

"Picking up a few groceries," Wendell said.

She closed her eyes and took a deep, rasping breath.

"Do you suppose there are days like this in heaven?" she asked.

"Every day," Wendell said.

"That's what I was just thinking," Selma said.

She looked at him. She chuckled, but that caused a fit of coughing. Wendell took her hand. It passed.

"I remember the first time I was here," Selma said. "August 1945, just after the accident."

"You brought daisies," Wendell said. "Tommy brought them up after you left."

"You weren't very sociable," Selma said.

"Then or now," Wendell said.

"Tommy and I had a nice talk that day, sitting right here," she said. "He told me."

"I remember thinking what an Eden this place was, hidden back in the trees," she said. "It felt like home to me, even then. You see what I'm driving at, Wendell?"

"Afraid you've lost me,'" he said.

"I married you for your property," she said, winking and putting a hand to her mouth to try and stifle a cough.

He smiled and shook his head.

"What an awful, shallow person I am," she said. "Are you appalled?"

"Terribly," Wendell said.

"Francis," Selma said. "You?"

"No, ma'am," Francis said.

"How could you be with a poor woman in my condition?" she asked.

"Not possible, come to think of it," Wendell said.

"After all, it worked out, didn't it," Selma said.

"Just fine."

"I love you, Wendell," she said.

"I know."

"I'm the luckiest girl in the world."

The sun inched toward the branches, the air cooling in the waning light. Selma started to shiver.

"We need to get you in," Wendell said.

"Just a few more minutes," she pleaded.

"No more than that," Wendell said.

"There's something I want to tell you."

"You should save your strength."

"I just realized this in the last day or so," she said. "I've loved you from the first time I laid eyes on you."

"It's probably the painkillers," Wendell said.

"You were my student. How illicit."

"Like I said, the drugs," Wendell said.

She looked over at him, beaming.

"I remember exactly what you were wearing," Selma said. "One of those dark red flannel shirts. Blue suspenders. And there was a bruise beneath your eye, from football, I guess."

"I'll be damned." Wendell said, shaking his head.

"This big, handsome boy comes walking in, towering over the rest. He wouldn't look at me. He looked so handsome, but so shy. My stomach did a somersault right then, the beginning of love."

"I've always said you have peculiar taste in men."

"It was intuition," Selma said. "I knew in a heartbeat that there was something special about you, something abiding in your heart."

She took his big hand in both of hers and placed it on her lap.

"What I didn't know was just how good you were," she said. "Until this last year. If anything, I underestimated you, Wendell."

He looked into the trees.

"You, too, Francis," she said.

Francis caught a tear with his palm.

"This year has been vindication of sorts for me, Wendell," she said. "I was right about you."

"Shush, Selma," he said. "You'll tire."

Wendell stood and lifted her. Francis held the door. Wendell climbed the stairs, laid her in bed, pulled the covers up around her thin shoulders, closed the curtains and left the room. His legs buckled at the top of the stairs. Wendell cried for the first time since her disease was diagnosed. Francis sat down on the top stair and put his hand on his shoulder.

Wendell changed in the last two days of Selma's life. There was hesitancy and worsening tremors that Francis attributed to her condition. Moments of ice in his eyes. The stony mask on his face for hours at a time. Through the fog of the drugs Selma noticed it, too.

"Wendell, what's wrong?" she whispered during a lucid moment.

"Nothing, Selma," he said.

"Please tell me," she said.

"Nothing to tell," he said.

On the last night, the sound of her labored breathing filled the bedroom. Wendell sat on the side of the bed and rubbed her arm. William and Francis stood on the other side. Wendell stopped rubbing, his eyes closed and his chin dropped for several seconds.

"Dad?" William asked.

When Wendell opened his eyes they were terrified, haunted.

"I know," Wendell said.

"Know what, dad?" William asked.

"I'm sorry," Wendell said.

"For what?" William asked.

"He'll come again," Wendell said.

William looked at Francis.

"Who will?" William asked.

"No one," Wendell said.

"Another dream, dear?" Selma asked.

She had opened her eyes and her voice was stronger than it had been in days.

"Mother!" William cried.

Wendell bent over her.

"You're shaking," she said. "Was it the war?"

"Nothing," Wendell said.

"Everything will be fine," she said.

"I know," Wendell whispered.

"I will always be with you."

"You will," he said.

"Will always listen to your bad dreams."

"Yes."

"You will tell me your dreams, won't you Wendell? You promised."

"I will," he said.

"So what was it?" she asked. "Please."

"Nothing."

"You are my knight in shining armor," she said. "Give me a kiss."

She closed her eyes as he bent to her. The wheezing intensified. Selma opened her eyes a few minutes later but stared into another world. The wheezing stopped after a few last tortured breaths and there was a terrible silence. William collapsed to his knees, clutching the side of his mother's bed and sobbing. Wendell seemed frozen. Francis left the room, walked down the stairs and sat down on the porch, a numbness filling him.

Too Far for the Past to Follow

Chapter 8

On a September Minnesota morning, Claire's heart had started to hammer the moment she opened her eyes, mostly from familiar dread. But on that first day of her freshman year of high school, something foreign was mixed in with the inner darkness. It was a flicker of hope, like a small candle in a drafty room, fragile, like it could be blown out at any second, but unmistakably there just the same. For the first time since that horrible night in her house two years earlier, maybe she could be just another messed-up kid, not that girl from the papers and television news who had been in the very next room when it happened. No more stares. No more whispers. No more sick jokes or nasty comments made just loud enough for her to hear.

Maybe today was finally the day.

She threw back the covers, took a quick shower, and put on baggy jeans and a loose-fitting sweatshirt that camouflaged her curves. She pulled her long, dark hair into a ponytail. She never wore makeup, nothing that might cause her to stand out.

Downstairs, her Uncle Jack scanned the paper as he finished a plate of scrambled eggs. He mumbled something about the price of gas.

"Morning," Claire said.

He didn't look up.

Aunt Sophie had her hands in dishwater, scrubbing a frying pan with one eye on the Today show that blared from a miniature television on the counter.

"Could I buy my lunch today?" Claire asked.

"Minced ham too good for you all of a sudden?" Sophie asked, drying her hands on a dish towel. She didn't take her eyes off the fat weatherman.

Claire made her sandwich, grabbed an apple from the refrigerator, and tucked both into her school bag. The sunny Minnesota morning was warm enough that she didn't need a jacket for her mile-long walk. She paused a block away, took a deep breath and made the sign of the cross. Inside the ancient brick building, she dodged other kids until she finally found her locker, where she dumped her extra notebooks and fell in with the river of students heading to their first classes.

A group of older boys formed a gauntlet at the bottom of the stairs. There were about ten of them, all wearing red varsity jackets with tan leather sleeves. They jostled and laughed as the river of students flowed in their direction and between them up the steps. Then she was in the middle of them, close enough to smell their cologne. She kept her eyes down and started to climb and was three steps up when she heard it.

"Now that is one sweet ass," one of them said. The others roared with laughter.

Claire froze on the steps and her cheeks filled with blood. Someone ran into her from behind. Claire turned and saw it was a very pretty older girl in a cheerleader uniform.

"Grow up, Richie," the girl said, smirking down at the boys. She turned to Claire. "Plan on standing there all day? Fucking freshmen."

The girl tossed one more glance toward the boys and hurried up the stairs past Claire. Claire followed her to the second floor, dizzy with relief. For the rest of that first day, through homeroom and all of her classes, no one gave her so much as a second glance. She was just another new kid.

The next day her heart throbbed again as she neared the boys by the stairs. One of them tossed a tube of Clearasil into the path of a girl disfigured by acne. The boys howled with laughter as Claire scurried by.

The day after that, the mob mimicked the speech impediment of a boy with thick glasses and two hearing aids, then tripped him as he got to the stairs. Claire was just glad it was him, not her.

So it went that entire first week, Claire ignored by that mob of boys and everyone else. Her hope grew with each passing day. If the boys by the stairs hadn't seen fit to mention it, if they had moved on, maybe everyone else had, too. Claire slept soundly that weekend for the first time since it happened, as if even the nightmares had grown tired of messing with her.

On the Monday morning of her second week, a voice from the gauntlet called her last name. When she looked up, the boys ripped open their varsity jackets to reveal white T-shirts smeared across the chests with what must have been ketchup. She dropped her books, and a folder full of papers splayed out across the floor. No one dared to help her retrieve them. The boys howled. The next day they brandished plastic knives, plunging them into their respective hearts when Claire trotted by. It went on like that for weeks, the ketchup stunt more than once, the knives. Then she heard it for the first time.

"Watch yourselves, boys," one of them said. "Here comes the spawn of the black widow."

Before long it was shortened to just one word, a nickname that spread from the mob into the student body more generally. By October of her freshman year, that's how Claire Calhoun was known at St. Barnabus Catholic School, by that one terrible word: "Spawn."

Claire had despised cigarettes because of the blue haze of smoke that filled the little home where she had spent her first twelve years. But that changed when she enjoyed her first actual puff, with girls named Margie and Lynette beneath a railroad trestle near the school. A day before that liberating drag, in October of their sophomore year, the three of them had found themselves together at the end of the field hockey bench. Field hockey was not optional for the girls at St. Barnabus and Claire learned that the two other girls despised the sport as much as she did.

Margie and Lynette appeared the next day at the table in the corner of the lunchroom where Claire sat alone with a tray of half-eaten fish sticks and some macaroni and cheese that she had barely touched. A copy of *Great Expectations*, an English class assignment, sat open next to what was left of her lunch.

"Hey, Spawn," Margie said.

"I wish you wouldn't call me that," Claire said.

"I wish they didn't call me 'Freak' either, but there it is," Margie said. "Gonna finish those?"

She picked up two half-eaten fish sticks, popped one in her mouth and handed the other to Lynette.

"You actually read that shit?" Lynette asked, tapping the book.

"I like Dickens," Claire said.

"Lynette likes dick," Margie said, and the two girls laughed.

"Gross," Claire said.

"Let's go, Spawn," Margie said. "The bell rings in a half-hour."

"Go where?"

"Out of this fucking hole," Margie said.

Claire froze. She wondered if the girls were setting some sort of cruel trap. But the two didn't seem like the type, dressed as they were in black from head to toe, with black makeup to match, like that rocker Alice Cooper. So Claire got up from the table, dumped the rest of her lunch in a trash can, set her tray on a pile of others, and followed Margie and Lynette from the cafeteria into a cold, rainy autumn day.

The railroad tracks were at the far side of a city park. The three of them trotted through a light rain. Beneath the trestle, Margie pulled out a pack of Kools, took one for herself, handed another to Lynette and extended the pack to Claire. Kools had been her father's brand.

"No thanks," she said.

"Suit yourself," Margie said, sparking her cigarette with a cheap plastic lighter, then handing the lighter to Lynette.

The two girls moaned as they took in their first large puffs. Margie let out the smoke through her nose, elegant twin plumes of blue. Lynette made a circle with her mouth and produced an expert series of smoke rings that wafted off into the gray day.

"Come on," Margie said to Claire, extending her Kool.

Claire finally took the cigarette, looked at it for a second, put it to her lips and took a short drag. The smoke tasted minty, a menthol. She almost fell over from the dizziness that hit her in a second. She steadied herself against a pillar of the trestle.

"Whoa," Lynette said.

Claire giggled.

"Keep it," Margie said, pulling out another cigarette and lighting it.

Claire's second puff was deeper. She coughed and tapped the cigarette lightly with her index finger, flicking away spent ash, imitating her mother, who chain-smoked Marlboro Lights when she and Claire lived together at home. Sun poked through the clouds. Claire admired the blue smoke that poured from her mouth. Dizziness was replaced by another feeling, foreign and wonderful, that started where her long black hair was pulled into a ponytail. It spread down her face, into her chest, down her legs, to the ends of her toes. Claire felt she might drift off into the low clouds.

Lynette dropped her Kool and stubbed it out with the toe of her black tennis shoe.

"We gotta go," she said.

Margie took one last drag. Smoke spilled out her nostrils as she followed Lynette toward the school. The two of them were several paces away when they turned to where Claire still stood beneath the trestle.

"What's keeping you, Mrs. Dickens?" Margie asked.

Claire took another puff and dropped her cigarette, stubbed it out and staggered after the others. She caught up, and they jogged through the rain toward the school.

"Talk about a lightweight," Margie said.

The next morning the three of them strolled past the mob and Margie flipped them off. They met again beneath the trestle at lunchtime. A few weeks later, Lynette produced a bottle, and Claire found the feeling from the vodka even more wonderful.

He appeared one night in her junior year. Claire heard the doorbell, expecting Margie and Lynette, but saw him instead, standing on the doorstep. His wire-rimmed glasses were covered in condensation. He wiped them on a shirt tail that stuck out from beneath his varsity jacket, which seemed a few sizes too big.

"I'm Larry," he said when she opened the door.

"From English class," Claire said.

"You're probably wondering what I'm doing here," he said.

"You can say that again," she said.

He took off his glasses, polished them again, and returned them to his nose. He looked at her, then over her shoulder.

"Would you be my date for the homecoming dance?" he asked.

"You've got to be shitting me."

"No, I'm not shitting you."

"Then you must be hard up," she said.

"I'd appreciate it if you would answer my question."

Claire surprised herself by what she said next.

"OK," she said.

The next day, Claire, Margie and Lynette hurried off to the trestle at lunch and passed around a joint that Margie had stolen from her mother. Claire was good and stoned before she told her friends about Larry.

"Claire Calhoun, the homecoming queen," Lynette said.

"Larry, the little fucking wrestler," Margie said.

"Some guys will do anything to get laid," Lynette said.

"He's not getting laid," Claire said, giggling with them. "I may be crazy, but I'm not easy."

Later, at home, Sophie's jaw literally dropped when Claire told her.

"What should I wear?" Claire asked.

"Leave that to me," Sophie said.

Claire tried on several dresses at Dayton's after school the next day. Sophie picked a dark red number that came to mid-thigh, fit snugly over Claire's behind, and accented her larger-than-average breasts.

"It's too tight," Claire said.

"It's perfect, trust me," Sophie said. "That boy of yours is a lucky man."

"It's a dance."

"If only your mother could see you," Sophie said.

"Mother wouldn't want to see me, in this dress or anything else," Claire said.

"Well who is to blame for that?" Sophie asked.

Like Claire needed any reminders.

Sophie helped Claire apply eye shadow for the first time that Saturday night. Claire stared at the finished product in the mirror. At the eyes now bordered in light blue. At the long black hair, typically lifeless and straight, that now billowed from Sophie's curling iron. At the long chin and neck. At the mounds of her chest. She jumped at the sound of the doorbell.

Larry wore a pale blue leisure suit with a red tie and presented her with a wrist corsage that was the same color as Claire's dress. Sophie placed a white wool wrap around her shoulders.

"The dance is over at eleven," Larry said. "I'll have her home right after."

"Don't worry," Sophie said, practically pushing them out the door, as if Larry might suddenly change his mind. "You two have a wonderful time."

Larry closed the door of his pickup after Claire slid into the passenger seat. She waited for him to say something.

"So," she said. "You wrestle."

"At one-twenty-six," Larry replied.

"One-twenty-six what?"

"That's my weight class," he said. "One-twenty-six."

"That's pretty small."

Claire weighed that much. She was also an inch taller.

"I still don't get this," Claire said.

"Get what?" Larry said.

"Like I said, you must be hard up."

"You are pretty underneath all that shit you and your friends put on your faces."

"Shit, is it?"

"And you have nice handwriting," Larry said. "And you always get good grades in English, but you never say a word in class."

"What's to say," Claire said.

"And you seem lonely," Larry said.

"Oh, please," Claire said.

He turned into the school parking lot.

They entered a long, brightly lit hallway where couples congregated. Claire felt ridiculous in her tight dress, the corsage on her wrist, the fancy white shawl. She thought of Cinderella but there was one huge difference. Cinderella enjoyed the attention at the ball. Claire wanted to turn and run back out the door.

The gym was dark, with paper streamers in school colors hanging from the ceiling. A band tuned its instruments beneath one of the basketball hoops. They sat with other members of the wrestling team and their dates. Larry brought Claire a plastic glass of punch. She relaxed a little.

The band started to play and couples got up to dance. Larry leaned over and asked, so Claire folded her shawl on the back of her seat and they headed for the floor. Claire had danced with Margie and Lynette when they were drunk or stoned but had never tried it sober. She attempted to imitate the way other girls moved their arms and slid their feet from side to side to the beat, a song by the Beatles. Larry was pretty tentative himself. The two of them were jostled by the other dancers. Back at their table after one song, he filled her glass.

The boy approached across the dance floor. He was very tall, and lean, and had thick brown hair parted in the middle. Unlike most of the others, he had shed his coat and wore his shirt sleeves rolled up to his elbows. His tie hung loose around his neck. He leaned down and shouted into Claire's ear above the music.

"I had to get a closer look," the boy said.

"At what?" Claire shouted back.

"At you," he said. "It's hard to believe."

"What is?" she asked.

"That you are the same girl."

Claire blushed, glad for the dark.

"Let's dance. Little Cavanaugh won't mind."

Claire looked at Larry, who shrugged. The boy put his hand on her back and guided her through the bodies to the middle of the floor. The band played the Rolling Stones. The next song was a ballad by Chicago.

"One more," the boy said.

61

Larry was watching them.

"OK," she said.

He closed in and put his arms around her, clinching his hands in the middle of her back. Claire put her hands on his shoulders. Larry couldn't see them through the bodies. Then it hit her.

"You're one of them," she said, trying to pull away.

He tightened his embrace.

"Hang on. We just have a little fun."

"Some fun," she said.

"Sorry, Claire," he said. "We'll be nicer to you from now on."

She relaxed.

"So, my name isn't Spawn."

"No, it isn't," he said.

He tightened his arms around her and his hands moved farther down her back.

"Larry Cavanaugh?" the boy said into her ear.

"What about him?" Claire asked.

"He wouldn't know what to do with a girl like you if he had instructions," he said.

"And you would, I suppose," Claire said.

"No instructions necessary," he said.

He pulled his head back a few inches, looked down into her eyes and smiled.

"I need a cigarette," Claire said.

"I've got something better in my car. Tell Larry you need to pee."

She pushed away from him when the song ended, leaving him smiling on the dance floor as she headed to the table where Larry sat with his friends.

"I need to use the ladies' room," she said.

The tall boy had put on a dark suit jacket and stood by the bathroom, smiling.

"We'll be back before Cavanaugh knows you were gone," he said. "My girlfriend, too."

Claire couldn't do it. She rushed through the door of the bathroom and saw a line of girls waiting to use the toilets. The boy was gone when she hurried back out the door. She forced herself back into the gym.

"Take me home," she told Larry.

"What's wrong?" Larry asked.

"Please," Claire said. "Home."

"We just got here."

She started for the door. She was outside and halfway to Larry's truck by the time he caught up.

"You forgot this," he said, handing her the shawl.

"Thanks," she said. "I'll walk home."

"My ass," Larry said.

"Really."

"I hate dances," Larry said.

Claire's breathing slowed on the short ride home. He walked her to the door. They faced each other in the dark.

"You OK?" Larry asked.

"I'm never OK," she said.

Larry scratched his head. Finally he exhaled deeply, a cloud pouring out of his mouth on the cold night.

"Well, thanks for going," he said.

"Sorry I was such a shitty date," she said.

"You were beautiful tonight," he said. "The other guys were jealous. That's a new one for me."

"Give me a break," she said.

Larry took off his glasses, cleaned them with his jacket, and put them back on his nose.

"That was Ned Peterson," Larry said.

"Who?"

"The guy you danced with."

"He supposed to be someone?" Claire asked.

"Leading scorer on the basketball team," Larry said.

"I could care. You wrestle, at one-twenty-six."

Larry smiled.

"I should go," Claire said.

He leaned in to kiss her but Claire turned her head. He gave her a stiff hug.

"See you around," he said.

Claire watched through a window as Larry walked slowly back to his truck, looking up at a nearly full moon in the autumn sky.

Chapter 9

The next Monday morning, Claire left for school without her black makeup.

"Must be love," Margie said as the three of them headed down the hall.

"Enjoy the dance, Claire?" a male voice asked.

Ned Peterson had sidled up next to her.

"It was fine," Claire said.

"I was hoping for another dance or two."

"We had better things to do," Claire said.

"Oh, really," Peterson said.

They had neared the mob by the stairs. Peterson winked at them.

"What might that be?" he asked.

"For me to know, and you to find out," Claire said.

Peterson laughed.

"Oh, I'll find out," he said.

He peeled off toward his friends. Claire walked faster to get by them. Margie and Lynette had to almost trot to keep up.

"What was that about?" Lynette asked.

"Nothing," Claire said.

"What an asshole," Margie said.

"Pig," Lynette agreed.

Claire didn't skip out at lunch because she didn't want to answer their questions about the dance or Ned Peterson. She craved nicotine all afternoon. Her hair was damp from a shower after field hockey practice, and it was getting dark when she started her walk home. About halfway, a car screeched up beside her—a new sports car. The window on the passenger side was down, and the driver leaned toward her.

"Need a lift?" Ned Peterson asked.

"No thanks," she said without stopping.

He crept along beside her in his car.

"Come on," Peterson said. "It's cold."

He stopped his car, jumped out, ran around to the passenger side and opened the door.

"At your service," he said.

No possible good could come from getting in Ned Peterson's car, but she did it anyway, sliding into the passenger seat, dumping her book bag at her feet. He got behind the wheel and reached across her, opening the glove compartment. He took out a bottle and handed it to Claire.

"This will warm you up," he said.

It was a nearly full bottle of peppermint schnapps.

"Go ahead," Peterson said. "Help yourself."

Claire unscrewed the cap and put the bottle to her lips, taking a quick sip. The clear liquid was delicious, like a menthol form of vodka. She passed the bottle to him and he took a large gulp and returned it. He slammed the car into gear and sped off down the street. Claire took a longer gulp at a stop sign, then another. He missed her turn. He punched an eight-track tape into the console, and a song by The Cars began to boom. He parked behind an abandoned warehouse at the edge of their St. Paul suburb. Claire took two more long slugs and passed the bottle to him. She slid down in her seat, her head spinning, a foot tapping to the beat of the music. Peterson reached back across her and put the bottle back in the glove compartment. He looked up and smiled, his face just a few inches away. Claire smiled back. He closed the distance and kissed her, softly at first, but more fiercely when he found her lips welcoming. A boy's tongue danced in her mouth for the first time and it wasn't nearly as nasty as she thought it would be. The music pounded. The windows fogged. Peterson and his tongue tasted like peppermint.

Then he slid his hand down her shoulder, onto her breast and squeezed, like he was testing the ripeness of a piece of fruit. Claire pulled back from his face, grabbed the hand and tried to yank it away, but Peterson kept it there and squeezed again.

"What are you doing?" she yelled above the music.

"You know what I'm doing," he said. "I don't need instructions."

"We've had our fun," Claire said. "Now take me home."

"Have another drink," he said.

She punched a button on the console, silencing the music.

"I'm sorry if I gave you the wrong idea," she said.

"I had the right idea," Peterson said.

"No, you didn't," Claire said. "I'm not a slut."

"That's not what I hear," he said. "I hear you take after your mother."

The words took her breath away. She started to cry.

"Please take me home," Claire said.

"Or what? Or I'll end up like your old man?"

Claire groped in the dark until she found the door handle. She tumbled to the ground as she tried to get out. She got up and staggered toward a distant streetlight. She heard his door open and close and footsteps echoing in the night as he jogged after her.

"Hell of a long walk," he said, grabbing her by the shoulders and jerking her toward him.

He forced his mouth onto hers. When she turned her face away, his left hand curled into a fist, coiled several inches from her head, and came smashing down across her right cheekbone. Claire's legs buckled and stars filled her head. Somewhere in the dark swirl of the night, she heard a car door open and close and tires screech as the vehicle sped off, leaving her lying on cold concrete and broken glass.

The spinning subsided after a few minutes, replaced by a fierce throbbing on the right side of her face. Her hand went to her right eye, and she cried out in pain. She got to her knees, and finally to her feet, supporting herself against the wall of the warehouse, taking her first steps toward the light. She again began to cry.

Claire walked for what seemed like hours. She hid behind bushes or trees each time a car approached on the dark, quiet streets, worried it would be him, ready to come back to take care of the other eye or worse. She finally saw golden arches in the distance, a McDonalds not too far from her home.

"Your eye!" Sophie said when she saw her. "What happened?"

"A stick at practice," Claire said. "I'm fine."

"Where are your books?" Sophie asked.

She pushed by her aunt and ran up the stairs to her room.

The next morning, she puked next to her bed.

"Jesus," Sophie said.

She left the room and returned with a bucket of soapy water, and bent over the mess.

"Next time, you clean it up," Sophie said, but by then Claire had returned to a dreamless sleep.

It was dark outside when she heard the doorbell.

"Your friends are here," Sophie said from behind a crack in the door. Claire pretended to be asleep.

The next day she could stand without nausea, but it felt like her heart had been moved to her right eye and was pumping there. Claire saw in the mirror that her eye was completely closed and had turned from dark purple to livid shades of red and blue. She went back to bed and stayed there until dinner time, when the smell of cooking meat came to her from downstairs. Claire realized she was famished. She put on a pair of sweat pants and a clean T-shirt, ran a brush through her hair, made her way downstairs and took her place at the table. Jack looked at Claire and shook his head as he passed her the potatoes.

But food made Claire feel better. Back in bed, she replayed what had happened. Getting in his car. Drinking like a fish. Kissing that asshole. She fell asleep and jerked awake, panting, jolted out of a new version of an old dream. Her father taunted her mother in their old living room. But Peterson somehow had found his way into the scene and was putting in his two cents.

"A couple of sluts," Peterson said in the dream.

Claire woke up.

The next morning, the colors from her eye had faded a little and the lid had opened a slit.

"Fuck," Margie said when she saw Claire at school.

"Who did that to you?" Lynette asked.

"I fell," Claire said.

"Bullshit," Margie said. "Tell us."

"Nothing to tell," Claire said.

Peterson stood with the mob, smirking at Claire as she drew closer. He tossed her book bag on the floor into their path. Claire bent to pick it up.

"She's not a spawn," Peterson announced to the others. "She's a prick tease cunt."

A human blur came from behind her. The second figure was a foot shorter than Peterson but went for his knees, yanking them out from under him and toppling his lean frame onto the floor. Larry Cavanaugh pinned Peterson's arms to his sides with his knees and hammered his face, two stiff blows with his left fist and two with the right, until Peterson's buddies intervened and the first nuns arrived to restore order.

"Apologize!" Larry screamed as he was pried away. "Or you'll get some more."

Margie and Lynette pulled Claire off down the hall. Word of Peterson's pounding spread through the school. Larry was suspended for a week. Peterson wasn't punished, but he wasn't at school the next day. When Claire next saw him, he was standing a little apart from the mob, glowering at her with swollen eyes that were roughly the same color as her own.

Claire passed the mob without comment from then on. The day Larry returned to school, he avoided her during English, so Claire waited for him after wrestling practice. He came out of the locker room with two of his teammates.

"Hi," Claire said.

"What happened to your eye?" Larry asked.

Claire approached him, put her hands on his shoulders and kissed his cheek.

"Thank you, Larry," she said.

Chapter 10

They sat near the front of the theater sharing a tub of popcorn and a large Coke. Claire couldn't help comparing Indiana Jones to the boy next to her. Harrison Ford was so dreamy in that hat, with that husky voice and that rakish smile. Larry had popcorn butter on his chin. He wore glasses, his freckles were visible in the light from the screen, and his short red hair was already thinning. But Larry had pummeled Ned Peterson for her. She passed him the Coke and Larry took a long slurp through a straw.

After the movie they shared an order of fries and another Coke at a bowling alley. The next Saturday, they saw the same movie again. The following week it was Arthur, the funny picture about a spoiled rich guy who didn't have to work and was drunk all the time.

Claire laughed so hard she thought she might actually pee her pants. They found their booth at the bowling alley and ordered fries.

"I love to hear you laugh," Larry said.

A few days later, she giggled when Larry stripped off his warm-up suit, revealing the black tights beneath.

"Get him, Larry," she yelled from her seat in the bleachers.

The other guy pinned him in less than a minute.

"Why didn't you tell me you were coming?" Larry asked after the match.

"I wanted it to be a surprise," Claire said.

"You knocked me off my game," Larry said.

"Sorry," Claire said. "But you were cute, anyway."

"I'm not supposed to be cute," Larry said.

A young woman approached her in the stands at the next match.

"You must be Claire," the woman said.

"Yes ma'am," Claire said.

"I'm Bridgett, Larry's older sister. Why don't you sit with us?"

Claire followed Bridgett down several rows and was introduced to two other sisters, Kate and Margaret, both also older, and Larry's mother, Mary, who said, "Larry says such nice things about you." None of them mentioned her eye, which had faded to a light blue, or that she had been the reason for Larry's suspension from school. They all cheered when Larry took the mat. His match was close throughout, and the crowd was on its feet at the end. Larry won a narrow decision, the referee raised his hand, and Claire and Bridgett hugged.

"Why don't you join us for Thanksgiving?" Bridgett asked as they waited for Larry afterward. "That would be OK, wouldn't it mother?"

"If you don't have other plans," Larry's mother said.

"Nothing special," Claire said.

Larry drove her home Thanksgiving night. They sat on a sofa in her living room, holding hands while half-watching an old movie in black and white.

"Your sisters think I'm damaged goods," Claire said.

"Huh?"

"I heard them talking today," Claire said.

"About what?" Larry asked.

"The oldest one, Shannon? And Margaret. They were doing the dishes and didn't think I was around. 'Damaged goods,' was their exact words. They thought that a girl like me was too much for their darling little brother to handle."

"That pisses me off," he said.

"Why? It's the truth."

"It is not."

72

"Come on, Larry. Of course it is. I was on the news, remember. I'm 'seriously fucked up,' as Margie puts it."

Larry released her hand and slid over so he could look at her. He opened his mouth but didn't speak. He looked toward the television.

"At least they think I'm pretty," she said.

"Stop it."

"In a Black Irish sort of way," Claire said. "I am you know, on my father's side. That explains the black hair."

"For Christ's sake," he said.

He stood and paced in front of the sofa. She thought he was about to storm out the door and a big part of her hoped he would. She wanted a cigarette and some booze. It had been weeks. He looked down at her, keeping his voice low so the adults upstairs wouldn't hear.

"That's over with," he said. "In the past."

Claire pushed up from the sofa and faced him, their noses only a few inches apart. Her voice rose. She didn't care if they heard upstairs.

"Are you that clueless?" Claire asked. "Past? What happened that night is with me every day."

She began to cry, which was the last thing Claire wanted to do. He took her in his arms. They stood like that for a long time as she wept on his shoulder.

"I should be with Margie and Lynette, getting drunk at lunch," she said. "If I were you, I would walk out the door right now and not look back."

"I'm not moving," he said. "Not an inch."

"Now you're just being stubborn," Claire said. "We've been friends a month and you haven't asked me a single question about it. Aren't you at least curious?"

"Curious about what?"

"Jesus," she said.

"It's none of my business," Larry said.

Claire pushed away and slumped back on the sofa.

"Right, Larry. In the past. You're just afraid to find out how terrible it actually was, how fucked up I actually am. I don't blame you. Who wants to really know he brought a nut job to Thanksgiving dinner with his family."

"I love you, Claire," Larry said.

His eyes pooled behind his glasses. His words caused a hitch in her breathing. Finally she laughed.

"Didn't see that coming," she said.

"I didn't either," he said. "But it's true."

"You're like talking to a mule."

"That's what my sisters say," Larry said.

"Love me? You haven't even kissed me."

Larry sat down on the sofa, raised his hand toward her face and lowered it. He raised it again to her chin and leaned in. His lips were rigid at first. She was the first to use her tongue.

Larry's mother had the idea. There were spare bedrooms with the older sisters gone, and everyone knew that Claire's living arrangement left something to be desired, that her aunt and uncle had taken her in only because they felt like they had to.

After high school, she got a part-time job as a receptionist at a hospital, and she and Larry both enrolled at the local junior college. Claire took a job at the town library when she graduated and Larry went to work at the auto plant where his father worked. Jack and Sophie were invited but didn't come to the wedding, making up some excuse. Larry's mother and sisters doted on her like a queen after she got pregnant. They named the baby boy Michael, after Larry's father.

In the fall of 1991, Larry lost his job at the auto plant. He was offered a job at a plant in Texas, but it would be that or nothing. The prospect of their departure cast a palpable gloom over Larry's family.

But as Claire started to sort through old boxes, paring things down, a different feeling tingled inside of her. She knew next to nothing about Texas but one thing was certain, no one would know her there. No more stares. No more whispers.

A week before they were to leave, Claire unfolded the top of an old cardboard box. Inside were dog-eared copies of her old Sherlock Holmes mysteries, moth-eaten pajamas and a newspaper, with the big black headlines and a front-page picture of Claire at twelve. There was the glare of flashbulbs as Claire was led away from her home by the lady detective. In the picture, Claire held a teddy bear beneath one arm. At the bottom of the box was the bear itself, its furry exterior paled by years of neglect and dust. Claire had hugged that bear on all those terrible nights, too many to count. Now she picked it up, hugged it again, but it no longer seemed to fit in her arms. She set the bear back in the box, patted its brown head, put the newspaper on top of the books and the clothes, and folded the box shut, like shutting the lid of a coffin. She carried the box to a trash bin near their apartment, paused, and hurled her past inside, atop the beer cans, rotting vegetables, and dirty disposable diapers. She wiped her hands on her jeans and walked away.

Chapter 11

They drove south through leaden skies and large flakes of snow, Larry in the U-Haul, Claire in the Impala with Mike strapped in the back seat. They pulled off the freeway in Kansas City and checked into a Motel 6.

The murk persisted across Oklahoma, but the clouds began to lighten in midday. Claire's pulse skipped when she saw a sign for Gainesville. Just as they crossed the Texas border, the western clouds parted into the most majestic sunset Claire had ever seen, rays piercing the lingering gray, seeming to confirm that this new life, so far from the old, would be just as radiant. They landed in another cheap hotel in Arlington, putting Mike down in the double bed next to his parents. Larry promptly crashed, exhausted from the road. Claire laid next to him, wide awake on their first night in the strange land, tingling at the idea of a place too far for her past to follow.

She met Lucille three days later.

"You're not from here are you, honey?" she had said, looking up at Claire over the top of reading glasses.

"The accent?" Claire asked.

"Let me guess," she said. "Wisconsin."

"Close," Claire said. "Minnesota."

"How long?"

"Just a few days. My husband has a job at the auto plant."

"More Yankee refugees," she said. "Says here that you have experience in libraries. And yes, we do have an opening."

Lucille put her in the racks at first, shelving books, but after a month she was promoted to the information desk. She and Larry found a nice two-bedroom duplex on a shady street, and convenient day care for little

Mike. They got sitters and started going back to the movies, and were invited to join a bowling league with people from Larry's work. They thought about visiting an animal shelter to rescue a mutt. They talked about having another baby. Claire bought Larry tickets to opening day at the Rangers' stadium, and he took a buddy from work. Even the old nightmares were intermittent, one every few weeks at the most.

Claire bought a telephone answering machine that first May because everyone seemed to be getting one. They went for a week without a message. Then Claire saw a blinking red light after work, and she heard a familiar voice when she pressed the button.

"Claire, it's your aunt," Sophie said. "Larry's mother gave me your number. Please call. I have important news."

Claire did not call back. The light was blinking again on the next day, and the next.

"Me again," Sophie said. "We really need to talk."

Claire waited until Mike was tucked in and Larry dozed in front of the baseball game.

"It's me," Claire said when Sophie answered.

"Claire," Sophie said. "I was beginning to worry."

"When have you ever worried about me?"

"I practically raised you, Claire, or have you forgotten?"

"You wouldn't let me," Claire said. "What's the big news?"

"It's about your mother," Sophie said.

"I figured," Claire said.

"She gets out in a few months, or at least she hopes she will," Sophie said. "Parole. Good behavior."

"I'm glad to hear it," Claire said. "Give her my best."

"She's dying to see that grandson of hers," Sophie said.

"Does she know she has one?" Claire asked. "You must have told her. I sure never got the chance."

"Little Mike is what, four now?" Sophie said.

"Just turned three," Claire said.

"Jack and I should send him something."

"Don't bother."

"Claire, I think your mother should come and live with you," Sophie said.

Claire steadied herself against the kitchen counter.

"Pardon me?" she said finally.

"When she gets out."

"That's what I thought you meant," Claire said.

"Jack and I plan on doing some traveling, and I don't think it would be fair to ask him again."

"You mean after what I've already put you through," Claire said.

"That's not what I meant."

"You've got to be joking. Mother? With me?"

"You're her daughter," Sophie said.

"Have you forgotten those trips to the prison when she wouldn't even see me?" Claire said. "All those letters I wrote to her? How many did she answer? Not one. And now you say she should come live with me?"

"God knows you owe it to her," Sophie said.

Claire hung up and unplugged the machine. The phone began ringing a few seconds later.

"Going to get that?" Larry asked from the sofa.

"Somebody trying to sell us something," she said.

"Oh."

She thought about cigarettes and tried to remember if she had any old packs stashed away. No such luck. She climbed into bed and watched the ceiling fan whirl above her in the dark. She finally fell asleep and plunged immediately into a dream. Claire's father and Ned Peterson were there, but this one took place in the living room of Claire's home in Texas. Claire's mother sat next to her on the sofa. Larry was in another chair, behind the sports page.

"If it isn't the best little whorehouse in Texas," her father said.

He and Peterson laughed. Claire woke up.

The next day, the old woman brought her usual stack of romances to the checkout desk and handed her library card to Claire.

"I'm sorry, Claudine," Claire said. "You'll have to take care of your fines first."

"There must be a mistake," Claudine said.

"That's not what it says here," Claire said. "Seventy-five cents."

"I can prove it," Claudine said, opening her purse and starting to dig inside.

"Oh, for Christ's sake, stop it," Claire said. "We go through this every other week."

Claudine took a step back. Claire dug in her own purse and pulled out three quarters.

"Here," she said. "I'll pay your damn fine for you. It's not worth arguing about."

Lucille had come up behind her.

"Claire, why don't you let me help," she said. "I'm sorry Claudine. Everyone has a bad day. We'll let the fine go this time."

"My word," Claudine said.

When Claudine had shuffled away, Lucille nodded toward her office.

"What in God's name?" Lucille said after closing the door.

"I'm sorry," Claire said.

"Are you ill? Did something happen at home? Is little Mike OK? Larry?

"Everything's fine," Claire said.

"Honey, it sure doesn't seem like it," Lucille said. "You're like a different person today."

"I'll apologize next time Claudine comes in."

"There's trouble in that pretty young face of yours," Lucille said. "But I guess everyone's entitled to a bad day."

Chapter 12

The next day, Claire followed her co-worker, Rachel out of the library when it was time for their afternoon break. Rachel lit up a Merit in the shade.

"Could I borrow one of those?" Claire asked.

"Didn't figure you for a smoker," Rachel said. "Kind of a goody two-shoes."

"Just when Lucille isn't looking," Claire said.

Rachel handed her the pack.

"Your secret is safe with me," Rachel said.

The cigarette was wonderful. She lit up another. She chewed Dentyne nonstop for the rest of the day. At home, she changed out of her blouse and brushed her teeth before popping in another stick of gum.

"Your hair smells like cigarettes," Larry said.

"This girl at work smokes like a chimney."

"Oh," Larry said. "Those burgers smell good."

The next afternoon, Rachel found Claire at the reference desk.

"I'm going out," she said.

"No thanks," Claire said.

"Back to goody two-shoes, then?" Rachel asked.

"Got busted last night by my husband," Claire said.

"Heaven forbid," Rachel said. "You know where to find me."

A week later, Claire carried Mike across the parking lot, through the sliding-glass doors, and was met by the bracing blast of cold air from inside the supermarket. She put him into the seat of a shopping cart and pushed it into the store. She picked up pork chops for that night's dinner. A loaf of bread. A gallon of two-percent milk. Frozen packages of hash browns, macaroni and cheese. Vanilla ice cream and chocolate syrup. Toilet paper. Laundry soap. Shampoo. She double-checked her list while they waited in the checkout line. The woman in front of them had half the store piled into her cart, so Claire picked up a magazine and began leafing through it.

Mike spotted the Hershey bars and made a lunge. He would have landed on his head if Claire hadn't caught him at the last second. She bumped the newspaper stand with her hip in the process, sending several copies of the *Fort Worth Star-Telegram* spilling onto the floor.

"Shit," she said.

Claire returned Mike to the cart.

"You sit still," she said.

A young store clerk came up to help with the mess. That's when Claire noticed him smiling out at her from the front page. She looked, and looked again, unable to believe her eyes. She wrote a check for her groceries, loaded the sacks into her car, strapped Mike in and drove off, remembering on the way home that the same paper would be waiting on their front step.

She put saltines in a plastic bowl and sat the boy down in front of Mister Rogers. Their paper was rolled with a rubber band around it. Claire took it inside and closed the bathroom door. She unfurled the paper and saw him, the same thick hair, combed high; the same kind smile; the same pale and delicate skin. First Sophie's bullshit call. Now Van Cliburn appearing out of nowhere.

She slumped down onto the toilet and read the story beside the photograph. It said that every four years, thirty of the world's finest young pianists came to Fort Worth for the Cliburn International Piano

Competition, which was to begin again that week. Cliburn lived in Fort Worth.

The fat blots on the paper were from Claire's tears. She jumped at the knock on the bathroom door.

"You OK in there?" Larry asked.

Claire took a deep breath and rubbed her eyes.

"Fine," she said. "Out in a minute."

"Got home a little early," Larry said. "You seen the paper?"

Claire put her head in her hands.

"I've got it," she said.

"In the bathroom?" Larry asked. "Didn't think girls went in for that sort of thing."

"I'll be right out," she said again.

She flushed the toilet to put him off. He was on the floor with Mike when she came out.

"Your eyes are red," he said.

"Just tired," she said. "Hot dogs OK for supper?"

They tucked Mike in about eight and Larry was dozing in front of the ballgame a half-hour later. Claire paced in their small kitchen, then slipped out the back door and walked down the block and back through the steamy evening. She opened one of Larry's beers and slugged it down, though she had never particularly liked the taste.

She took two more gulps of another beer before pouring the rest down the kitchen drain. She thought of Rachel and her cigarettes. Larry stumbled out of the living room on his way to bed. Claire took his place on the sofa and turned on the television. Van Cliburn's face popped up on the news and she shut it off. She lay down next to Larry about midnight, listening to his snoring, watching the ceiling fan. The next thing she knew, Larry was coaxing her awake.

"Another bad dream," he whispered, stroking her hair.

Claire couldn't remember it, whatever it was.

"OK," she said.

He was snoring again within seconds. Claire's T-shirt and pillow were both damp. Claire got out of bed and walked to the kitchen for a glass of water. She gulped it down and thought again of Rachel and her sublime cigarettes. Claire tiptoed into Mike's room and found him crowded into a corner of his little bed, his thumb in his mouth. She wanted to pluck up his chubby little body and hold him, but Mike stirred as she stood over him, rolling onto his back as if he didn't want to be bothered. He stuck his thumb back into his mouth and dropped back off into a deep sleep.

Claire walked to the living room, falling onto the sofa. She was about to get up and turn on the television, but a vision flooded her brain and she couldn't move. She heard footsteps, her father's voice, her mother's sobbing.

"I'll leave when I'm damn good and ready," her father said. "I'll leave when I get what I came for."

It was like Claire was watching herself in a movie. She saw herself slipping out of her childhood bed, taking the bear along for courage, and cracking her door just enough to see them in the living room. Her dad had his back to her as he walked toward Claire's mother. He tossed a six-pack on the floor. Claire's mother wore her yellow pajamas and her hair down around her shoulders. She tried to fend him off with the piano bench.

"Please, Rory," she cried. "You'll wake Claire."

"Fuck Claire," he said.

Little Mike was at the living room door until his father carried him away. Larry returned, and knelt on the floor next to her, but when he tried to reach out, she slapped him, caught him flush on the cheek with her open hand. Larry grabbed both of her arms.

"Claire, wake up. You're scaring the baby. It's just a dream."

"It's true," Claire sobbed.

"What is?" Larry asked.

"Everything," Claire said.

Larry helped her up onto the sofa and sat next to her, rubbing her shoulder as she quietly whimpered.

"Can you walk?" he asked.

"Walk where?"

"To the bedroom," he said.

"I want to see Mike."

"Let's let him sleep."

"Why?"

"We don't want to upset him any more tonight," Larry said.

He wiped her nose with a tissue and lifted her to her feet. He steadied her as she stumbled to the bedroom.

The alarm went off at seven. Claire heard the gush of the shower and Larry humming, as usual. She hated him then only slightly less than she hated herself. She wanted to be dead. She eventually made it to the kitchen where Larry and Mike were eating cereal. Larry had dressed the boy, combed his hair and packed his bag for day care.

"I thought I could take him today," Larry said.

Larry looked exhausted and worried but didn't mention the weirdness of the night before. Claire was twenty minutes late to work. She followed Rachel out the door at break time, but did not have to bum a cigarette. Claire opened her own pack of Kools.

"I've created a monster," Rachel said.

Claire felt better with the first puff.

"You smell like smoke," Larry said that night.

"There's a reason for that," Claire said.

"Which is?"

"I've been smoking" Claire said.

"Why this all of a sudden?" Larry asked. "You know it's bad for you. It's a horrible example for Mike."

"He doesn't need to know why mommy smells like a chimney," she said. "Sorry to freak you out last night, by the way."

"It was just a bad dream," he said.

"Yeah," she said. "Just a dream."

She smoked more than a pack a day after that. One lunch hour, she went to a store that sold pianos and laughed when she saw the prices.

"Why are you so fucking shaky lately?" Rachel asked one day while they were smoking.

Two-and-a-half crazy weeks after Van Cliburn popped back into the picture, on a Saturday morning, she felt Larry sitting on the side of her bed, his index finger tucking a strand of long black hair behind her ear. He was smiling but looked haggard.

"Why don't we build in the country?" Larry said.

"Build?"

"Our house," Larry said.

"Our house," Claire said.

"We could get a pony for Mike," Larry said. "Some goats to keep the grass down."

"Goats."

"Let's go for a drive. Let's go find our place in the country."

He kissed her on the forehead and disappeared from the bedroom. By the time she got up, Larry was washing cereal bowls. She ate half a piece of toast, buckled Mike into the car seat and got in beside her husband. He drove south out of Arlington, into the country where hills of scorched brown grass rolled off toward the horizon.

"Some place with trees, don't you think?" he asked.

Claire was desperate for a cigarette. Larry found a Golden Oldies station on the radio. They drove into a little town—post office, cafes, drugstore, clothing store, a tavern—weathered buildings of brown brick. There was a blinking red light at the intersection with a larger road, and a green sign with a white arrow pointing toward Dallas. Larry turned that direction onto a road lined with auto body shops and feed stores. A small private road disappeared into a large cluster of trees. By the private road stood a homemade sign that made Claire's heart thunder the moment she saw it.

The letters were stenciled in black against peeling white paint.

"Used pianos for sale," the sign said. "Cheap! Free delivery!"

She read it twice before Larry drove by, thinking her eyes had deceived her.

Chapter 13

So she lied to Lucille and drove back herself. She missed the turn on her drive back, and when she finally found the right road back to Arlington, cars and pickups inched along past orange construction pylons and sweating men in hard-hats who worked hot tar into potholes. "Do you follow Jesus this close?" said the bumper sticker on the van that crept along in front of her. It seemed a question directed specifically to her. Maybe her insanity had been brought on because she and Larry hadn't been to Mass since they had arrived in Texas. That would change. Get me through this horrible day, get me to day care on time, and we'll be in our pew every Sunday. Regular confession. The works.

She pushed in the cigarette lighter and popped another Kool from the nearly empty pack. After two long puffs, she crushed it out in the ashtray.

OK. No more smoking, either.

It was ten after four when she pulled in. She dashed from the car, leaving her purse on the seat and keys in the ignition, tearing open the front door of the place, which smelled of dirty diapers. Miss Dawn was seated behind the front desk and talking on the telephone.

"Never mind, Mr. Cavanaugh," Miss Dawn said, "Here she comes now."

Claire needed a moment to catch her breath.

"I'm so sorry I'm late," she said. "Construction everywhere."

"Your boss at the library said you had gone home at lunchtime, not feeling well," Miss Dawn said. "When you didn't answer, I figured I better call your husband. Are you feeling better?"

"Just now on the phone, what did you tell Larry?" she asked.

"What I told you," Miss Dawn said. "Is that a problem?"

"Of course not," Claire said. "And I am feeling better, thank you."

"Let's go get your little guy."

"Mommy, aren't you listening?" Mike asked from the back seat. "I sing my new song for you."

"Of course I'm listening, sweetheart," she said. "It's wonderful. You're such a good singer."

She started the pork chops and felt her pulse settle as the meat started to sizzle. She was stirring flour into the grease for gravy when she heard the back door open and close. A few seconds later, she felt him standing in the doorway to the kitchen. She glanced up and tried to smile. His freckled face was flushed. Her heart galloped and Claire knew her own face was turning red.

"You shouldn't be cooking if you don't feel well," Larry said, setting his lunch pail down on a counter. "Mike and I can fend for ourselves."

"I'm fine," Claire said.

"Miss Dawn told me you left work at lunch," Larry said.

"I didn't want to worry you," Claire said.

"What was it?" Larry asked.

"Bad cramps, is all," Claire said. "I feel much better now."

"You didn't mention them this morning," Larry said.

"They came on all of a sudden," Claire said.

She turned away from the bubbling gravy.

"What gives, Larry? You don't believe me?"

"You were late getting Mike," Larry said, folding his arms, the red deepening across his freckles. "That might have been reason enough to give me a call."

"I'm sorry," Claire said. "One little mistake and you give me the third degree."

"One little mistake?" Larry said. "You haven't been yourself for three weeks. It's like I woke up one morning next to a different person. Now these so-called cramps and late to day care and no call to me?"

"So you notice then," Claire said.

"Notice what?"

"Me. The way I've been lately. Never would have thought."

"What's that supposed to mean?" he asked.

"You just don't want to know," Claire said. "Never have."

"Know what?"

"God," Claire said.

"You've been out of sorts."

"That's what you call this?" Claire said. "Out of sorts?"

"Now might be a good time to take a week and go back to Minnesota for a visit," Larry said. "Mike would like the train."

She stared at him. A visit to Minnesota. That was his remedy. The gravy was starting to burn.

"Are you going to get that?" Larry asked.

"Get it yourself," Claire said, walking past him toward the bedroom. "Mike's watching TV."

The sound of the slamming door echoed in the house. She stretched out on their bed, watching a whirling ceiling fan. She had never felt so exhausted. She fell asleep.

The duplex smelled of burned food. Her first thought upon waking was of the old man, someone out of a dream. Maybe he was. Maybe Claire imagined the whole thing. Then she remembered the rest. Late to day care. The scene with Larry. A trip to Minnesota. Real. Her life. The ghosts had followed her down the interstate after all, had tracked her down in Texas, and she would have to deal with them, alone. She would cook pork chops, and collect fines because that was her life, until the last little bit of her sanity drifted away from her like smoke from her cigarettes. In the meantime, her mother could go screw herself. Live on the street as far as Claire was concerned. Claire could have kept her out of prison. It was her fault. Tough shit.

She got up and changed into a clean T-shirt and shorts. She combed her hair and brushed her teeth. Mike was on Larry's lap while the two of them watched baseball on television.

"I'm sorry," she said.

"It's OK," he said.

She sat down next to them. Larry put his arm around her.

"I bet Mike would love the train," Claire said.

Chapter 14

He made his way to the information desk, standing over her with his hands clasped behind him. Sweat dotted his white shirt. His bow tie was askew.

"I hope you don't mind me intruding," Wendell said in a voice so soft that Claire could barely hear. "I was troubled by how you left the other day, wondering if there was anything else I could do."

"Jesus," Claire whispered. "How did you find me?"

"You mentioned where you worked," he said. "I can see that I've upset you. I won't take any more of your time."

He turned, keeping his eyes to the carpet as he limped toward the sliding doors and out into the hot noontime. Claire ignored a ringing telephone. She bolted from her chair and jogged toward the door.

"Jesus H. Christ," Rachel said.

Claire didn't notice the blast of Texas summer air as the doors slid open and she ran from the air conditioning, looking first toward the parking lot on the right, then down the street to the left where she saw the old man shuffling down the sidewalk more than a block away. He stopped and dug in his pocket, pulling out his keys to unlock the door of a shiny black pickup. He paused before opening the door, as if he had just remembered something, staring at the pavement by the side of his truck. Claire yelled his name and he turned and looked up the street in her direction. Out of breath at the end of her sprint, she rested her hand on the hood of Wendell's pickup, but recoiled from the searing heat.

"Shit!"

Claire struggled to rein in her breathing. He hadn't moved from the door.

"What in the fuck do you think you're doing?" she asked.

The inside of Wendell's pickup had a clean, piney smell. The fact that the truck was new consoled Claire somehow. He looked over at her every few minutes, but mostly he kept his eyes on a middle-aged couple sitting on a park bench in the shade, feeding bread crumbs to the ducks.

She heard the gentle hum of the pickup's engine and the whisper of the air conditioner set low. The dreadful moment out in the street came back to her, when the world started to spin and a strong arm caught her as she was headed for the pavement. She held a handkerchief, sodden and crumpled, his initials stitched in one corner. Her shoulder strap and seat belt were buckled. Her library ID card dangled from a white shoelace around her neck. Claire slid down in her seat, hysteria reduced to the occasional spasm.

"I should thank you," she said finally.

"Just rest," Wendell said.

"I'd be a puddle in the street if it weren't for you," she said.

"I'm to blame," Wendell said. "If I kept to my own business, you'd still be back at the library, tending to yours."

Claire smiled.

"Maybe they'll give us adjoining rooms in the loony bin," she said. "How long have we been here?"

Wendell's gold watch sparkled on his thick wrist. He had rolled his shirtsleeves to the elbow.

"Twenty minutes, give or take," he said. "It's a quarter of one."

"Where are we?" Claire asked.

"The library's just around the corner."

"You're a dear man," Claire said. "Strange, but dear."

Claire closed her eyes and tilted her head back against the headrest, feeling strangely weightless and peaceful. She must have dozed and was chilled when she opened her eyes. She opened her door and stepped into the midday heat, walking slowly toward the bench near the pond that had been vacated by the middle-aged couple. She slumped there and a half-dozen hungry ducks swam expectantly in her direction, waddling onto the shore at her feet, quacking. She heard the door of the pickup open and close. A few of the ducks headed toward Wendell as he limped toward the bench.

"It's near one o'clock, Claire," he said. "You might want to be getting back."

"Come sit," she said. "The heat feels good, don't you think?"

Wendell waded through the ducks and sat down at the far end of the bench, leaning forward with his elbows on his knees and his hands clasped. Neither spoke for a long time.

"I really could use a cigarette," she said.

"I can't help you there," he said.

"I'm supposed to have quit, anyway."

A cardinal warbled and they looked into the trees to try and find it. A few more minutes passed before Wendell spoke.

"It's your story that brought me here because I knew there was one," he said finally. "Call it nosiness. Concern, maybe. Something wicked was behind your trip out to my place the other day, and behind all those tears just now. Maybe you have someone else to talk to, but that didn't seem to be the case."

Claire's eyes again filled.

"There's no time like the present," she said.

"Beg your pardon?"

"To tell you my story."

"Is there time?"

"I can't hold this anymore," Claire said. "The library will have to wait."

"Missing work might only make things worse."

"I just don't know where to start."

"If your mind's made up," Wendell said, "why don't you start at the beginning."

Chapter 15

Minnesota 1978

The doorbell rang just after Claire and her mother had returned from Mass. Claire beat her mother to the door and found a small old man standing on the front step. He wore a plaid jacket and matching hat pulled down low against the rain. A leather bag was slung over his shoulder.

"Hello, young lady," the man said, tipping his hat when Claire opened the door. "I was looking for a young woman named Elizabeth. I hope I have the right address."

Her mother came up behind her.

"Mr. Fitch!" she cried. "I had no idea you would come so soon."

"At your service," he said, bowing again. A fat raindrop dangled from the brim of his hat.

Claire's mother pulled him inside by his lapels and swept him into a long embrace. He patted her on the back.

"I'm so sorry about Audrey," she said as he held her.

"Thank you," Mr. Fitch said.

"I can't believe she's gone. I feel terrible."

"Hush," Mr. Fitch said. "We'll talk later."

She finally released him.

"You must be Claire," the old man said, turning to her and extending a thick, liver-spotted hand that was freezing cold when Claire shook it. He was no more than a few inches taller than she was. "There's something in here for you, if I'm not mistaken."

He dropped his bag and took out a large brown bear with button eyes and a red ribbon around its neck. He held it toward Claire.

"Your manners, Claire," her mother said.

"Thank you, sir," Claire said.

"You're more than welcome, my dear," Mr. Fitch said, bowing again. "I'm delighted to find that you favor your mother."

"Do you think so, Mr. Fitch?" Elizabeth said.

"Very beautiful this child is, even if her mother is much too thin. You look tired, my dear."

"Just older," she said. "It's been so long."

"So it has," he said. "But what a fine reunion, you and your gorgeous child and this old man."

"I'll make you some tea with lemon, like you used to take it," Claire's mother said as he took off his damp hat and coat. "It's a dreadful day."

"First things first, Elizabeth," he said. "So where is this dinosaur you told me about?"

"Please call me Lizzie, like before," she said.

He spotted the piano himself and lifted the leather bag.

"Eleven years, you say," he said.

"Almost to the day," Elizabeth said. "Claire will be twelve next spring."

Mr. Fitch walked to the piano, lifted the cover and struck a soft note.

"Is your homework done?" her mother asked Claire.

"Yes, mother," Claire said.

"Then read," she said. "Mr. Fitch has work to do. Then he and I need some time to catch up."

Through the door of her room, Claire heard Mr. Fitch tinkering at the piano, and when the tinkering stopped, there were bursts of shared laughter from the dining room table. She had never heard her mother laugh that way. Claire tried to listen through the door but caught only snippets, nothing to explain why this stranger appeared out of the autumn mist to transform her mother.

The laughter finally stopped.

"Come say goodbye," her mother told Claire through the door.

Mr. Fitch was again dressed for the weather when Claire came out of her room. Elizabeth pulled a crumpled twenty-dollar bill from a coffee mug in a kitchen cupboard.

"Don't be silly," he said, and they hugged again.

Tears had left jagged trails in the makeup Claire's mother had put on that morning for church.

"To know you are playing again is payment enough," Mr. Fitch said. "And you young lady, you must, too. The music is in your blood."

"Thank you, Mr. Fitch," Claire said, holding the bear.

"You're welcome, my dear."

He pulled his collar up against the cold.

"Call me again in a few weeks, Lizzie," Mr. Fitch said. "It will need an adjustment. Greet your husband for me. So sorry that I missed him."

"How can you ever forgive me?" Elizabeth asked. "How can Audrey?"

"Just don't be such a stranger," he said.

"I won't."

"You sure you're well?" he asked.

"Positive," Claire's mother said.

"Well then," he said, and slipped out the door.

Claire's mother stood at the window looking after the old man as he disappeared into the afternoon mist.

Claire's father showed up one afternoon six months later wearing assembly line coveralls and gold-rimmed sunglasses with mirror lenses. He threw open his arms when she stepped down from the school bus.

"Doll," he said, grinning.

"Hi, daddy," Claire said.

"How about a hug for your old man?"

He held Claire tightly to his chest, smelling like sweat, Brut deodorant and stale beer. He kissed her loudly on the cheek.

"Surprised?" he asked.

"Did something happen?"

"Why would you say that?"

"You haven't been home since Saturday."

"I'll be home more often."

"Where do you stay?"

"Never you mind."

"Why aren't you working?" Claire said.

"So many questions. Can't a guy buy his favorite girl an ice cream cone?"

"Mom will worry."

"I've talked to her," he said. "She says go ahead. "

"She did?"

"Would I lie to you?"

"I guess not."

As they walked, their breath poured out in clouds on the cold, rainy spring day. He hummed a country-western song, a tall, thin man with dark sideburns. Like a young Elvis. His black hair shone from the April mist as he opened the heavy glass door of the ice cream shop.

"Vanilla or chocolate?" he asked.

"Chocolate, I guess."

"Chocolate it is."

He handed Claire a huge cone, and took a Styrofoam cup of coffee to a corner booth.

"Don't make a mess," her father said.

"Yes, daddy," Claire said, licking desperately.

He blew on his steaming coffee and slurped loudly, looking out the window into the dark day, still wearing his sunglasses. He took another loud sip of his coffee and smiled at her.

"So, what's your favorite subject in school?" he asked.

Claire had a mouth full of ice cream.

"English," she said after swallowing. "Sister Rosalie says I'm one of the best readers."

"No kidding. What do you read?"

"Sherlock Holmes," Claire said. "They're scary sometimes, but exciting. I'd like to visit London someday."

He finished his coffee with a loud slurp.

"What's your worst class?" he asked. "Let me guess. Math."

Claire hesitated.

"Catechism," she said.

"That's a new one," he said.

"The teacher is so old and mean," she said. "Yesterday she slapped Billy O'Malley across the face for throwing spitballs. Tommy Briggs was the one who threw them, but Billy didn't squeal."

"Good for Billy," her father said. "If it's one thing I can't stand it's a squealer. You never squeal, do you Claire?"

"No."

"Good," he said.

Claire was relieved to finish her ice cream. He pulled a pack of Kools from his breast pocket, tapped one from the pack, and lit it with a disposable lighter, blowing a cloud of smoke toward the ceiling through one side of his mouth. He leaned toward Claire. The smell of stale beer fouled the air between them. She saw her reflection in his glasses—dark hair spilling out from beneath a red stocking cap, a red scarf still around her neck. He lowered his voice.

"There's something I've been meaning to ask you," he said.

He took another long pull on his cigarette, looking back out the window, blowing smoke out through his nostrils. Two kids whizzed by on bikes.

"Anybody else been spending time at the house while I'm not around?"

"Anybody else?"

"Yeah," he said. "Anybody?"

"I guess so," she said.

"Who?" he asked.

"Aunt Sophie and Uncle Jack come over sometimes," Claire said. "They didn't use to."

"Besides Sophie and Jack. I mean like another man."

"An old man," she said. "Mr. Fitch."

"Huh? His wife used to teach your mom piano," he said.

"He works on it," Claire said.

"He what?"

"He tunes our piano."

"That worthless pile of boards? Why? Nobody else, though?" he asked. "Say, at night after you're in bed?"

"No, daddy."

"When you come home from school?"

"No."

He leaned back and turned again toward the window, which had begun to fog at the bottom. His stabbed his cigarette out and lit another.

"Your mother's different lately," he said, speaking to the window. "Why is that?"

He took off his glasses, revealing a large purple welt, yellowed in the middle, which bulged beneath his left eye.

"An accident at work," he said. "Now tell me."

"Tell you what, daddy?"

"Christ! Are you listening? Or are you just stupid," he said.

Her eyes burned.

"Tell me."

"Her music," she said.

"Music?"

"She plays piano like an angel."

"And how would you know?"

Claire was too afraid to answer.

"She's playing the piano again?"

"Yes."

"For how long?"

"Since last year," Claire said. "Before it snowed."

"Jesus H. Christ. Where does she find the time?"

"Every day," she said.

"That explains Mr. Fitch."

"Maybe," Claire said.

Tears crowded back into Claire's eyes and trickled down her cheeks.

"We need to go," he said.

"Thanks for the ice cream, daddy."

He was already out of the booth.

"The fucking piano."

Claire had to run to keep up with him. Her father knelt at the bus stop.

"Don't tell your mother about any of this, you hear?" he said. "Don't say you've seen me at all."

"You said…"

"You don't squeal, isn't that right, Claire?" he said. "Get on home."

She watched the dented Ford screech away. Claire ran home through the damp and found her mother waiting.

"My God," she said, hugging her in the doorway. "I've called everywhere, to the school, to Karen's house. I was about to call the police. You've never done this before."

"I went over to Ruth's house, Ruth Schmidt's," she said.

"Never again, Claire! I was worried sick. You're all I've got, don't you understand that?"

"I'm sorry mama," Claire said.

She was about to tell the truth about her father's visit when her mother spoke again.

"It's OK, my love," she said. "Just never again."

Chapter 16

Claire slid down the bench. Wendell laid an arm lightly around her shoulders. He smelled of starch and aftershave.

A young mother and her little girl came up from behind them to feed bread crumbs to the ducks. From the edge of the water, the mother stole glances at them.

"It's after two," Wendell said.

"I don't care," Claire said.

"I don't want to cause worse trouble," he said.

"You didn't cause anything," Claire said. "Can you believe my dad?" She lifted her head.

"Buying me a bloody ice cream cone, then the interrogation. And then my mother at home. 'You're all I've got.' Sometimes I think they were made for each other. I guess we should go."

Claire wrapped both hands around Wendell's arm as they stood. It was surprisingly muscled for a guy his age. Wendell opened and closed Claire's door, then walked around the front of his pickup and climbed behind the wheel.

"There's more," Claire said. "A lot more."

"I figured," Wendell said as he slowly pulled away from the curb.

"Will you listen?"

"I'm listening already."

"You can't abandon me now," she said.

"I won't," Wendell said.

He stopped outside the library and reached across Claire into the glove compartment, fishing out a dull yellow pencil and an old receipt. His hands trembled as he placed the receipt on the dashboard. He could barely scribble out seven numbers because of the tremors.

"Call anytime," he said, handing her the piece of paper. "I don't sleep much anymore."

She put the receipt into her purse and checked her makeup in the rear-view mirror.

"Adjoining rooms in the loony bin," she said, trying to smile but again close to tears.

"Neighbors for sure," Wendell said.

Claire ran up the steps. She turned and waved, then hurried through the sliding doors.

"I covered for you," Rachel said. "Told Lucille you had a long errand to run. But you are weird."

That night, with Mike in bed and Larry snoring in front of a baseball game, Claire sat at the dining room table and rummaged through her purse. She finally dumped it onto the table—plastic coin holder, lip gloss, brush, small mirror, nail file, a small tin of Tylenol, old Kleenex, a book of matches, a single stick of Dentyne. She picked through the clutter until she found the receipt with the numbers written in Wendell's palsied hand.

Claire refilled her purse and looked in on Larry. She dialed the number from the telephone next to her bed, counting fifteen rings before she hung up the first time, and ten more when she dialed his number a few minutes later. She put the number into a drawer near her bed and sprawled out across the mattress.

Larry stumbled into bed at eleven, kissed her, and was snoring again within minutes. Four sleepless hours later, Claire slid out of bed and tiptoed into the kitchen. She had his number memorized by then. Wendell answered on the second ring.

"I've been calling," Claire whispered. "I was getting worried."

"I've been out," Wendell said.

"This girl I work with lied for me," Claire said.

"That's rarely a good thing."

"Rachel probably thought I had been kidnapped by this handsome old man in the bow tie."

Wendell kept silent.

"You still there?" she asked.

"Don't have many places to go at three in the morning," Wendell said.

"Are you a kidnapper?"

"I am many things," Wendell said. "A kidnapper isn't one of them."

"Nut job, then. Just like me."

"That's closer to the truth."

For several seconds there was silence.

"Maybe we should say goodnight," Wendell said.

"When I came out to your place the other day, I was late getting to day care, and they called my husband at work. He was wondering why I was late."

"So you told him," Wendell said.

"No," Claire said. "Not about today, either. The whole piano business has been my little secret. I know. I'm a complete whack job."

"You're not," Wendell said.

"Yes, I am."

"You are a delightful young woman."

"You say that now. You haven't heard the rest of my story."

"But keeping things from your husband?" Wendell said. "I guess it's none of my business."

"He doesn't want to know," Claire said. "Never has. I can't blame him."

She took a deep breath.

"Come to supper tomorrow night," she said.

"Beg your pardon?"

"Unless you have other plans," Claire said. "Or maybe it's just a bad idea."

"Supper with you would be fine," Wendell said.

"Really?"

"What time would you like me?"

Chapter 17

Claire diced fresh strawberries, dumped them into two heaping bowls of Wheaties and put them in front of Larry and Mike.

"Strawberries," Larry said. "What's the occasion?"

"No occasion," she said.

"Daddy's loved strawberries from the time he was your age," Larry said to Mike.

"I thought I'd cook a roast tonight."

"Jesus," Larry said. "You've already won wife of the year."

"You're sweet," Claire said.

"But on a work night? Sunday would give you more time in the kitchen."

"I don't mind," Claire said.

"And it's damn hot outside to be running the oven," Larry said. "The AC runs nonstop as it is."

She took a sip of juice and a deep breath.

"I was hoping to invite a friend," she said.

"Tonight?"

"If you don't mind," Claire said.

"Who?" Larry asked.

"A lonely old man."

He looked up from his cereal.

"Say again."

"A widower who comes into the library," she said.

"A widower from the library," Larry said.

"You'd like him," she said.

"First time we've had company over since we've been down here and it's an old stray from work?"

"I wouldn't put it like that," she said.

Anger replaced her guilt.

"Just forget it," Claire said.

She got up and left the table. Larry followed her into the bedroom.

"Hell, honey," he said. "If it's that important to you. I just don't understand....Well, anyway."

"You'll like him," Claire said.

"You said that already," Larry said.

"His name is Wendell."

Claire had thawed the roast overnight. Before she left for work, she slathered the meat with horseradish, and cut carrots and onions into the pan, setting it in the refrigerator. That afternoon, back from day care with Mike, she set the meat in the oven and put on a light blue sundress. She pulled her hair back.

"Look at you, all dressed up," Larry said when he got home. "Should I put on a tie?"

"Slacks would be nice," she said.

He came out after his shower wearing khakis and a button-down shirt.

"You look very nice," she said. "Thank you."

He grabbed a beer from the refrigerator, took it to the living room and opened the sports page. Claire looked at her watch and at the clock on the oven five minutes later. She put water on to boil the potatoes. She checked her watch. She took the roast from the oven and put in a tray of buns to bake. She checked her watch.

The doorbell rang at exactly half past six. Claire nearly dumped a full pan of boiled potatoes.

Claire beat Larry to the door. Wendell stood out front holding three yellow roses. Claire opened the door.

"Right on time," she said. "Come in."

"I've never understood what was fashionable about being late," Wendell said.

"These are my boys, Larry and Mike. This is Mr. Wendell Smith."

Larry was a head shorter. He shook Wendell's hand.

"Welcome to our humble abode," Larry said.

"From our garden," Wendell said, handing Claire the roses.

"They're lovely," Claire said, hugging Wendell with one arm.

Wendell bent to Mike, who hugged his father's leg.

"Hello young man," he said. "Something smells awfully good in here."

"How about a beer," Larry said. "Bud OK?"

"I've got lemonade," Claire said.

"A beer would be fine," Wendell said.

"I'll get it. You guys make yourself comfortable," Claire said. "Supper's almost ready."

Claire hurried off into the kitchen, returning with a can of beer for Wendell and a fresh one for Larry. She took away Larry's empty. Wendell sat on the sofa. Larry took the recliner and Mike crawled up into his father's lap. Claire returned to the kitchen to mash the potatoes, straining to hear what was said in the next room.

"Claire said your wife just passed," Larry said. "Sorry to hear it."

"Last fall," Wendell said. "It started as breast cancer."

"A damn shame," Larry said.

Larry belched from the beer.

"Excuse me," he said. "Sounds like you're quite the reader."

"A reader?" Wendell said.

"A regular at the library," Larry said.

Claire froze over the potatoes.

"Not sure I'd say a regular," Wendell said. "It's a nice cool place in the summer."

"Claire said you two have gotten to be buddies," Larry said.

"Nice that she would think so," Wendell said.

"I figured she'd be too busy to make friends at the library," Larry said.

There was silence for several seconds.

"I ask a lot of questions," Wendell finally said. "She tries to humor me."

Claire dashed for the living room.

"Wendell, why don't you take a seat at the table," she said. "Larry, could you cut the meat? Supper is about ready."

Wendell's roses sat on the table in a long vase next to burning candles. Larry put Mike in his booster seat and led them in the Catholic blessing. They filled their plates with beef, potatoes and gravy, corn, squash and fresh rolls. Little Mike continued to stare at the stranger with the shaking hands.

"Claire, you've outdone yourself," Larry said.

"Mighty fine," Wendell said.

"Larry's mother taught me this recipe," Claire said.

"You ought to taste her pork chops," Larry said. "So what part of Arlington are you from?"

"Actually, I live in a little place to the south called Bisbee," Wendell said.

"Don't they have a library in Bisbee?" Larry asked.

Wendell paused and cleared his throat.

"No," he said.

"Can you get a library card here?" Larry asked. "Being from out of town?"

"You can if your town doesn't have a library," Claire lied.

"Handy," Larry said. "Bisbee. That sounds familiar. Have we been there, Claire?"

Claire dabbed at her lips with a napkin.

"Maybe," she said, helping Mike with a spoonful of mashed potatoes. "On one of our drives."

"We've been out in the country lately," Larry said. "Driving here and there. I think it would be nice to have a house there. I'd like to build our own place."

"I might be able to help you," Wendell said.

"How's that?" Larry said.

"My family's been in the lumber business for seventy years," he said.

"You don't say," Larry said.

"I'm retired, but I can get you a good price on materials and carpenters you can trust."

"I'll be goddamned," Larry said.

"Larry, your language. Little ears," Claire said, but for the first time that day she felt herself relax.

"Get this man another beer," Larry said.

Soapy water drained from the kitchen sink. Wendell leaned against the counter, a damp dishtowel over his shoulder. Claire had shooed Larry out of the kitchen, telling him to go watch the ballgame. She put Mike to bed before she and Wendell cleared the table and did the dishes. It wasn't long before she heard Larry's snoring, like clockwork. All was going according to plan. Claire brewed decaffeinated coffee.

"You've got a beautiful family," Wendell said.

"I'm very lucky."

"Larry is a fine fellow," Wendell said.

"Good as gold," Claire said.

"This isn't right," Wendell said.

"It needs to be this way for now."

"You sound certain about that."

"Could you tell Selma everything, Wendell? There must have been things that you saved for the priest, so to speak."

Wendell turned abruptly, folding the towel on the counter.

"Well, did you?" she asked. "Good listener, you say, but did you?"

"No, I didn't tell her everything," he said finally.

"And why was that?"

"I should be going," Wendell said. "It was a nice evening."

"Oh no you don't," she said.

Claire led him to the dining room table. The candles had burned down to stubs.

"Sit down, Father Smith. Larry will be out for a while."

"I need to…" Wendell said.

"Listen," she said. "You need to listen."

Chapter 18

Minnesota 1979

Mr. Fitch was the first to arrive. His black shoes were freshly shined. Claire wore a new yellow dress, bought with her mother the day before.

"You are a vision," he said.

"Thank you," Claire said.

"A surprise, your mother said."

"Sorry," Claire said. "I promised not to tell."

She led him to her father's recliner. The sun was nearly down, and the room was dark except for candles that Claire's mother had lit here and there, and a small lamp on the piano.

"Your seat," Claire said.

"And this mysterious mother of yours?"

Claire laughed and skipped away to the door of her parents' bedroom. Inside Elizabeth Calhoun was shoeless, dressed in a white slip and dark brown nylon stockings. She paced with a cigarette between her fingers. She wore her long dark hair in braids, which Claire had never seen, tucked into a roll behind her head. There was fresh red lipstick, a hint of color on her cheeks, blue on her eyelids.

"Mr. Fitch is here," Claire said.

The doorbell rang again.

"Sophie and Jack are on time for once," Claire's mother said, crushing out her cigarette next to four or five other butts. "Come back when they're ready."

Jack and Sophie followed Claire to the sofa.

"Do you remember Mr. Fitch?" Claire asked, following her mother's instructions.

"It's so good to see you again, Leonard," Sophie said. "Has it been since Audrey's funeral?"

"Too long," Mr. Fitch said. "Jack, how are things in the insurance business?"

"Keeps a roof over our heads," Claire's uncle said.

Claire returned to her mother, the eyes of their guests following her.

"They're ready," Claire said.

Elizabeth had put on a sleeveless black dress that fell just below the knee.

"Do you remember what to say?"

"Yes, mother," Claire said.

"Go."

Claire slipped from the room and walked to the piano.

"Ladies and gentleman," Claire said. "I present to you, Elizabeth Calhoun, playing Rachmaninoff's First Sonata for piano in D minor."

The bedroom door opened and Claire's mother strode into the room.

"My God, Lizzie," Sophie said.

Claire sat at the end of the sofa next to Sophie. Jack joined the clapping when Sophie elbowed him. Elizabeth walked to the piano, turned and bowed deeply. She sat on the piano bench and pulled it closer to the keyboard. Her slim, beautiful back was straight as a ruler, head erect, hands motionless on her lap, still as a statue. She brushed the keys with her fingertips, as if dusting them. She lowered her head, and with her left hand played the first soft notes of a performance that went on for twenty minutes. The music was quiet and tender one minute, loud and angry the next. During the softest parts, Elizabeth again lowered her face to within inches of the keyboard, caressing the keys more than playing them. Then her fingers raced up and down, pounding the notes, until the music built one last time, and she hit the closing chord, pulling her fingers away as if the keys were suddenly hot. Her small audience stood and clapped, then rushed to embrace her. She collapsed against Mr. Fitch and began to sob.

Elizabeth pulled a shawl around her shoulders as they took turns praising her. Sophie hurried back and forth between the dining room table and the kitchen, clearing away plates and coffee cups. Claire sat across from Mr. Fitch.

"What got you playing again, my dear?" Mr. Fitch asked.

Elizabeth looked out the open window into the spring night. The flame of a candle danced on the table in the soft breeze.

"But you know," she replied.

"I have my suspicions," he said.

"Audrey," Claire's mother said. "When you called and told me she had died."

"I guessed as much," Mr. Fitch said.

"I hadn't even known she was sick, which made it worse," Elizabeth said.

She looked at Claire.

"None of this makes sense," Elizabeth said.

"Not really," Claire said.

"Claire has been my little angel these last months," her mother said. "My audience of one. But there are so many things you don't know."

Sophie came in from the kitchen.

"She doesn't need to know," she said.

"Know what?" Claire asked.

"About your grandfather, for starters," Elizabeth said.

"Christ help us," Sophie said.

"He was gone before my first birthday," Elizabeth said. "Sophie was older. She actually remembers him."

"Nothing to remember," Sophie said.

"I got his dark skin and hair. So did you, Claire," Elizabeth said.

Elizabeth took a long drag from her cigarette.

"Anyway. So daddy takes off," she said. "Nobody knew where. Several years later, mother is killed on a motorcycle. I went to live with Sophie and Jack, though they were just newlyweds at the time, and the last thing they wanted was a snot-nosed kid to take care of. I was seven. Are you following, Claire?"

She nodded.

"And who should live just across the street," Elizabeth touched the hands of Mr. Fitch, "but this lovely man and his equally lovely wife, the piano teacher who took the poor orphan girl under her wing."

"The girl with the amazing gift," Mr. Fitch said.

"She always said so, didn't she," Elizabeth said.

"She did," Mr. Fitch said.

He chuckled, looking at Claire.

"Other girls your mother's age were in love with Elvis Presley. But this one? She cut out news stories of Van Cliburn and taped them to the wall above her bed. I still remember the headline: 'American wins in Moscow.' And the photograph of that Texas boy and Khrushchev."

"Lord, I had almost forgotten," Sophie said. "Van Cliburn."

"Who?" Claire asked.

Elizabeth stubbed out her cigarette, walked to the living room, opened up the piano bench and grabbed two magazines from the stack of sheet music. She put old copies of *Time* and *Life* in front of Claire. On the covers of both was a tall young man at the piano.

"This boy came from a small town in Texas," Elizabeth said. "Out of nowhere he goes to Russia and wins their most important piano competition, playing Russian music, no less, their best-loved composers, Tchaikovsky and Rachmaninoff. The next day, he was on the front page of every newspaper in the world. There he stood next to Nikita Khrushchev, their leader. This was a time when everyone thought

Russian missiles would fly in our direction any second. That seemed a lot less likely after Van won in Russia."

Mr. Fitch shook his head at the memory.

"They gave him a ticker-tape parade in New York City," he said. "Hard to imagine a pianist that popular these days."

"I was thirteen," Elizabeth said. "Mrs. Fitch started playing Van's recordings when I had finished my lessons. I begged her to teach me his music. She finally gave in. I wrote Van a letter once and he wrote me back. Before you know it, I got a scholarship to a famous music camp called Interlochen."

Claire's mother tugged the shawl closer.

"Then I disappeared, didn't I, Leonard," Elizabeth said. "After everything you had done. Then years later you call to say she had died. Was I thinking she was going to live forever?"

"She was only sixty-six, Lizzie," Mr. Fitch said. "You couldn't have known."

"Of course I could have."

She lit another cigarette. Twin streams of smoke again poured out of her nostrils.

"It was criminal."

"You did what you needed to do," Mr. Fitch said.

"No," Jack said. "She could have sent me after Rory Calhoun with a two-by-four. Rory Calhoun, for Christ sakes."

"Stop it, Jack!" Sophie said. "That's Claire's father."

"Where is he tonight, by the way?" Jack asked.

"Working late, like I said," Claire's mother said.

"Right," Jack said.

"So you began to practice," Mr. Fitch said, steering talk in a different direction.

"When you called about Audrey, it took a week for me to get the nerve to start playing," Claire's mother said. "But yes."

"What now?" Mr. Fitch asked. "Carnegie Hall?"

A faulty muffler puttered into the driveway and the sound died. Jack and Sophie exchanged glances and Mr. Fitch looked from one face to the other. Claire's mother stared at the ashtray and tugged at the shawl.

"Of all the nights," Elizabeth whispered.

The front door opened, the floor creaked, and Claire's father appeared at the doorway holding a hard-hat in one hand and a six-pack of Budweiser in the other. Claire hadn't seen him since the afternoon at her bus stop a week before.

"Jesus Christ," he said.

"Jack, let's leave," Sophie said.

She patted her sister on the back.

"It was a lovely evening, Liz. Let's do it again soon."

"Oh, let's," Claire's father said. He touched the braids on his wife's head. "What the fuck have you done to your hair?"

Jack stood and slowly put on his jacket, glaring at Claire's father, who blocked the doorway. The two men faced each other.

"Haven't changed, Rory," Jack said. "Still the charmer."

"Feeling a little left out, is all," he said, smiling.

"Excuse us," Jack said.

Rory shuffled to his left. Jack and Sophie passed without a word, walking through the living room and out the front door. Mr. Fitch rose.

"I'm Leonard Fitch, Mr. Calhoun," he said, hand extended.

"I know who you are," her father said, ignoring the extended hand.

"Could you mind your manners, for once," Claire's mother said.

"Shut up!"

The old man blushed and turned to Claire's mother. They embraced, but quickly, and didn't speak.

"Goodnight, Claire," Mr. Fitch said, and walked past Rory.

The front door opened and closed. Claire's father put the beer in the refrigerator. He tossed his hard-hat on the kitchen table, and it slid toward Claire, spinning and rocking.

"You two look like a couple of expensive streetwalkers," he said.

"Claire, it's time for bed," her mother said. "I'll be in to say goodnight."

"Yes, mother," Claire said, rising from the table.

"No goodnight kiss?"

He grabbed Claire's arm and kissed her loudly on the lips.

"Sweet dreams, honey."

Claire ran to her bedroom. She grabbed her bear and slid beneath the covers, still in her dress. Claire buried her head beneath her pillow, trying to separate herself from the ugliness about to take place outside. Curiosity got the better of her fear. She lifted the pillow.

"I spoiled your little party," her father said.

"I played for them," she said. "It was like the last twelve years had never happened, and I can't tell you how many nights I've wished that were true."

"You ungrateful bitch," he said. "I oughta throw your skinny ass out in the street. Then who would pay your bills, buy your food, your fancy dresses that make you both look like whores."

"You'd be doing me a favor," she said.

"Then you'd just run off to your boyfriend," Claire's father said, "you good-for-nothing slut. I know you're off screwing somebody else, and when I find out who it is, he's dead."

Elizabeth began to laugh.

"My boyfriend," she said. "As good as dead."

"Try me," he yelled.

Claire heard a magazine drop to the living room floor.

"Have at him."

"It's an old fucking magazine," he said.

"Not the magazine," she said. "The boy on the cover."

"You're crazy."

"Van Cliburn. My lover."

"You're out of your fucking mind."

"You're nothing but a worthless drunk. Claire answers the phone when your barflies call here for you. Did you know that? And the day you tell her to lie to me again is the day we're both gone. Understand me?"

"The little shit squealed after all."

"I'm telling you Rory," she said.

"Just try and leave," he said.

The front door slammed, and the muffler roared back to life in the driveway, the sound fading as he sped off down the street. Her mother stayed up smoking. Claire didn't sleep. Not long before the sun came up, her father's car puttered back into the driveway, the door opened, and she heard quieter voices this time, coming through the wall from her parents' room. In a few minutes, Claire heard groans, and thought for a moment he was hurting her, but then their headboard began to pound against the wall.

He was gone when she got up. Her mother stayed in bed for the rest of the weekend and was still there on Monday morning when Claire ate a bowl of Cheerios and walked to the bus stop for school.

Chapter 19

Wendell had seemed agitated when he first sat down, but when she resumed her story, his gaze never wavered. He listened with his hands clasped in front of him on the table. His watch glinted in what was left of the candles. Larry's snoring lightened.

"She never came in to say goodnight," Claire said. "Funny how that has stuck with me. Her out there smoking all night, you'd think I might have occurred to her in there somewhere. Just fighting with him, and smoking, and then that business in the next room."

"A little girl all alone," Wendell said.

"I looked up Interlochen the other day," Claire said. "The place my mother talked about. It's a very famous summer camp for music. Only the best get to go. That means..."

"Don't blame yourself," Wendell said.

"But instead of Interlochen, or Carnegie Hall, she gets knocked up."

"I said don't," Wendell said.

Claire smiled.

"But I got her back good," she said. "I guess that's for another time. Or has my nuttiness scared you off, too?"

"It's not nuttiness," Wendell said. "It's an abomination."

"Such a big word," she said. "One of Selma's?"

"Likely."

"It gets worse."

He looked away.

"Thank you for dinner," he said.

"So I have creeped you out."

"It's just hard to find words," Wendell said.

"But Selma always had the right words for you," Claire said.

"Even she..."

"What?"

"Nothing," Wendell said.

"You are a wonderful listener," Claire said. "A wonderful priest."

Larry coughed in the next room and resumed snoring.

"Let's let him sleep," she said. "I'll tell him you said goodbye. He'll want to talk to you about our house in the country."

"Any time he's ready."

Claire took his hand as they walked through the grass toward his pickup. There was a hot breeze, stars and a half-moon. The night buzzed with cicadas.

"Drip, drip, drip," Claire said when they stood by his truck.

"Beg your pardon?" Wendell asked.

"My story," she said. "Out it comes, drip, drip, drip. I should just skip to the end. But as long as I have it to tell, I have a reason to see you."

"You never need a reason," he said.

"You feel like my best friend," she said.

He looked down at her in the darkness. A car drove slowly by. Claire raised Wendell's hand to her lips and kissed it. She dropped his hand and put her arms around his waist. He gently separated himself.

"I need to be going," he said.

"My priest has a long drive home," Claire said.

"Not your priest," he said. "Your friend."

"That you are," Claire said.

She watched the pickup's taillights disappear down the street.

Chapter 20

On the fateful day when it all changed, when it all went to shit, Francis had finished the loading and rumbled next door to pick him up. They had just chugged back through the front gate when Francis saw the car coming down the road through the trees from the other direction.

"Expecting somebody?" Francis asked.

"Who would I be expecting?" Wendell replied.

Francis stopped in front of the car. A dark-haired young woman sat behind the wheel looking up at them.

"I'll just be a minute," Wendell said.

He jumped down and limped over to her window. They talked for a minutes. Francis checked his Timex.

"She's looking for a piano," Wendell said when he was back in the cab.

"Don't tell me," Francis said.

"Selma's damn sign," Wendell said.

"Everyone around here…"

"She's not from around here," Wendell said. "Arlington."

"Of all the foolish things," Francis said.

"I'm going to invite her back for something cold to drink."

"You're pulling my leg," Francis said.

"All the way from Arlington," Wendell said. "That damn sign."

He limped back to the car. The girl said something and nodded. Wendell climbed back into the cab.

"Back up," Wendell said. "She'll follow us. You could probably use a drink yourself."

"We've got work to do," Francis said.

"Sorry," Wendell said. "I can't help you today."

But that wasn't the shocking part—surprising and damn aggravating, but not shocking. Francis inched back through the trees to the house. Wendell jumped out to help her from the car. He brought the woman, who turned out to be not much more than a girl, around to Francis' side of the truck.

"This is Claire," Wendell said when Francis rolled down his window.

Francis looked once, then twice. Selma stood below him, a young Selma, the one that tutored him after school, the Selma who sat in Wendell's pickup that bizarre morning in 1946. This girl could have been her twin.

"Howdy," Francis said, though he could hardly get out the word.

"You going to join us or not?" Wendell asked.

"Some folks still have work to do," Francis said.

He put the truck into gear and rumbled off through the trees, stopping before he got to the main road. Grief washed over him. Then fear. Francis thought about driving back to the house to take one more look, make sure his eyes were not playing tricks. But he had a big load on his truck, and he was late. And it was a hallucination. Had to be.

Francis finished work at five and drove back to Wendell's. He was not waiting on the porch swing, as usual. Francis found him inside, sitting in his wicker chair, staring out the window into the long shadows of early evening. Francis turned on a lamp.

"What's keeping you?" Francis asked.

"You go on," Wendell said. "I'm not hungry."

"Since when," Francis said.

"I need a favor," Wendell said.

"I don't do favors on an empty stomach," Francis said. "Let's get on over to Lilly's."

"Tomorrow, I want you or one of the boys to take that piano sign down and haul it off to the dump."

"What's the goddamn rush?"

"Don't want any more visitors."

"You mean like that girl today."

"She came all the way from Arlington."

"So you said," Francis said. "Foolish, if you ask me."

"No one's asking you."

"That was Selma's sign," Francis said.

Wendell stood.

"It needs to come down," he said. "You won't do it, I will. Like I said, I'm not hungry. You go on."

Wendell walked down the hall and up the stairs. Francis heard the door to his bedroom open and close. He thought about following Wendell and giving him a piece of his mind. Instead, he drove off to Lilly's and sat alone at the corner table where he and Wendell had taken almost every evening meal for the past six months.

"Where's your sidekick tonight?" Lilly asked.

"Wendell's a little under the weather," Francis said.

"I hope it's nothing serious," Lilly said.

"Old age, I figure," Francis said.

"Are you OK, Francis?" Lilly asked. "You're looking a little blue in the gills, yourself."

"I'll have the meatloaf," Francis said.

Francis set the foil-wrapped plate on Wendell's dining room table and climbed the stairs. He opened his bedroom door when there was no answer. The day's last gray light filtered in from a window. Wendell sat in the old chair by the bathroom.

"The hell's wrong with you?" Francis asked, though he knew.

"There's a reason that door was closed," Wendell said.

"You're making a hell of a lot out of that silly girl's inconvenience," Francis said. "Or maybe it's something else."

"It's none of your concern," Wendell said. "I'm tired."

"Suit yourself," Francis said. "Lilly sent meatloaf."

"That was kind of her, but I'm still not hungry," Wendell said.

"I'll take care of that sign tomorrow," Francis said.

He stepped out of the room and shut the door behind him, loud enough to make a point. The girl had been no hallucination.

The next day, Francis wedged apart the sign with a crowbar, and pushed the warped boards onto the truck bed. He drove back to the lumberyard and hurled everything into a distant corner of the wood lot, not willing to part with it altogether because it had been Selma's. Wendell was still in his wicker chair that night, unshaven and unwashed, staring off, looking pretty much as he had after Selma had died.

On Thursday, two days after the girl showed up, Francis had been out at lunch picking up a prescription for his blood pressure, and decided to check in on Wendell whether the old bastard deserved it or not. As Francis approached the road through the trees, Wendell pulled out in his pickup and drove past him in the other direction. He wore a white shirt and a bow tie.

Francis pulled a U-turn and took off after Wendell, following him through town, and north out into the country. After forty minutes he nearly lost Wendell in Arlington's midday traffic. Wendell slipped through one intersection on a yellow light and turned left. When Francis finally got the green, he drove down two blocks and saw Wendell's truck parked at a meter. The old man shuffled up toward the front door of a huge building of brown stucco, the Arlington Public Library.

He parked a few vehicles behind Wendell's truck, and it wasn't more than a few minutes later that Francis watched him come limping back from the library. Then the girl, that same one it appeared to Francis, came rushing out after him. She burned her hand on the hood of his truck, pointed at Wendell and screamed something. Then sobs came over her. Wendell steadied her with an arm around her shoulder and led the young woman around to the passenger side of his truck. The two of them drove off. This time Francis didn't follow.

Chapter 21

Wendell took off again the next day, just before six in the evening. Francis saw him from the road that time, too, and had a good idea where Wendell was headed, or at least who he was headed to see. Francis avoided Lilly's that night because he didn't feel up to her questions. He stopped at a new fast-food place in town that served fish, and ate half of a deep-fried filet of something or other and a few French fries, before taking a plastic cup of root beer out to his truck. He drove to the pond and sat at the top of the hill as the sun went down.

It was full dark when he got to Wendell's place. His pickup wasn't there and there were no lights in the house. Francis went home to feed his cat and was back within an hour. By then, Wendell's truck was parked in front, but there were no lights on inside. Francis let himself in, checked the living room and kitchen, and climbed the stairs to Wendell's bedroom. The barn was empty, too.

There was only one other place within walking distance and when Francis drove over he found the front door of the lumberyard unlocked. A light burned in the woodshed out back. Wendell sat on a stack of two-by-fours near the big electric saw, letting a palm full of sawdust run between his fingers. He wore khakis and a nice shirt, dressed for an evening. Wendell didn't look up.

"They should have took your keys when you sold this place," Francis said.

"I've always loved sawdust," Wendell said. "The smell of it, the feel of it in your hand."

"If it's sawdust you wanted, why didn't you say so," Francis said. "I could have brought some over and saved you the walk."

"Maybe I needed the walk," Wendell said.

"Maybe you did," Francis said.

"And I didn't come for the sawdust," Wendell said.

"What then?" Francis asked. "It's near midnight."

"She came here, you know, to this very spot. Like she owned the place, as always."

"Who you talking about?"

"Who the hell do you think?"

"Your wife," Francis said.

"She wasn't my wife at the time," Wendell said. "It was a day or two after I got home from the war. I was standing right there cutting plywood when I smelled her perfume. She stood about where you are now, wearing this dress and smiling."

"Before I started working here, then," Francis said.

"She said she had loved my speech at the high school, though I didn't say three words."

"I was there that day," Francis said. "Quite a crowd to see you home."

"I called her Miss Sanchez then," Wendell said.

"We all did."

"I'm standing here filthy with sweat, covered in splinters, and she's looking fresh as a daisy."

"Like she always looked," Francis said.

"She said she was glad I had come home alive," Wendell said. "She brought me a book of poems."

"That's something she would do," Francis said.

"I read them, too, every last one."

Wendell scooped up another handful of sawdust from beneath the saw, and returned to his seat on the boards. He still had not looked at Francis.

"Maybe that was the day I fell in love with her," Wendell said.

"You were in love with her a long time before that," Francis said. "We all were."

"She deserved a hell of a lot better than me," Wendell said.

Francis walked over to the saw, bent and scooped up some sawdust himself.

"Spare me," Francis said.

"I don't remember asking for company," Wendell said, watching flakes of sawdust trickle to the cement floor.

"When have you ever?"

"What's that supposed to mean?"

Francis turned toward the door, took two steps and stopped.

"You ever wonder why I didn't marry?" Francis asked. "Maybe because no woman would have me. Another reason is that I never really needed to, with my sisters and you and Selma around. I had plenty of family. But then there's this, a notion that just came to me. There was no woman who could compare to Selma and she was taken. So you had the best female on this planet, and I'm not much in the mood to listen to you bellyache about it."

Wendell dumped the rest of his sawdust and stood.

"I followed you to Arlington yesterday," Francis said. "I saw you out in front of the library with that girl. I saw her go to pieces."

Wendell took a step toward Francis.

"You did what?"

"You don't want me to repeat it," Francis said.

"If you weren't such a pathetic old bastard, I'd march over there and knock you into next week."

"Then tonight you disappear again," Francis said.

"You followed this time, too?"

"Didn't need to," Francis said. "Hot date?"

"I had supper with Claire, her husband and little boy," Wendell said. "Sound like a date to you?"

"So you say," Francis said.

"We've been friends a long time, but there aren't enough years for this kind of bullshit. I'm helping that girl through a rough time."

"Then why are you sitting here alone, thinking about your wife? Sounds like you're feeling guilty about something."

"Get the hell out."

"I'll tell you something else I'm not in the mood for," Francis said. "I'm not in the mood to have you soil your wife's memory by mooning after a girl young enough to be your goddamn granddaughter. Whether she looks like Selma or not."

Francis walked away from him, and stopped at the door to the office.

"You want a ride home?" he said.

Wendell didn't answer.

"Suit yourself," Francis said.

Young Enough to Lift a Board

Chapter 22

Rachel Livingston was the Ivy League-educated author of three critically acclaimed novels and a collection of short stories. In the summer of 1992, she succeeded John Dutton as the English Department chair at Texas Tech University, which was widely considered a coup for Texas higher education. One Tech faculty member was less than elated, however. William Smith did not sleep much the two nights before the first meeting with his new boss.

Livingston was a tall, elegant woman who made no attempt to disguise the gray in her shoulder-length brown hair. Her handshake was manlike.

"Coffee?" she asked.

"No thanks," William said.

He sat down across the large desk that until recently had belonged to Dutton, William's longtime friend.

"How do you stand this heat?" she asked.

"I go to Colorado for a few weeks every summer," William said.

Livingston opened a thick file on her desk, chitchat over, and glanced at the document lying on top. It was a photocopy of William's short story, published fourteen years earlier in an obscure literary journal.

"I read this last night," she said, picking it up. "Nice."

"Thank you," William said.

"I can't help but wonder," Livingston said. "Any other ideas? Maybe a novel just dying to get out?"

"I've had some false starts here and there, but nothing has really grabbed me lately," he said.

She took a long sip of coffee from a red cup that had Harvard spelled across the side in white letters. She exhaled slowly.

"I'll be honest," Livingston said. "I'm going to create one of the finest English Departments in the country and I'm not saying you won't be part of that. But one story in nearly twenty years? A writer of your talent?"

She studied the next document in the file.

"It also seems you've been indiscreet in your personal life," she said.

"You'll have to explain," William said, though she really didn't.

"Relationships with three young women who were students at this university," she said.

Fire spread across his face.

"They were graduate students," William said, his words sounding foolish even to him. "And none of them were in the English Department."

"It's OK to inflict broken hearts on other departments?" Livingston asked.

"Of course not," William said.

"Now I hear you're involved with a member of the English faculty," Livingston said. "Olivia Tyler."

"I don't see how that's any of your business," William said.

"It is if it causes the least bit of disruption in my department," Livingston said.

"Why don't you just say it," he said.

"Fair enough," she said. "Dr. Dutton was your mentor, friend, poker buddy, maybe even protector, from what I'm told. But it seems to me that Dutton did you a real disservice by not holding you to higher standards. He spent a good deal of time looking the other way where you are concerned."

"I'm a damn good teacher," William said. "Ask my students."

"I suspect that one reason for your popularity is your reputation for, how shall I put it, somewhat less than rigorous course requirements," she said.

William stood.

"I think I've heard enough," he said. "I'm tenured."

"There are ways around that, unpleasant as they might be. As I said before, you could be part of what I'm trying to build, but that's up to you. Publish. Raise your academic standards. Behave yourself. We'll talk again when you get back from the mountains."

That night they went to dinner at a quiet Italian restaurant where Olivia tore through three glasses of Chardonnay. She laughed loudly when William described his encounter with the new department chair.

"I fail to see the humor," William said.

"Your famous bimbos have come back to roost," Olivia said.

A young couple at the next table glanced in their direction. She laughed again and took another long slug of wine.

She had short dark hair, full lips, high cheekbones, huge brown eyes, and was as smart as she was beautiful, a Stanford graduate who taught feminist literature. She didn't shave her legs or armpits, her protest against antiquated social customs and the enslavement of women. William got used to the body hair because of those cheekbones, extraordinary breasts, and her insatiable sexual appetite. He could not get used to her cruelty, especially when she was drinking.

"I thought I might get some understanding," he said.

"I'm a woman who will stand up to you, not some doe-eyed coed," she said. "Finally you can pick on someone your own size."

"I'm not picking on anybody," he said. "I thought we were trying to have a relationship."

"Fucking, more like," she said.

She set her empty wineglass down and looked fiercely across the candle-lit table, challenging him somehow.

"Fuck you, Olivia," William said, rising from his chair, dropping his napkin on his plate and a five dollar bill on the table. "For the tip. You can get the bill. Wash their fucking dishes, for all I care. Consider it another act of liberation."

Eyes of other diners followed him to the door. William slid into the driver's seat of the Miata, its top down on the pleasant summer night. When he got home, he upchucked fettuccine alfredo into the bushes by the front door. Forty-five years old and alone again.

He unlocked his front door, plopped down onto the sofa, put his head in his hands and wept in the darkness. He paced the length of his living room, blowing his nose with a dishtowel and weeping some more. The sobbing returned when William thought of his mother, dead just six months.

A ringing telephone woke him. He stumbled from the sofa into the kitchen to answer it. It was that old bastard, Devos.

"This is not a good time," William said.

There was no immediate reply and for a moment, William thought Francis had hung up. But then he heard the nasal breathing on the other end.

"It's about your dad," Francis said.

"That much I figured," William said.

"I thought you'd want to know."

William felt more queasiness and pain at his temples. He took two deep breaths.

"What is it, Franny?"

"Last week he told me to tear down your mother's piano sign," Francis said.

That silly piano business. That ridiculous sign.

"I did it," Francis said. "It's lying in a heap in back of the yards."

"That's why you're calling?"

More nasal breathing.

"There are other things, though I don't quite know how to spell them out," Francis said.

"Why don't you try," William said.

"Last Friday night, I found your dad sitting by himself in the woodshed by the saw."

"Doing what?"

"He said he was thinking about your mom," Francis said.

"What's your point?"

"He doesn't come to Lil's," Francis said. "When I go check on him a lot of the time he's not at home. I figure he's out at the pond by himself. Where else could he go? Or I find him sitting in that chair of his, doing nothing. I think it has something to do with that girl."

"What girl?"

"I guess I haven't mentioned her," Francis said.

"No," William said. "You left her out."

"A girl drove out to the place last week. Your dad and I met her when we were heading out on a delivery. The piano sign brought her. The next thing you know, he's asking me to tear down the sign. I've barely seen him since."

"What are you trying to say, Francis?" William asked.

"This girl looks like a Mexican, very pretty," Francis said.

"You've got to be kidding," William said.

"The image of your mother, when she was younger," Francis said.

"Oh, for fuck sakes," William said.

"I think he's been seeing her," Francis said.

"You're imagining things," William said. "He's ancient."

"Son, I know your dad," Francis said. "Ever since that girl showed up, he hasn't been right."

"What do you want me to do?" William said. "I haven't talked to him in two months."

"You're his son. I just figured I should let you know."

William rubbed his forehead.

"So he's got a new friend," William said. "A young woman."

"Young enough to be his granddaughter," Francis said.

"Not sure I see the harm."

"I should have known better," Francis said.

The memory came to him in that gauzy space between tortured sleep and anguished wakefulness. He and his mother were sitting next to each other on matching rocking chairs on the front porch. Wendell was watching television inside.

"It's hard to let you go," Selma said.

"I should stay here and keep working for dad," William said. "Stay closer to you. Go to TCU. You'll be too lonely with just him for company. His moods."

"I can handle his moods," she said. "He reads me poetry. You know how much he loves me. We're going to take some trips. I'll be just fine."

"Lubbock is a long ways away," William said.

"I'm making it difficult for you. That's horrible of me. This is your time. It's just that I love you so much."

"I love you, too."

"And I'm so proud of you, the young man you've become. So is your father."

"Please, mother. Dad hasn't said five words to me in the last year, except to tell me how I screwed up again at the lumberyard," William said. "And the way he looks at me when college comes up, studying English. He should just come out and say he thinks I'm queer."

"He thinks nothing of the sort," Selma said.

"I'm afraid he does."

"You're too hard on your father."

"Maybe I'm not hard enough," William said, rocking faster.

"He's a very good man, William," Selma said. "Loyal and loving and decent. But he was in the war and…"

"Lots of men were in the war," William said.

"There is so much you don't understand about him," Selma said.

"Maybe you should help me," William said.

"Maybe I should."

William drove to the campus after a sleepless night, unlocked his office, and sat down at his desk. He laid his face against the cool glass of the desktop, trying to quiet the pounding in his head. There was a knock at his door. Rachel Livingston was wearing a sundress and holding a briefcase. William hoped she didn't notice the redness in his eyes.

"I see you've taken our little chat yesterday to heart," she said. "Working on lesson plans for next semester, no doubt."

"Yes, Rachel," William said. "I've taken our little chat to heart."

"I'm glad about that," she said.

"I quit," William said.

He stood and strode past her.

"William," she said.

"I'll be back in a few weeks to clean out my office," he said.

Chapter 23

The night after Wendell came to dinner, Claire slept soundly for the first time in nearly a month. She had managed to unburden herself to him, first in the park, then at her kitchen table. It amazed her that he seemed to understand, as if he had heard it before.

Larry took Mike for a haircut the next morning. Claire misdialed Wendell's number the minute they left. Someone from the Bisbee post office answered. She dialed more slowly the second time, but the phone just rang and rang and rang. There was no answer on Sunday, either. Or Monday. Claire called again after work on Tuesday, and he finally picked up.

"Hello, stranger," Claire said. "Remember me?"

"Of course I do," Wendell said.

He sounded even more tired than usual, more tense.

"I've been calling since Friday," she said. "You need to get one of those machines."

"I've been out a good bit," he said.

"Find yourself another girlfriend?" Claire asked, forcing a laugh.

"I've been with my wife," Wendell said.

"Your wife?"

"At the cemetery."

"I'm sorry," Claire said.

Claire groped for words.

"Wendell, what's wrong?" she asked.

"What's right?" he replied.

"I know. Six months ago you lost the love of your life," Claire said. "I should be listening to you, not the other way around."

"Like I told you, I don't have much to say," Wendell said.

"That's not true," Claire said. "Selma had been your teacher. I want to hear all about her and your son."

"The less said about him the better."

"Why?"

"He'd probably say the same about me."

"I don't believe that," Claire said.

"Ask him yourself, then," Wendell said.

"Maybe I will someday," Claire said.

"No time like the present," Wendell said.

"On a Thursday night?" Larry asked. "It will be Mike's bedtime by the time we get down there."

"It seems important to Wendell," Claire said. "His son is visiting."

"Will his son be around this weekend, too?" Larry asked. "We both have to work Friday morning."

"You could talk to him about our house," she said. "Like I said, it seems important."

They left before six and drove into the little town forty-five minutes later. Larry chattered happily about his job, saying he expected a promotion and a raise. Claire had a hard time listening through the pounding in her ears.

"Turn left here," Claire said, pretending to study written directions. She knew too well how to get there.

Larry pulled onto the highway toward Dallas.

"A half-mile down, in the trees on the left," Claire said.

They passed the junkyards and body shops. The thicket came into view, but the piano sign was no longer beside the road. Had she imagined the whole thing?

"Looks like this is it," Larry said, turning into the trees.

"I guess so," Claire said.

"A doggone jungle," Larry said.

Larry drove through the trees and the gate.

Claire saw Wendell stand from the porch swing as their car approached. He met them at the bottom of the front steps and shook Larry's hand.

"Hello again, big fella," Larry said. "Quite a place you've got here."

"I appreciate your making the drive," Wendell said. "How's the little man?"

"You remember Mr. Smith," Claire said to Mike, who was standing at her knee.

The boy waved up at Wendell. Just then Francis emerged through the front door. She had not been expecting him.

"This is the young lady I told you about, Francis," Wendell said.

Like they hadn't met on the first day. Francis was in on it, too.

"Howdy," Francis said, nodding tersely, but not looking at her.

"Hello," Claire said.

"And her husband, Larry," Wendell said to Francis. "The little fellow is Mike."

Francis shook Larry's hand.

"It's a pleasure," Larry said.

The front door opened again and a third man stepped onto the porch. He was tall and broad, with the same square jaw and gray eyes as his father. But his graying hair touched his shoulders. He wore a baby blue shirt untucked over khaki shorts. Flip-flops clucked as he lumbered down the porch steps. His eyes found Claire the moment he came through the door.

"I'm William," he said, extending his hand.

"Claire Cavanaugh. This is my husband and son."

William shook hands with Larry, tapped Mike on the head and turned back to Claire.

"Dad said a nice young woman and her family would be our guests," William said. "He didn't say beautiful young woman."

Claire found it difficult to breathe.

"We're all fond of your father," she said.

"Clearly, to drive all the way out here on a Thursday night."

"And so sorry about your mother," Claire said.

"Thank you. Let's hope the meal is worth it. Drinks? Larry, I hear you're a Bud man. Right there in that cooler."

Wendell handed Larry and Francis beers as William disappeared inside. He came back a few seconds later with a glass of red wine and a cup of lemonade for Mike.

"I thought you might prefer a nice cabernet," William said to her. "I know I do."

"Thank you," Claire said.

Did anyone notice the size of her first gulp? She took another.

"I'll tend the grill," William said, disappearing again.

They sat in an awkward silence until Larry spoke up.

"Wendell, I wouldn't have expected a lumberman to have such a green thumb.

"Selma had the green thumb," Francis said.

Wendell glared.

"Selma?" Larry said.

"My wife," Wendell said. "That's one area where Francis and I might agree. What you see is her doing."

"Took her years," Francis said.

The men sipped their beers.

"So Francis, what's your business?" Larry asked.

"Wendell's dad hired me at the lumberyard right out of high school," Francis said. "Been there ever since. I worked for Wendell when he took over. Or I should say, I did all the work, he got most of the money."

"I seem to remember hauling a few boards myself," Wendell said.

William came through the door.

"Dinner is served," he said.

Claire had been holding her breath. When she stood she was dizzy from nerves and wine.

Wendell sat at one end of the table, with Larry and Francis on one side. Claire faced them on the other, next to Mike, who was propped up in an ancient high chair. William poured Claire more wine and took his seat opposite his father at the other end of the table.

"Francis, could you do the honors?" Wendell asked. "Or would that be too much to ask?"

Francis crossed himself. Larry, Claire and little Mike did the same. William and Wendell bowed their heads.

"Bless us O Lord, and these Thy gifts which we are about to receive, from Thy bounty, through Christ our Lord, amen," Francis mumbled.

"Amen," they said in unison.

Food was passed.

"Eat up, dad," William said. "You look like a broomstick. Has Lilly finally cut down on her portions?"

He asked Larry about the auto plant and listened as Claire's husband laid out his dream of a new home.

"Your dad said he could help us," Larry said.

"He's forgotten more about lumber than most will ever know," William said.

Claire decided to try and join the conversation.

"Wendell says you teach college English," she said. "That would be my dream job. I've always been a big reader."

"Actually, I quit on Tuesday," William said.

"You what?" Wendell asked.

"I quit," William said. "I guess I forgot to mention that."

Everyone but Mike stopped eating. Wendell cleared his throat.

"Why, if you don't mind me asking?" he said.

"Tired of the politics. Tired of the students. Tired of Lubbock," William said, smiling. "You name it. Just tired."

"Just like that?" Wendell said.

"Just like that," William replied.

Wendell and Francis exchanged glances.

"What do you propose to do?" Wendell asked.

"I don't really know," William said. "Need any help over at the lumberyard? I'm still young enough to lift a board. Hell, Franny, look at you."

Mike looked from one adult face to the other. Claire spooned potato salad into his mouth.

"Dad, you have a surprise of your own," William said. "I don't see mom's piano sign."

"It was an eyesore, and we weren't selling pianos," Wendell said, looking at his plate. "Francis hauled it away."

"It's been an eyesore since the day you built it," William said.

"What business is it of yours?" Wendell asked, his jaw muscles tensing.

"Of all her wild schemes, that one might have taken the prize," William said. "Claire, I wish you could have known my mother. She was going to save the world, one way or another. Dad, tell Claire about her little piano business."

"Some other time," Wendell said.

William raised his wine.

"To mother," he said.

Larry raised his beer, but Wendell and Francis stared at their plates.

"Dad, how did you end up at the Arlington library?" William asked. "That's quite a bit out of your way."

"Beg your pardon?" Wendell replied.

"Where you met Claire," William said.

Wendell's eyes stayed on his plate but his cheeks burned. He finally looked down the table. He cleared his throat.

"I met Claire before I ever saw her in the library," he said.

Claire wiped grease from Mike's cheeks with a napkin, swallowing against her panic.

"Where was that?" William asked.

"Claire drove out here one day on her lunch break looking for a piano," Wendell said. "She had seen that damn sign. Since she came all that way for nothing, I invited her in for a glass of cold tea."

"How about that," William said.

"That's why I told Francis to take care of it," Wendell said.

"What?" Larry said.

"God," Claire whispered.

"You've been here before?" Larry asked.

"Just that once," Claire said.

"Wait a minute. Was that the day of your so-called stomach cramps?" Larry said.

"I guess," she said.

"Long drive if you weren't feeling well," Larry said.

Claire stared at her plate and the table started to spin. Larry's voice saved her from fainting.

"And you thought we needed a piano so bad that you lied to everyone and drove all the way out here by yourself?"

"I guess," Claire said.

"And why is that, Claire?" Larry asked.

"I wanted to surprise you and Mike," Claire said.

"Mission accomplished there," Larry said.

"It was a mistake," Claire said.

"The mistake is that I found out," Larry said. "You all must think I'm a fool."

"Please, Larry," Claire said.

"What else aren't you telling me?"

"We can talk later," Claire said.

"At least one person has the decency to tell the truth," Larry said. "I thank you for that, Wendell."

"She meant no harm," Wendell said feebly.

"So tell me, Wendell," Larry said. "What else don't I know?"

Wendell stared at his plate.

"Francis?" Larry said. "You in on this, too?"

"That's enough," Claire said.

"I would agree with you there," Larry said, turning toward Wendell. "And you were in our home."

He pushed back from the table, grabbed Mike out of his chair and headed for the door. Wendell stood and spoke to Claire who seemed paralyzed at the table.

"I figured something like this would happen," he said. "Keeping Larry in the dark."

She finally pushed back and rose.

"I think you meant it to," Claire said. "That's why you asked us to come in the first place."

She headed after her husband and son. Wendell followed them onto the porch. Larry fumbled in the dark, strapping Mike into his car seat.

"How could you?" Claire said to Wendell.

"He deserved to know," Wendell said.

"That was my decision," Claire said.

"It's time you were on your way," Wendell said.

"You've got that right," Claire said.

They rode home in silence with Mike asleep in the back seat.

"I'll get him," Larry said when they pulled up to their duplex.

He lifted Mike from his car seat, carried him inside and put him to bed. Claire watched as Larry changed into shorts, grabbed his pillow from the bed and headed for the living room sofa. Claire shut the door to the bedroom, relieved to be alone, left to the shame of what she had done to her husband. But as minutes passed and the pounding in her temples began to settle, anger returned. Larry had his share of the blame for what happened at Wendell's. He had never wanted to listen, never had the guts to face up to her truth. Wendell did.

Sometime after midnight, the sound of her husband's snoring came to her from the other side of the door. She picked up the phone by their bed and dialed. Wendell answered on the first ring.

"Were you sleeping?" Claire asked.

"No."

"You were right to tell the truth."

"I know I was," Wendell said.

"I'm a terrible person," Claire said.

"I'm glad you're home safe. I'd like to say goodnight."

"But I need to talk to you," Claire said.

"I'm tired, Claire," he said.

She heard a dial tone.

Chapter 24

Francis and William were left alone at the table.

"You're a bastard," Francis said.

"I'm here because of you," William said. "You called me, remember?"

"You meant that to happen," Francis said.

"They were obvious questions."

"You already knew the answers to them," Francis said. "I told you on the phone. No need to embarrass your dad like that."

"You're feeling sorry for the wrong guy," William said. "That poor schmuck, Larry."

"You think this is funny," Francis said.

"I don't find many things funny these days," William said. "But if I did…"

Francis stood and dropped his napkin by his plate.

"Hasta mañana, Franny," William said.

He heard the front door open and close and poured himself more wine. William looked around at the half-empty plates, leftover potato salad, corn and rolls, at the grandfather clock. He took his glass into the living room, stopping in front of his graduation picture that hung next to the Army portrait of his father. It had been another of her attempts to bring them together. William headed down the hall and onto the porch. Wendell was sitting on the swing in the dark.

"Still hot," William said, leaning against the railing.

"Have you no shame?" Wendell asked.

"You seem pretty enamored of this girl."

"Go back to Lubbock," Wendell said.

"Why is that?" William said.

"It's none of your goddamn business."

"Lying to Claire's husband?" William said. "Francis thinks something is strange, too. He was the one who called me."

"Figures," Wendell said.

"He says you've been acting funny since Claire first showed up."

"That old bastard should mind his own business, just like you," Wendell said.

"That old bastard is the only friend you've got."

Wendell stood.

"What you did tonight, embarrassing our guests…"

"I'll apologize," William said.

"Lot of good it will do," Wendell said.

"Franny is right," William said. "Claire looks an awful lot like mother when she was young."

"What has that got to do with anything?" Wendell asked.

"You tell me," William said.

Wendell stomped down the front steps and off toward his truck. The engine fired up and William watched the truck's taillights disappear into the trees. Where the hell did he think he was going at this time of night?

He took his father's place on the swing, finished his wine in a long gulp, and pulled a can of beer from the cooler at his feet. The night was still. Sweat bubbled on his forehead and trickled down his back. He drained the first beer, got another, and drank it in sips.

He thought of their summer ritual from his high school years. William would come home from work at the lumberyard, bathe and eat dinner with his parents. He and his mother would do the dishes, pour themselves glasses of tea or lemonade, and leave Wendell in front of the television.

William remembered the buzz of cicadas on those summer nights, the sound of her voice as they sat beside each other on the porch swing. She went on about novelists and poets, and students, and general gossip at the school, talking to William as she would an adult. William told her everything. Their only disagreements on those summer nights concerned his father.

"Where he is concerned, I couldn't crap right if I had two butt holes," William said one night.

"That's not true," she said.

"Please, mother. I'm not an idiot."

Decades later, after the debacle with Claire's family, William hurled half a can of beer into the night and pushed himself up off the swing.

William returned to the air conditioning and stumbled up the stairs, drunk. He paused at the door to his parents' bedroom, then opened it. He groped for the light switch and flicked it on. The bed was unmade. Wendell's reading glasses sat on the bed stand next to a glass of water.

He opened the door to her closet and the scent of his mother nearly buckled his knees. He pulled a cord, and the small space was filled with light from a naked bulb on the ceiling. Her skirts hung on one side of the closet, blouses and sweaters on the other, exactly as she had arranged them for nearly fifty years. High heels and pumps were next to the pair of old sneakers on the floor. A black purse hung from a nail just inside the door. Four sunbonnets were in a row on the far wall, over the stacks of sweat pants that she wore gardening.

The cardboard box was pushed against the back wall. He pulled it out and unfolded the top. He reached in and pulled out Selma's favorite serape, bright red and blue, a gift from her grandmother. He put it to his nose but smelled only mildew. Beneath the serape were old grade books and a thick anthology of poetry. At the bottom, he found a notebook with a ball-point pen clipped to the cover. He took it from the box and opened it to the first page, seeing a date and his mother's elegant handwriting. In the light from the bulb, surrounded by his mother's clothes and her scent, he began to read.

Chapter 25

September 27, 1987

It's a lump. No denying that any longer, a lump in my left breast. I felt it for the first time a few weeks ago after a bath, and thought I was imagining things, or that it was just a gland flaring up. But it didn't go away, and at risk of sounding alarmist, I've been around too long not to know what that could mean. I'm seeing my doctor in Fort Worth tomorrow. So far as Wendell knows, it's just a regular checkup. He will insist on driving me, as gallant as ever, and until I hear what the doctor has to say, I won't tell my husband otherwise.

But this certainly gets a girl to thinking. Well, not a girl, exactly. I turn sixty-seven on my next birthday, and too many people don't get near that length of years. But closing in on seven decades, with a lump on my breast, maybe it's time to start asking a few questions. What is my story? What has my life really been about? For so many years in the classroom I've been happily devoted to the tales of Dickens, and Tolstoy, Conrad, Fitzgerald, Hemingway and Mailer. But have I neglected my own? Someone asked Thoreau why he so often wrote about himself, and he said, "There is no other person I know so well," or something to that effect. Is it too audacious to suggest that if it's true for Thoreau, it must be true for me?

This old notebook is left over from my teaching days. It's been sitting in the drawer by the telephone for God knows how many years, now handy for this old bird with a lump on her left breast who is finally ready to set down her own story.

It concerns this home in the trees, so unlike the place in San Antonio where I grew up. It is the story of raising my only son. But most of all it is the story of the man I lie next to in bed every night, listening as he whimpers and thrashes in his sleep, though not as badly now as in the worst times. My story and Wendell's story are one, as it should be when a couple has been married for nearly a half-century. I have a lump on my breast. It's high time I got around to telling my story. And his.

■

I was hot and very nervous that summer day in 1943, when I grabbed my purse from the seat of my father's Packard and hurried toward the entrance, nearly changing my mind several times on the way. My favorite charcoal skirt was wrinkled from the long drive up from San Antonio. I ran a brush through my hair that was tousled because I had driven with the windows open on the warm Texas morning. I wore a long-sleeved white blouse with lacey frills at the neck because my mother always said that first impressions were important, but the blouse was dotted with perspiration.

The school was quiet and mercifully cool. A prim-looking secretary looked up from behind a small desk in the reception area. Melvin Harrison himself appeared in the door of an office at the far end of the room. He was a bearish man in his sixties, with thick tufts of white hair combed back on a very large head.

He smiled broadly.

"Miss O'Leary is it?" he said. "Why don't you step inside?"

He moved a pile of books and folders from a chair so I could sit down and was still smiling when he took a seat behind his desk, pulling a lamp closer to better read my application.

"Is there something you aren't telling me?" he said. "Miss O'Leary."

"My father's name is Sanchez," I replied. "He owns grocery stores in San Antonio. My mother was an O'Leary."

"Why don't I see the name Selma Sanchez on your application?"

"If I had used that name, you and I wouldn't be sitting here," I said.

"I see," Mr. Harrison said.

"You've done very well," he said. "It's been some time since I've seen an academic record this impressive. This is Bisbee, Texas, after all."

"Thank you," I said.

"You're more than qualified to teach here," Mr. Harrison said. "But young lady, do you have any idea what you would be in for?"

"There were hard times that way at the university," I said.

His smile faded.

"This isn't the University of Texas. For darn sure this isn't Austin," he said. "Let me be blunt: Too many Bisbee folks think Spanish people belong in the fields with a hoe in their hand, not in a classroom teaching white children. Do you hear what I'm saying?"

"Yes, sir," I said. I smoothed my skirt, leaned toward him, and forced myself to look him in the eye. "I hear what you're saying."

"Why subject yourself to such aggravation, my dear?" he said. He had taken up a pipe from an ashtray and chewed on the mouthpiece.

"That's a good question," I repeated. "Maybe it has something to do with what my mother told me one night when I was sixteen. She is a bit of a rebel herself. Her own father still won't speak to her because she married a Mexican. So one night my mother sat me down at our kitchen table and she said to me, 'Selma, darling. You're getting to an age when important decisions must be made. And I really have only one piece of advice for you.' Do you know what she said to me then, Mr. Harrison? My mother said, 'When the world expects you to do one thing, do just the opposite. I can tell you from my own experience that your life will be so much more interesting and meaningful that way. Just have a thick hide when you do.' That's what she said, Mr. Harrison, pretty much word for word."

It was the first time I had told that story to anyone, let alone a prospective employer. When I finished, Mr. Harrison put down his pipe, pushed my transcripts to the side and smiled.

"Well then, my dear, you're hired," he said. "Maybe it's time I start doing a little of the opposite myself. I retire in two years anyway."

The principal stood and extended a hand. We shook on the deal and shared a giggle, as if we had just conspired to set in motion a most diabolical plot, which I guess we had.

I'm told it was no coincidence that the most popular hairstyle among Bisbee High School girls in the fall of 1943 was not the uplift favored by movie stars like

Rosalind Russell but the simple ponytail. That was generally the way I wore my hair, pulled back into a mass that fell halfway down my back. Some of the boys snuck up behind me in the halls and gave that hair a little tug, which I didn't really mind, because from my first day, I adored my students at Bisbee High, and most of them adored me back. I might have looked like a Mexican, and some of those students no doubt carried bigotries into my classroom. But Bisbee students clearly weren't used to a teacher so inspired by her material, a teacher who would pace the room from front to back, through the rows of old wooden desks, reciting poem after poem by heart, and after a while my enthusiasm was contagious.

Sure, they grumbled when I assigned them the sonnets of Shakespeare, Milton, Yeats, or the Lake poets. But then I would wander the room, spouting line after line of Wordsworth or Coleridge from memory and I guess they figured if I had memorized so much, the least they could do was read the poems themselves.

It was that love of my students that sustained me in those first few months, when I was ostracized by every one of my colleagues at Bisbee High except a heavy-set young biology instructor named Hazel Miller. On the second day of school, Hazel brought her lunch to where I was sitting alone in the faculty lunchroom. She was a third-year teacher who had been pretty well ostracized herself. She wore tent-like dresses to disguise her heft, and her body odor was particularly disagreeable after a hot day in her biology lab. To make things worse, her complexion was like that of a suffering adolescent. In short, we were both pariahs because of the way we looked.

Hazel was the only teacher who would speak to me, at least until sometime around Christmas of my first year when, one by one, the others realized I would not be driven away by their cruelty. Eventually, the conversations continued when I walked into the teacher's lounge and occasionally I even sat to join in.

But I would always be grateful to Hazel, and, as a result, willing to endure her lack of personal hygiene and propensity for gossip. Indeed, it was from Hazel that I learned on August 17, 1945, of my future husband's terrible misfortune.

The date was easy to remember because Japan had surrendered two days before. I had heard the bulletin on the radio in my apartment, and I remember the celebrations in Fort Worth, Bisbee and across the nation. Just a few months earlier, as the spring term ended, I overheard senior boys hoping that the war would last long enough so they could enlist and enter the action. I wondered how those boys could think that way after all the military funerals in the last four years, twelve in Bisbee alone. Four of the casualties had been my students.

So the nation danced and our boys would have to find their adventure in other ways. There would be no more military funerals in Bisbee, no more young lives cut short. Or so I thought that morning of August 17, when the telephone rang in my apartment.

Usually Hazel's gossip was small-time stuff—which student was dating whom, who was flunking what. This news, however, was anything but trivial, for no one was talked about more in Bisbee than Wendell Smith, the high school football legend who went away and became a war hero.

In my first year of teaching, Wendell made all-state as a fullback and middle linebacker on Bisbee's district champion football team. It seemed every conversation that year contained at least passing mention of the Smith boy's latest exploits. He was a massive young man, well over six feet tall and thickly muscled from his neck to his heels. Wendell was also reasonably good-looking, with a strong jaw and unruly brown hair he was forever brushing away from brooding gray eyes.

I had found it strange that a young man so talented on the gridiron and so attractive off of it would also be so withdrawn. Wendell never seemed to speak more than one short sentence at a time, even to his football buddies. Most girls found him as unapproachable as Olympus. Wendell seemed to prefer to keep his distance from everyone but his brother Tommy, who was three years younger. It was said that Wendell Smith never smoked or drank, never used an expletive stronger than damn. After school and on weekends, he worked late into the night at his father's lumberyard. No one in Bisbee was really all that surprised by the newspaper accounts of his heroism in the Battle of the Bulge.

That was what made Hazel's telephone call so shocking.

"You're not going to believe this," she began. "Wendell Smith and a soldier buddy missed a turn and drove their car off a cliff on the Jacksboro Highway. It happened sometime after two in the morning. Wendell's in Harris Hospital in Fort

Worth and they say he has one foot in the grave. Donna Wells just called and told me."

I guess I was speechless, because the next thing I remember was Hazel's voice on the other end of the line.

"Selma? Are you there?"

"That can't be true," I said

"But it is," Hazel said, and I hated the relish in her voice.

"My God," I said.

"And that's not all," Hazel said. "Wendell was in the back seat when the car crashed, and Donna says he was not alone. A woman was with him, and there was another girl in the front seat with Wendell's buddy. Donna said she heard Wendell and this other fellow had been drinking in the honky-tonks up and down Jacksboro, and they hooked up with these two hussies. Donna heard that they were prostitutes, but she can't be sure. But one thing that is for sure is that the car was full of empty beer bottles. Donna has a cousin who works as a policeman in Fort Worth. He was the one who told her. Selma, are you there?"

"How badly are they hurt?" I asked.

"All four of them are critical. Donna said Wendell has internal injuries and possible brain damage."

I hung up the phone, which rang again a few seconds later.

"Are you OK, Selma?" Hazel asked.

"I'm fine. Enjoy the rest of your vacation."

I hung up again and fell onto my sofa. I closed my eyes, considering Hazel's tendency to exaggerate. After several deep breaths, I stood and dialed Mr. Harrison's home number but there was no answer. I tried to rein in the thoughts and memories swirling inside my head.

I replayed Wendell's speech at the high school just the month before. The auditorium had been packed a good half-hour before the soldier and his family arrived from the train station in Fort Worth. I had helped distribute hundreds of small American flags, and later I watched the young soldier in his snappy green uniform shift awkwardly from foot to foot as Mr. Harrison and the mayor sang his praises.

Wendell was so much thinner than I remembered him, and he seemed close to tears while making his own short speech, which somehow confirmed my suspicion that he was more shy than arrogant.

I had first laid eyes on him two years before. Wendell sat in the rear of the class, towering above the rest of the students, and seemed to spend a lot of time looking out the window as I lectured. But his papers were promptly submitted, and his essays, carefully written in an almost feminine hand, were often thoughtful and fresh.

One afternoon that first fall, I spotted Wendell seated alone in the shadows, on the wooden bleachers of the empty gym. He was bent forward, his elbows resting on his knees, holding open a thin book with dog-eared pages. Wendell moved his lips when he read.

He snapped the book shut when he heard my footsteps, and hurriedly stuffed it between two other books as if he'd been caught with a dirty magazine.

"Don't you usually work for your father after school?" I asked him.

"I'm waiting to talk to coach," Wendell said, straightening.

"What were you reading, Wendell?" I asked.

"Nothing that would interest you."

"Why don't you let me be the judge of that," I said. "Show me the book or I'll assign you detention. What would your mother say?"

I was laughing by then. Wendell blushed deeply. He took out the book and handed it over with downcast eyes.

"Romantic poetry," I said. "You don't mean to tell me you've been listening in class after all?"

"Yes, ma'am," Wendell said.

"Which poem were you reading?"

"I'd rather not say."

"Why?"

"It was Wordsworth," Wendell said.

I opened the book to where it was marked.

"You've made my day."

"That one reminds me of this pond where I go fishing," Wendell said.

165

I returned the book to him.

"Daffodils,'" I said.

"Yes, Miss Sanchez," he said. "That's what it's called."

"I love that poem, too," I said.

"Yes, ma'am."

"Well, goodbye," I said. "I hope coach doesn't keep you waiting."

"Goodbye Miss Sanchez," Wendell said.

I replayed that meeting dozens of times, wondering what other poems tugged at Wendell's heart. I was so relieved when he walked into the gym for his hero's welcome on that summer day in 1945, back from the war, safe and sound. Or so I thought.

After Hazel called, I sat on the sofa in my little apartment and tears ran down my cheeks. I had wept at the funerals of my other students killed in the war. But this time was somehow different, more personal. Internal injuries. Brain damage. Prostitutes. Beer. 'Daffodils.' Wendell Smith had one foot in the grave, or maybe he didn't. Maybe there were prostitutes and beer, maybe there weren't. I was so terribly sad.

The Smith place was close to the family lumberyard on the east side of town, at the end of a gravel road that led off the highway into a huge thicket of trees. I missed the turn on my first trip by.

The road through the trees was very bumpy and I started to think I had come to the wrong place. But a large white house eventually appeared. I parked next to a new-looking Ford pickup, gathered a bouquet of daises from the seat beside me, and made my way up onto the wooden porch. Two rocking chairs sat side by side overlooking a large vegetable garden. Loud swing music played inside.

"Just a minute," a young male voice yelled from somewhere inside when I knocked at the front door.

Tommy Smith appeared in his stocking feet, wearing a dirty white T-shirt and denim work pants. He was chewing, holding a half-eaten bologna sandwich. He hurriedly swallowed when he saw me.

166

"Miss Sanchez," Tommy said through the screen door.

"Hello, Tommy," I said. "How are you?"

"Fine, I guess," he said. "You?"

"I'm fine, too," I said. "But I'm up to my elbows, getting ready for you students."

"Don't remind me."

"I have you in American lit this year," I said. "You gonna take it easy on me?"

"Not a chance."

Tommy laughed, and realized he was holding his lunch. He set his sandwich on a table inside the door and joined me on the porch, leaning back on the railing with his arms folded. He was shorter than his brother, but built with the same impressive sturdiness and had the same wavy brown hair. The similarities seemed to end there. In my brief experience—teaching Tommy in one class the year before—I found that he was as talkative and engaged in class as Wendell had been withdrawn.

"You're not here to talk about school," Tommy said, nodding toward the flowers.

"No, Tommy. I guess not," I said. "Could I say hello to your brother?"

"He sleeps most of the time," Tommy said. "Doctor says that'll probably be the case for a few weeks. To tell you the truth, even when he's awake, he's not in much of a mood for visitors. Mr. Harrison's been by a couple of times. Guys he played ball with. He won't see any of them."

"Please give him these. And tell him how sorry I am about the accident."

"I'd be glad to Miss Sanchez," Tommy said.

He turned and opened the screen door, but paused and let it slam shut again.

"Could I offer you a sandwich?" Tommy asked. "I've got thirty minutes before I'm due back at the yard."

"No, thank you," I said.

"Lemonade? There's some made."

"I'd like that."

"I'll need all the brownie points with you I can muster. Have a seat in one of those rockers."

The screen-door slammed again. I sat down and listened to the birdsong and the soothing rustle of leaves. Tommy returned, still in his stocking feet, carrying two glasses.

"Thank you, young man," I said. "Quite a place you've got here."

"It's quiet," Tommy said. "Lots of shade in the summer, which helps cool things off."

He sat in the other rocking chair, crossing his ankles in front of him as he sipped.

A thin squirrel with too much energy for such a hot afternoon nibbled on a nut by the front wheel of my car, studying us over his shoulder, and zipped up the long thin trunk of a nearby oak.

"Where are your parents?"

"Dad's at the yard. Mom's at the beauty parlor."

"I've never had the pleasure of meeting your father. But your mother hasn't missed a teacher conference. She's very nice."

"I'm partial to her myself," Tommy said. "But I worry...after everything."

I stopped rocking and set my glass on the porch railing.

"How is he, Tommy?" I asked.

"The doctor says his body will be fine after a while," he said.

A tear made a crooked path down his cheek.

"Is there anything I can do?"

"Erase the last year and a half," he said. "Wendell's problems didn't begin with that crash. He was a different guy the day he got off the train from the Army."

He rubbed the tear with his palm and sniffed.

"I should be getting back to work," he said.

"A second ago you told me you had plenty of time," I said.

"I just remembered something I have to do."

"This is your first assignment," I said. "Sit down and tell me what's on your mind."

He took a nervous sip of his lemonade.

"We went fishing right after Wendell got back," Tommy said. "Out at the pond he took off his boot and showed me one of his feet. He had lost three toes on one foot and two on the other from the cold. It was awful."

He ran his hands through his hair.

"I'm sure it was," I said.

"I made the mistake of telling dad about Wendell's feet. I guess he thought he could keep missing half of his toes a secret. When he found out I told that was it. Not another word from him about the war ever since. Not to me. Not to my mom. Not to anybody that I know of. Unless you consider how he talks out loud in his sleep. I'd shake him to wake him up, and not twenty minutes after he fell back asleep the nightmares started again. After a while, I got so tired myself that I had to start sleeping on the sofa downstairs."

Tommy stood and put his hands on the railing, leaning forward, looking into the trees.

"Wendell started drinking, though he had never touched a drop before," he said. "He'd stay at the bar until ten or eleven every night, then come stumbling up the stairs to bed and pass out in his clothes all night and not say two words to anybody the next morning."

Tommy returned to his rocker.

"You think that things can't get any worse," Tommy said. "Then one day about the time the Japs surrendered, a buddy from his Army outfit comes into the lumberyard. I'll never forget how this guy was wearing this bright-colored Hawaiian shirt, and this fancy straw hat. You don't see many of those around here. Wendell was behind the counter in the office and didn't seem to recognize him at first. But when he did, my brother looked like he'd seen a ghost. I remember the guy's name. It was Kendall Crawford.

"'Kendall Crawford. What are you doing here?'" Wendell says.

"'Some greeting for an old Army buddy,'" this other fellow says.

"My brother tells this Crawford he was busy and to state his business. Crawford says that he didn't drive all the way over from Shreveport for nothing. Shreveport,

that's what he said. 'The least you could do is join me for a beer. And I've got a proposition you might be interested in. Has to do with what went on over there.' This guy is smiling like a hyena, and I could tell Wendell wanted to strangle him. But then Wendell took off his work apron and walked around the counter and out the door with this Kendall Crawford. That was the last we saw of my brother until my dad got the call in the middle of that night."

Tommy stood and hurried back inside, returning an inch taller because of his work boots. We walked down the steps together and then to my car. Tommy pulled open the driver's side door.

"Thanks for the drink," I said

"Wendell wasn't killed that night in the car, but he might have been better off if he had been," he said. "I miss my brother, Miss Sanchez. Does that sound strange? He's laying in a bed right up those stairs. I hope that someday he finds his way home."

I touched his cheek. The gesture unleashed a sob in the boy, then another and another. I put my hand behind his head, guiding it to my shoulder, holding him there while his body was bent by grief.

Chapter 26

November 9, 1989

(Two years since I last wrote here)

A week ago, Wendell's brother died of a heart attack. Tommy had been jogging in Waco, getting ready to coach one more season of high school football, and just like that, he was gone.

This has been a devastating time for us all. But I've been so proud of my husband. I was worried that the tragedy would pitch Wendell off into one of his deep spins. But he's surprised me. He's been such a quiet comfort to Fay, and their two daughters, Helene and Beth. But now Tommy has been laid to rest next to his parents, and all the company is gone, and Wendell is alone on the porch with his memories and I wonder whether his heart is up to what is to come.

My cancer is back. I don't know that for a fact, but there is a lump on my right breast this time, and blinding headaches like I've never had before. When the cancer spreads, the brain is one place it spreads to. I can't tell Wendell, at least not yet. Not so soon after Tommy. So I'll say I'm going shopping and sneak off to the clinic in the next few days, and have the doctors there tell me what I already know. The cancer has returned with a vengeance, and now it's just a matter of time. Wendell has just lost his beloved brother, and his wife is dying, and how much suffering is one wounded heart expected to endure?

.

One afternoon in the fall of 1946 I saw him standing in front of the trophy case. Almost everyone else had gone for the day. He turned and hobbled down the hall in my direction.

He was thin and his hair was long. An angry red scar started on his forehead and made almost a half-circle around his right eye. He dragged his left leg like it was heavier than the right.

"Good afternoon, Miss Sanchez," he said.

"You look an awful lot like an old student of mine," I said. "What brings you here after all this time?"

"I came for a visit," Wendell said.

"Coach is gone for the day. Mr. Harrison, too."

"I came to see you."

His face flushed and he looked down the stairwell a few feet away, as if pondering an escape in that direction.

"What on earth for?" I asked.

"Tommy said I should thank you for those flowers."

"Really. When did you start listening to your little brother?"

Wendell glowered before lowering his eyes.

"I'm sorry it's taken so long," he said. "I've been indisposed, but you knew that."

"That's all anyone talked about around here for weeks, your accident. But it's funny how the world moves on."

Wendell turned down the stairs. I followed him two steps.

"There's only one person I know of who still brings your name up at all," I said. "Care to guess?"

Wendell stopped.

"Tommy Smith," I said. "We talk about you every week, or Tommy talks and I listen."

"Tommy," Wendell said.

"He knows the war was terrible, and it caused you to do some things when you got home that you wouldn't have done otherwise," I said. "He doesn't blame you for that. But he doesn't understand all the hours you spend lying alone in your room, or how you push him away when he tries to talk to you."

"He should walk in my shoes."

172

"Maybe you should quit worrying so much about yourself."

An angry silence hung between us.

"Tommy, huh," Wendell said.

"Tommy."

"I talk to him every day," he said.

"He says he's lucky if you say good morning."

"He's lying."

"How many of his ballgames have you been to this fall? He's doing pretty well, though he might not make all-state like his big brother."

Wendell began to shake and his face reddened.

"I'll be going now," he said, hobbling down the steps.

I called after him.

"There's another reason why I want Tommy to talk to me. I care about you, Wendell. There are things inside of you that you're determined to hide from the rest of the world. Things that you might not even know are there."

I heard his footsteps clomp down the stairs. A few minutes later I found myself in front of the trophy case and its large photograph of the young man in the white jersey, helmet tucked beneath one arm, football in the other. ``Wendell Smith, All-State, 1943," the caption read. Wendell had seen that same photograph that afternoon, too, had compared that robust image there with the devastation mirrored back at him in the glass.

At the time I was living a half-hour drive away, in an apartment in Fort Worth. I pulled into the lot of my building and parked, and grabbed my purse and schoolwork out of the back seat of my Packard. When I straightened, Wendell was standing behind the car with his hands in his pockets. I nearly dropped my books. He was pale and breathing heavily.

"What in the world are you doing here?"

He didn't answer, just stood there looking at me.

"You're scaring me," I said.

His breathing started to calm.

"You had no damn right to talk to me that way," he said finally.

"How did you find me?"

"I followed you," he said.

"That's not right," I said.

"You have no idea what it was like."

"I don't suppose I do," I said, leaning against my car as my own heart settled. "But maybe you should consider another possibility. All this tip-toeing around your suffering isn't doing you all that much good. I just had this idea."

"An idea?"

"Maybe what you need is—how should I put this—a swift kick in the pants," I said.

"A what?"

"A swift kick in the pants."

"A what?"

"You heard me," I said. "No one else seems up to it. Bend over."

"Like hell."

"You quit feeling sorry for yourself, or you're getting a swift kick from me, heels and all."

Wendell laughed out loud, a strange sound if ever there was one. An old woman walked past us with a small dog on a leash, looking at this tall young man and this Mexican woman, laughing in the parking lot.

"I'm hungry," I said. "Your butt can wait."

Chapter 27

I felt him in every nerve ending. Our hips grazed when I put the tamales into the oven and our hands touched when I showed him how to roll dough for tortillas. I tried to remind myself he had been my student just two years before.

"My Grandmother Sanchez taught me to cook, which was a good thing, because my mother was never much interested," I said.

I placed the tortillas into a hot frying pan and a starchy aroma filled the apartment.

"Mother grew up in Boston, the daughter of a crooked Irishman who made a fortune doing God knows what. He sent her to college at a place called Smith, an important school for girls on the East Coast. She studied English, like I did, and wanted to be the next Willa Cather or Edith Wharton. Her father had other ideas. She should marry the son of one of his cronies. Not my mom. One night she stole a fistful of cash from his wallet, snuck out of the house, and caught a train heading west. She changed trains in Kansas City, and woke up in San Antonio. She found work as a secretary for a lawyer, who was a friend of my father's. That's how they met."

Wendell leaned against the counter, towering over me, listening. For the first time I saw a hint of light in those big gray eyes.

"I'm their only child," I said. "People say I've got my father's skin and my mother's stubborn and flighty disposition. I can't say that I disagree, can you? This is almost ready. Set these on the table, will you?"

I took two plates from a cupboard. Beethoven was on the Victrola. We ate tamales, tortillas and beans. I filled his plate twice.

"Thank you, Miss Sanchez," Wendell said.

"My name is Selma."

"I know."

"Say it."

"Selma."

"Much better."

I raised my glass of water.

"To your continued recovery," I said. "Or a kick in the pants, whichever comes first."

He raised his water glass and touched mine.

"Grama's recipe seems to agree with you," I said.

"It's very good," he said. "Different than what I'm used to."

"What should we talk about?" I asked. "I confess that I don't know much about football."

"I'm not much of a talker," he said.

"England," I said. "You've been there, and I can only dream of going. When I think of England I see fog, bobbies, Big Ben. Did you visit London?"

"On a three-day pass with a buddy," Wendell said.

"Tell me about it," I said, pushing my plate aside and leaning toward him on my elbows.

"There was a bombed-out building on every block, roofs and walls missing. The buildings were old. It was foggy, like you said. People drive on the wrong side of the street."

"So I've heard," I said.

"Until we shipped out to France we stayed in these old barracks in the country," Wendell said. "We'd go on long marches through the hills almost every day. The weather was cool, and there were sheep everywhere. The British must use a lot of wool, I figured."

"Or eat a lot of lamb," I said.

Wendell smiled and took another bite.

"Wordsworth was from England," I said.

"You said so in class."

"So you were listening."

"What made you think I wasn't?" Wendell asked.

"You spent a lot of time looking out the window."

"I was afraid you'd call on me and make me look dumb."

"You needn't have worried. You knew more poems than anyone else in class, which was a little surprising. Football star and all."

"My mother read poems to Tommy and me when we were little. Some of it stuck, I guess."

"But do you like poetry, Wendell? Tell me the truth."

"Some of it."

"So who's you favorite poet?"

"Probably the same as yours," he said.

"Not Wordsworth," I said.

Wendell took a sip of water.

"You were reading Wordsworth in the gym that day," I said. "Daffodils.'"

"Yes," he said.

"Be still my heart."

"There's another one of his poems that I like even more," he said. "It talks about meadows and streams, which I'm partial to."

"See if this sounds familiar," I said.

"There was a time,

When meadow, grove and stream,

The earth and every common sight,

To me did seem,

Apparell'd in celestial light,

The glory and the freshness of a dream."

"That's the one." Wendell said.

"It's called 'Ode, Intimations of Immortality.' One of Wordsworth's most famous."

"I like it. That's all I know," Wendell said.

"I have a favorite line in that poem," I said.

Wendell looked at me across the table.

"It goes like this. 'No more shall grief of mine the season wrong.'"

That's the moment I decided I was going to kiss him.

177

We cleared the table, washed and dried the dishes. I told Wendell about San Antonio, how as a little girl I used to dash up and down the aisles of my parents' grocery stores. Wendell told me about his favorite place, the little pond out of the Wordsworth poem where he and Tommy fished, how quiet and peaceful it was out there in the hills. With the dishes put away, I took his hand. He looked at me with alarm and his palm was sweaty, but he didn't resist when I led him to the sofa.

"Please sit," I said.

I wondered if he could hear the pounding of my heart. I knelt next to him on the sofa, putting my hands on either side of his face. The alarm was still in his eyes, but he made no effort to escape.

"Easy, soldier," I said. "There's nothing to worry about here."

The first kiss was a soft one. I pulled back and looked into his eyes. Alarm had been replaced by a surprising and endearing vulnerability. I leaned in to kiss him again and this time he took me in those strong arms. I pushed his body down onto the sofa, draping my body over his. Our mouths remained joined, more desperate each second.

Wendell's head was on my lap. I massaged his scalp through his shaggy hair, tracing his scar with the nail of my index finger. I decided not to ask about it.

"It was the second week of February and the weather was warmer than it had been," Wendell said. "First thing that morning, the lieutenant comes up to me and says, 'Smith, why don't you take a little walk down the road through those trees. Come back and tell me what's on the other side.' He always made it sound so easy. A little walk.

"It was sunny and the ice on the road had turned to slush. I got to the edge of these woods, and I slipped off the road, making my way from tree to tree to try and keep from being seen by the enemy. The next thing you know, German soldiers pop out from the trees all around me, a whole platoon of them at least.

178

"But you know what? Every one of those men dropped their weapons and threw their hands in the air. They had had enough of war, too, evidently. They just up and surrendered to me. I didn't really know what to do. But without me saying a word they lined up in single file. I pointed toward the road with my rifle and they turned and walked. You should have seen the lieutenant's face when I got back. The next thing you know, he's putting me in for a medal."

A little candle flickered on the coffee table. He was smiling in its light.

"The war hero," he said, and we both laughed.

He asked for some water but when I returned from the kitchen with a glass he was fast asleep. I covered him with a blanket and kissed his forehead.

Lying in my own bed a few minutes later I began to hear his snoring. My bedroom window was open because the night was warm and a breeze puffed my curtains. I wanted no part of sleep. I wanted Wendell next to me.

When I heard a strange whimper I hurried into the living room and found him upright, quivering, the blanket lying in a ball on the floor. I sat next to him and put my hands around his arm.

"Wendell, what's wrong?" I asked.

"I'm awfully sorry, Sergeant," he said.

The teapot whistled. I brought two steaming cups to the kitchen table, where Wendell was slumped in a chair. Every light in the apartment was burning, as if I thought brightness might dispel whatever nightmare Wendell had just endured.

"Drink this," I said.

He just stared.

"Wendell, please," I said.

"I need to be getting home," he said. "You have school."

"Don't be silly."

He patted his pockets.

"Where are my keys?" he asked, looking terrified. "There they are."

He started for the kitchen, where he had spotted his keys on the counter. I pressed him back in his chair.

"Tell me about your dream," I said.

"What dream?" he asked.

"There was a sergeant," I said. "You said, 'I'm sorry, Sergeant.'"

"I need to be going."

"When I was a little girl, my mother always made me tell her when something was bothering me, no matter what it was. She said it would make me feel better, and it always did. One of her favorite sayings was, 'Anything mentionable is manageable.' What was his name, this sergeant?"

"Newby," Wendell said softly.

"Newby."

"I never even knew his first name," Wendell said. "He was a fine man, though, Newby was."

"I bet."

"He took shrapnel in the leg a few days after D-Day, and they shipped him back to a hospital in England. He was assigned to train us after he got out. We looked up to him, though he probably wasn't more than twenty-five. And he had seen combat, knew what it was like."

Wendell straightened and took a sip of tea.

"One day at our camp in England, I saw a wallet on the ground outside the mess tent. It had about fifty bucks in it, and a few pictures, but no ID. I took it to Newby. He put a notice on the company bulletin board saying that the wallet had been found, and that the owner had me to thank for its return.

"That's the only reason I can figure that he called for me. We had been up there about a week and were taking a hell of a pounding from the German artillery. Newby's foxhole took a direct hit. The guy in the hole with him had his head blown clear off. Medics dragged Newby out and started to work on him. Parts of the shell had gone in his belly and out the back, and his insides were lying open. I heard him yelling my name.

"I ran over and he motioned for me to come close. I knelt down in the snow and put my ear by his mouth. 'Wendell,' he whispered. 'There's a big favor I've got to ask of you.' 'Anything, Sergeant,' I said.

"He said, 'There's cash in my money belt. Make sure it gets back to my wife and kids.'

"I said, 'You take it to them yourself. You're gonna be fine.'"

"'Please. For my wife and kids.' Then he died. I never took that belt to his family. I stood up and went back to my foxhole, more concerned with how cold I was. Just now I understood how much I let Newby down. I saw his face in that dream just now, and all that blood in the snow and the stench of his insides. The last human he saw... I don't feel that good."

I knelt next to him on the floor and leaned my elbows on his knees. My words were paltry, meaningless.

"He would have understood," I said.

Wendell stood.

"Thanks for supper," he said.

He limped out the door, closing it softly behind him. I was still on my knees next to his empty chair when I heard the engine of his pickup roar to life outside and rumble off down the street.

Chapter 28

William found him in the barn the next morning, sitting in a lawn chair while sharpening a mower blade with a heavy gray stone.

"Still drink this stuff?" William asked.

Wendell eyed his son suspiciously, then set down the blade and stone and took the mug of coffee. He blew on it and sipped.

"That mattress is probably older than I am," William said. "But it's always nice to be back in the old room."

William sipped from his own mug as he looked around the barn. Rakes, shovels, an axe and several orange extension cords were neatly hung from the walls. A riding mower was parked behind the Ford pickup truck that had been in the family since the 1940s. Wendell's toolbox sat in one corner next to a workbench. Plastic bags of mulch, fertilizer and plant food were stacked by the toolbox.

"Sleep well?" William asked.

"As well as an old man sleeps," Wendell said.

"I heard you on the telephone last night," William said. "Briefly."

"I was talking to Claire," Wendell said. "Trying to clean up your mess."

"I'm sorry about how that turned out," William said. "They seem like good folks."

Wendell set his mug on the cement floor and retrieved the mower blade.

"I'm busy here," Wendell said.

William sat on a sawhorse.

"We haven't always seen eye to eye," William said.

"Have we ever?" Wendell asked, and he swiped the stone down the blade.

"We have something pretty important in common though," William said.

"If you're referring to your mother…"

"She always wanted us to get along," William said.

"It's a little late for that," Wendell said. "I think even Selma knew as much."

"She never gave up on us," William said. "Maybe she was right not to."

"Maybe she wasn't," Wendell said.

"She always said you loved me in your own way."

William sipped his coffee.

"See if this rings a bell," he said.

Wendell looked up at him.

It is not now, as it hath been of yore;

Turn whereso'er I may,

By night or day,

The things which I have seen I now can see no more.

The rainbow comes and goes,

And lovely is the rose.

"It's Wordsworth," William said. "Years ago I memorized the whole ode. It impresses women."

"You will never change," Wendell said.

"I knew you used to read poetry to her," William said. "But last night I learned that you might even love it yourself. Curious to know how I found out?"

"I suspect you'll tell me," Wendell said.

"Last night I was in mom's closet."

"You have no business in there," Wendell said.

"I found an old notebook of hers," William said. "Inside was her memoir."

"Her what?"

"Her life story" William said. "I started it last night. I guess you haven't seen it."

"Maybe I wasn't meant to," Wendell said. "Maybe you weren't meant to, either."

"How else was I to learn that you loved poetry? I always figured I inherited that from Mom."

Wendell dropped the blade on the cement and the sound echoed in the barn.

"I'm going in," Wendell said.

"Let me make you some breakfast," William said. "Like I said last night, you're looking thin."

"I'm not hungry."

Wendell stood and took a few steps.

"Someday, I'd like to hear more about Sergeant Newby," William said.

"Who?"

"Newby," William said. "Your sergeant."

"Jesus, Mary and Joseph," Wendell whispered.

"He was in mom's story. He sounded like a hell of a guy. I'm truly sorry about what happened to him."

"Why are you doing this to me?" Wendell asked.

His lips quivered and he stuffed both hands in his pockets. Wendell cleared his throat and started to say something, but stopped.

"The hell," he said, and hobbled from the barn.

William took his place in the old lawn chair and picked up the sharpening stone and the blade. He gave the blade a few more strokes, then dropped them both back onto the floor. He walked back to the house and cleaned up the dishes from the eventful dinner of the night before.

He was dozing on the living room sofa a few hours later when he heard a car pull up. Claire's blue Impala parked next to his Miata.

"William," she said when he answered the door.

"Not working today?" he asked.

"I took the day off."

"To spend with dad, I guess," William said.

"I see his truck. Would you tell him I'm here?"

William joined her on the porch.

"I want to apologize," William said.

"Maybe last night was for the best," Claire said.

"You think?"

"But I didn't drive all the way here to talk to you about last night," Claire said. "I came to see your dad."

"What's going on, Claire?" William asked.

"Your father is helping me through a hard time," Claire said.

"He's helping *you* through a hard time," William said.

"That's what I said," Claire said.

"My mom hasn't been dead six months. She was his life."

"I know," Claire said.

"He had been doing OK. But he's lost ten pounds since you showed up and his mood has gone to hell, not that he was ever particularly chipper."

"Please, William. Tell him I'm here."

"Or is that all just coincidence?" William asked. "Do you know you look a lot like my mother?"

"He mentioned that once," Claire said.

"Oh, he did, did he?"

"What are you trying to make this out to be?" Claire asked.

"Why don't you tell me?"

"I can see now why your father feels the way he does," Claire said.

"About what?"

"About you."

Anger rose into his throat. He was about to send her on her way.

"He's in his room," he said. "I think it's best that you wait out here."

Wendell limped down the stairs and out to the front porch. William watched them through a window. Claire sat down on the swing, looking upset. She stood and grabbed Wendell's arm before trotting down the porch steps and back to her car. The Impala kicked gravel as it sped toward the gate. Wendell stood looking after her, came back inside and headed up the stairs. A few minutes later, he picked up his keys from the kitchen counter and walked past William without speaking. Wendell drove off through the trees, going after her, William thought.

Chapter 29

The night after the disaster around Wendell's table, little Mike forced Claire from a leaden slumber just after seven, standing at the side of her bed and tugging on her arm. Larry snored on the sofa as Claire walked through the living room.

"I'll make you guys some pancakes and bacon," Claire told her son.

In a few minutes, the bacon sizzled on the stove and the aroma that Larry loved filled the home. Claire smeared a pancake with butter, covered it in maple syrup and cut it into small squares, setting it in front of the boy, who waited hungrily, plastic fork in hand. She put a plate with pancakes and crisp bacon in Larry's place.

"Larry," she whispered to him at the sofa. "Your breakfast."

He rolled over.

"What's wrong with Cheerios?" he asked. "Why should this day be any different?"

"I just thought..."

"You just thought bacon would..." Larry said. "You must think I'm a fool."

He got up and disappeared into the bedroom. Claire heard the toilet flush and the shower run. Larry came out dressed for work in blue coveralls. He walked into the kitchen, kissed Mike on the top of his head and continued out the back door, ignoring the plate of food. The boy's eyes followed his father. Claire listened for the sound of his pickup. When she didn't hear it, she found Larry sitting on the back steps, quietly crying.

"You want to talk?" Claire asked.

Larry sniffled and rubbed his nose.

"You've got someone else to talk to," he said. "I guess that was Wendell you were on the telephone with after we got home last night. Like a couple of teen-age girls, you two. Or maybe it's something else."

"Don't be ridiculous," she said.

"Ridiculous," Larry said. "Now there's a word."

Her heart had plummeted when she saw him crying. But now anger rose.

"Is it any wonder," she said.

"Wonder what?"

"That I need someone to talk to," Claire said. "Sometimes the world involves more than movies and sports scores. Not that you'd ever care to admit it."

"Sneaking around with an old man," Larry said. "Talk about twisted."

Claire laughed.

"No argument there," she said.

Claire sat down next to him.

"There's a limit to how much of this shit I'm gonna take," he said.

"Don't blame you," Claire said.

"It's like you could not give a crap," Larry said. "Could care less how I feel."

"Larry, there are things I need to talk about," she said. "Things you don't want to hear. You've made that plain enough over the years. Wendell has offered to listen. It's as simple as that. Whether I care about you or not has nothing to do with it. And I do."

"You have a funny way of showing it," he said. "Now what?"

"I'm going back out there," Claire said. "Soon as I can arrange it. To talk."

"Fine by me," Larry said.

He paused.

"But I'm not sure I trust you with Mike," he said. "Not with the way you've been acting."

"Excuse me?" she said.

"You need help," Larry said.

"I'm getting help."

"From Wendell," Larry said. "Some help."

He removed his glasses and rubbed his eyes. He sniffled.

"I'll take Mike to day care," he said. "Go on. Do what you feel like you have to do. But there's no guarantee we'll be here when you get back."

He opened the back door.

"Say hello to the old man," he said.

Larry strapped Mike into his car seat. Claire bent to hug him before they drove away. She felt a strange relief, a sense of freedom when they were gone. She took extra time with her hair and makeup and she dug in the glove compartment of the Impala, where there were two cigarettes left in a crumpled pack of Kools. She smoked them both on the back step and drove to a convenience store to buy a fresh pack. She lit another cigarette, smoked half, and crushed her cigarette out on the step.

Construction was heavy on the road to Wendell's. She smoked one Kool after another. Her throat was raw. The whole drive she thought about the rest of her story, what she so desperately needed to get off her chest.

Chapter 30

Minnesota 1979

The nuns lived on the other side of a swinging door on the third floor. Claire and the other elementary school students at St. Barnabus wondered whether they ever took off those ugly black and white habits, and whether they actually had hair beneath the penguin costumes.

But they never had to wonder about Sister Rosalie, who taught English and social studies. She was much younger than the rest of them, still in her twenties, and the only one who did not wear religious clothing. Instead, she had a small wardrobe of cheap but colorful dresses. She was short and plump and jolly and loved kickball. It seemed Sister Rosalie loved lots of things, including the kids in her classes.

That's probably why Claire had begun to confide in the nun about the state of things at home. That Monday after lunch, Sister Rosalie found Claire sitting alone beneath a cottonwood tree and lowered herself to the grass.

"I'm dying to hear," Sister Rosalie said. "Was it wonderful?"

"Like a dream," Claire said.

"Tell me."

Claire described her mother's new dress, her hair, the candles, the Rachmaninoff sonata, the happy tears and cake when it was over.

"I wish I could have been there," Sister Rosalie said.

"But then my dad came home drunk."

"I prayed that wouldn't happen," Sister Rosalie said.

"He said mom and me looked like whores in our dresses."

"Please tell me he didn't," Sister Rosalie said. The color drained from her fat cheeks. "Mary, mother of God."

"It's OK," Claire said.

"No, it's not OK," Sister Rosalie said.

"I didn't know what the word meant," Claire said. "I came in this morning and looked it up in the dictionary in the library. I was looking under the H's. Karen told me it started with a W. She asked me, 'Why do you want to look that up, anyway?' I said, 'Oh, no reason.'"

Sister Rosalie grunted as she rose to her knees.

"Come here," she said.

Claire's first sob was muffled by Sister Rosalie's chest, but her weeping was loud enough that other kids on the playground turned to stare. By the time she had cried herself out, the playground was deserted except for the two of them, sitting beneath the tree on that beautiful spring afternoon.

Sister Rosalie took a Kleenex from her purse and held it to Claire's nose. The principal walked toward them across the playground, but Sister Rosalie waved her away.

When the weeping was done, Claire and Sister Rosalie talked some more.

"Why don't you wear that black thing on your head like the rest of them?" Claire asked.

Sister Rosalie nibbled on a long blade of grass and was plucking petals from a dandelion. She laughed.

"A wimple," she said. "What nuns wear on their heads. A funny word, don't you think?"

"So why don't you wear one?"

"Would you want to?"

"No. But that's what nuns wear, and you're a nun," Claire said.

"I eat with them. I pray with them. I sleep with them. But I don't have to look like them," she said, smiling. "And I don't have to act like them. My Lord, Claire, you'd think they had been nailed to the cross, not

Jesus, the way they walk around all day with their long faces, grumpy as old mules. Service to God should be a joyful thing, not a penance. So let them waddle around in those awful-looking black clothes. For my money, the Lord prefers me in red."

"Why did you become a nun?" Claire asked. "You don't seem like the type."

"Can you keep a secret?"

"I promise."

Sister Rosalie lowered her voice.

"Jesus told me to," she said.

"Jesus?"

"Clear as a bell."

"You're fooling with me."

"Nope. When I was sixteen," Sister Rosalie said. "I didn't have a lot of friends, probably because I was a little heavy. But mother always said that Jesus loved me just the way I was, and I never doubted that was true. I imagined him calling me Rosie, his pet name for me. In my mind I'd say, 'Thank you, Jesus. I love you just the way you are, too.' Jesus would think that was funny, coming from a kid.

"That summer, my parents took me to this cabin on Lake Superior. I got up early one morning and walked along the water as the sun came up. There were seagulls and little waves coming up on the sand. I walked down the shore until I came to a huge rock. I sat down and thanked Jesus because for some reason that seemed to be the happiest moment in my life.

"And I swear to God he answered me. It seemed as clear as the two of us talking now. 'I'm glad, Rosie,' he said. 'Since you're in such a good mood, I've got a big favor to ask. The sisters need help. The nuns.' That was it. I closed my eyes and pictured him sitting next to me. In my mind, he was barefoot, his feet sticking out from his long white robe that looked like it had just come off the clothesline. He had long brown hair and a brown beard, such a handsome man.

"Well, who was I to say no to Jesus," Sister Rosalie said. "You know what I mean?"

"Brown hair...beard...handsome," Claire said.

"I still see him."

"And you still talk to him?"

"Every day. How do you think I put up with those nuns? Jesus keeps me sane."

Sister Rosalie slumped against the tree and pulled a long sprig of grass from her mouth.

"Will Jesus talk to me?" Claire asked.

"Have you asked him?"

"Not exactly."

"Why don't you? Someday he will."

"Talk to me?"

"I'm sure of it."

"I don't know where to find him."

"Keep an open heart, Claire. And he will find you."

They stood and Sister Rosalie held Claire's hand as they walked across the playground. Other kids stared when Claire returned to her desk. Karen sat next to her in the second row of the bus, like always, but was unusually quiet.

"You missed catechism," she said finally.

"Yeah, I got upset," Claire said.

"About what?"

"Stuff," Claire said.

"Mills said you went psycho today," Karen said finally. "He says you've always been a little weird. I told him to shut his fat mouth."

"Thank you for that," Claire said.

"Are you in trouble for missing school?" Karen asked.

"Sister Rosalie was with me the whole time. If I get in trouble, I guess she will, too."

The bus stopped. Karen and Claire set off down the sidewalk.

"Don't worry," Claire said. "I'm not psycho."

"OK," Karen said.

Claire started to say something else when familiar music came from the direction of her house. She sprinted down the sidewalk, ran up the driveway to the back door, and sneaked in like she used to so she would not disturb her mother's playing. From the kitchen Claire could see her mother at the piano. Her long black hair was down around her shoulders and uncombed, but she wore her new black dress, and bright red lipstick, and a dreamy smile. Her eyes were almost closed. There was an expression on her face, a smile, unlike any Claire had seen before.

Claire saw the rest when she tiptoed to the living room. The sofa and her dad's chair had both been toppled. The television was still on its metal stand, but the picture tube was smashed in, with a large jagged hole in the middle of the glass. The floor was covered by bits of paper that looked like confetti.

"Oh my God, mother," Claire said. "What happened?"

She didn't answer. She just kept playing with that strange smile on her face. She had come to a quiet passage of the Rachmaninoff sonata and was playing it over and over, like a record that had gotten stuck.

"It was him, wasn't it?" Claire asked.

She stepped around the fallen furniture and looked at the shreds of paper on the floor. Here and there she saw musical notes. But on other pieces there were words, and fragments of advertisements, and Claire knew that her father had not spared her mother's cherished magazines. She looked over at her mother again and saw the three tiny pieces taped to the piano. Claire moved closer to see what they were. On one piece was a tiny human eye; an ear was on another; a tuft of red hair on a third—all that remained of Van Cliburn, her lover.

197

Claire went to her room and closed the door, found her bear, and got into bed in her school clothes.

"Find me, Jesus," she whispered.

Chapter 31

As she was about to fall asleep three nights later, Claire heard the muffler of his car as it sputtered into the driveway. The front door squeaked open. By the sound of things, her mother was standing between the kitchen and living room.

"Get out!" she shouted.

He laughed. The air in Claire's bedroom seemed to get hot and thick, like on a summer day just before it rained. It was hard for her to breathe.

"I pay for this fucking hole," her father said.

"Get out!"

He laughed again.

"How's your boyfriend?" he asked. "I heard he was a little torn up."

"I'll call the police," she yelled. "I should have called them on Monday."

"And tell them what?" he asked. "That your husband is a drunk? Not a crime, last I checked. Besides, I've got something I know you want. It's right here. Suck it."

"You bastard!"

"Such language," he said.

"No more chances. When Claire's out of school we're moving in with Jack and Sophie."

"That's a good one."

"It's already arranged," she said. "Three weeks and we're gone. And I'd no sooner sleep with you again than I would bang a street bum."

"You won't last a week without me," he said.

"Jack will support us until I find a job. We'll make it somehow. And if you don't leave, I'm calling the police."

"I'll leave, but not until I get what I came for."

Claire heard his first footsteps and the terror in her mother's voice.

"Don't," she cried. "Claire's asleep."

"I'll be quiet then," he said.

"Please leave," she said.

"Like I said, when I get what I came for," he said.

Claire's mother began to weep.

The sounds of her mother's crying faded, like she was walking away down the street. Another sound took its place, the whisper of leaves in a light breeze. Claire waited to wake up, waited for the sound of the leaves to disappear so she could hear what was going on between her parents. But the leaves became louder, as if a storm was blowing in. She finally sat up to look out her window, but when her feet hit the floor she felt dewy grass instead of linoleum.

She called for her mother, but there was no answer, no sound except the wind, which continued to blow stronger. Claire's hair swirled in her eyes. The wind suddenly stopped and she saw wisps of cloud skipping like great feathers past the face of a full moon. Claire thought it was strange that she didn't feel afraid, not even a little. In fact she felt an incredible peace, happiness, standing alone in her bedclothes in the middle of God-knew-where, looking up at the moon. She heard a man's voice.

"Quite a time you've had, young lady," he said.

Claire spun and saw him sitting in the moonlight with his legs crossed, next to a big rock.

"You scared me," she said.

"I apologize, Claire," the man said. "You've had enough fear for one night."

"Who are you?" Claire asked. "How did you know my name?"

"I just assumed you'd know," he said.

He wore something white. Shoulder-length dark hair. Dark beard. Long thin nose and large dark eyes, an extremely handsome man about thirty years old.

"Jesus," she said.

The moon grew fuzzy.

"No one will believe me," she said.

"One person will."

"Sister Rosalie said we would meet one day."

"Rosie was right," he said.

"How did I get here?"

"I brought you."

"How?"

"Through the Father who does all things."

"What does that mean?"

"It's magic," he said. "The magic of love."

He was silent for a while, as if giving her a chance to let his words sink in.

"I've been praying to meet you," she said.

"I know," he said.

"I was starting to think that you wouldn't come," Claire said. "And that Sister Rosalie was a little off her rocker. And if you did come, I figured you would come to me, not the other way around."

Jesus smiled and patted the ground next to him. When Claire sat, he took a thick blanket and tucked it around her shoulders. He touched her cheek with the back of his fingers.

"Now rest. You're safe here. You'll always be safe here."

"Where is here?" she said.

"Here is wherever I am," Jesus said.

The wind made a low gush through the trees. The sky had lightened from black to a dark blue with the dawn beckoning. Jesus looked toward the sky. The stars had started to vanish.

"Close your eyes," he said.

She curled up next to him and went to sleep. The next voice Claire heard was a woman's.

"Come, sweetheart," the voice said. "You need to wake up."

Claire opened her eyes, but Jesus was gone. The woman was sitting on the side of her bed. A pistol dangled from a holster on her shoulder. A gold badge was clipped to her belt, gleaming in the light outside her bedroom door, where strange men walked back and forth. One was in uniform. The woman on her bed had short black hair. She rubbed Claire's arm.

"Where's Jesus?" Claire asked.

"In heaven, we can only hope," the woman said.

"He was here a second ago," Claire said.

"Who was, honey?" the woman asked.

"Jesus."

"I see."

"Who are you?"

"My name is Sandra. I'm with the police."

"What?"

"We need to get you up and dressed," she said. "Your aunt will be here shortly. Then we can all talk."

"What happened?"

"Please honey, let's get your clothes," Sandra said. "You can take your bear if you'd like."

"Where's my mom?"

"You can see her later."

"Where's Jesus?" Claire asked again.

This time the woman didn't answer. Instead she looked toward a short, fat man in a suit and tie who had walked into the room.

"She's been dreaming," Sandra said quietly.

"We need to get her out now, Sandy, even if we have to carry her," the man said.

"She was just getting up, sergeant," Sandra said, smiling down at Claire, who pulled away when the woman tried to touch her cheek. "Weren't you, Claire. Please."

"I'll let you handle it," the man said.

"The sooner you get up, Claire, the sooner you can see your mother," Sandra said.

"Is my dad still here?"

Sandra rummaged around in Claire's drawer. She fished out a pair of pants, socks, and a sweat shirt. Then she spotted Claire's tennis shoes, and brought them to the bed. She set the clothes in a neat pile.

"We'll give you some privacy."

Sandra turned on a lamp and shut the door. Claire mindlessly pulled on the pants and sweat shirt, and put on shoes without socks but didn't tie them. She just sat on the side of her bed. Claire kept waiting for her mother to walk in, or Jesus, even as Sandra came back into the room.

"Why don't you take your bear," she said.

Claire picked up her bear. Sandra took her other hand and led her out.

"The kid's on her way out," Claire heard a man say in a hushed voice.

Two more men in uniforms looked down at Claire with grim faces as Sandra walked her past them. The door to her parents' room was closed, but Claire could hear movement and voices inside.

"Mom?" Claire yelled out.

"Soon," Sandra said.

"Is my dad in there?"

Sandra tugged a little harder on her arm.

"Who's in their bedroom?"

They reached the front door. Claire looked for her mother in the living room but saw only another man in a suit, sitting in her father's chair, smoking a cigarette and writing in a small notebook.

The cool night air felt good on Claire's face. Three police cars were parked outside with their lights flashing. Neighbors were huddled in groups on the other side of the street. She saw Karen, standing in her bathrobe with her mother and father. Claire waved at her and Karen started to wave back, but her mother grabbed her hand. Her dad's car was still in the driveway.

Sandra tugged at her hand and they walked toward a car that sat with its engine running. It was parked behind an ambulance that also had its lights flashing. Flashbulbs popped in the night. Sandra opened up the back door.

"Slide in honey," she said. "I'll be with you in a minute."

"They'll pick her up at the station," Sandra said to the man behind the wheel. "I'll ride in back with her."

Sandra got in beside Claire and patted her hand. The back door of the ambulance was open. It was empty but full of white light.

The car pulled out slowly. The people in the street followed the car with their eyes. As they drove down the block, she turned and looked out the back window at all the lights flashing in the night.

Chapter 32

The next Monday morning, the day after Easter, Jack drove the three of them downtown. The huge building smelled of cigarettes and body odor. Sophie pulled her along as Claire looked around at men in suits huddled with small groups of dazed-looking people. Sophie squeezed Claire's hand as they crowded into an elevator for the ride up. When they got out, a tall thin man in a navy blue suit and gray cowboy boots rose from the bench near the elevator, lifted a briefcase, and walked quickly toward them.

"You must be McLeish," Jack said.

"Michael McLeish. At your service."

Dark-rimmed glasses slid halfway down the man's long, pointy nose. His dark-blond hair was thin on top but longish on the sides, spilling down over his ears.

"Mrs. Thompson, I presume?"

He extended his hand to Sophie.

"And you must be the famous Claire, the novelist in waiting,'" McLeish said, smiling broadly. "And you're every bit as pretty as advertised. How are you this morning, young lady?"

"Fine," Claire said.

"Fine will do," he said. "I bet you're anxious to see your momma, aren't you?"

"Yes, sir," Claire said.

"Well, everyone, just follow me," the man said.

He walked off so quickly that they had to jog to keep up. At the end of the corridor a very fat man in uniform stood outside a door. The officer nodded toward McLeish, unlocked the door and held it as the four hurried past into a little room where florescent lights burned from a low ceiling. Claire saw her the moment they entered, sitting at the far end of a long table, a cigarette burning in a metal tray in front of her. Her mother wore bright orange coveralls with County Jail stenciled across the front. She rose and took Claire into her arms. Claire felt the bones of her mother's thin back through the jumpsuit, which smelled of cigarettes. Her hair smelled fresh, though, as if newly washed, and she wore makeup. She looked Claire in the eyes and pulled her back into an embrace. She took Claire's cheeks in her hands.

"Just look at you," she said. "What in the world would I do without you? God how I've missed you. Have you missed me?"

"Of course she has," Sophie said.

"They said you killed dad," Claire said.

Claire's mother paled and her mouth fell open.

"That's what we're here to talk about," McLeish said.

"Can you come home today, mother?" Claire asked. "I want to go home."

Elizabeth looked over Claire's shoulder at her lawyer, then at Sophie.

"That's where I come in," McLeish said. "Let's all have a seat."

Claire's mother took her hand and led her to the end of the table. The lawyer sat beside them, across the table from Jack and Sophie. Elizabeth's hand was frigid as she held Claire's tightly beneath the table, as if to keep her from getting away. She held another cigarette in her other hand. McLeish lit it. Elizabeth took a deep drag and tapped the cigarette on the ashtray.

McLeish lifted his briefcase onto the table, snapped it open and briskly pulled out a yellow legal pad and an expensive pen. He clicked the pen several times and pushed his glasses up his nose with his index finger, looking around the table at each of them.

"Elizabeth will be arraigned upstairs in forty-five minutes," McLeish said.

Claire's mother looked down at her and tried to smile but there was nothing but terror in her brimming eyes. Jack and Sophie nodded.

"The charge will be second-degree murder, to which we will enter a plea of not guilty," McLeish said.

All three adults gasped.

"There's not a chance in hell they can make that stick, but this case has gotten a good bit of press," McLeish said. "The cameras will be waiting outside the courtroom today, hoping to get a shot of my client and the little girl everyone has been hearing so much about. Unfortunately, publicity tends to make prosecutors unreasonable."

McLeish smiled.

"The good news is that they've agreed to bond," McLeish said. "With Claire to take care of, and solid citizens like her sister and brother-in-law nearby, with her lack of priors, it wasn't hard to convince them that Elizabeth is not what you'd call a flight risk."

Another smile.

"Fifty thousand," McLeish said.

"You've got to be shitting me," Jack said.

"I'll tell you how this works," McLeish said. "You pay a bondsman fifteen percent, and he puts up the rest. They keep your fifteen percent when Elizabeth shows up for trial. That's only seventy-five hundred."

"On top of the ten grand for your retainer," Jack said. "Jesus."

"If you can't post bond, I'll file for a speedy trial," McLeish said.

Sophie shot a sideways glare at her husband.

"You'll have a check by this afternoon," she said

"Then Elizabeth will be home by supper," McLeish said.

Claire thought of sleeping in her own room, even if her dad had been stabbed to death just a few feet away. It would be easier for Jesus to find her again and take her back to the rock, away from everything. When he did, she never wanted to come back. By now Jesus had risen from the dead.

McLeish pushed his glasses up his nose.

"Time for brass tacks. I hesitate to talk about this in front of the young lady, but I think it's important that Claire knows the score. Does everyone agree?"

The three adults nodded. Jack sat up in his chair.

"I have to tell you folks," McLeish said. "We've got a few problems. Problem numero uno is this: Rory Calhoun was asleep when he was killed. We know this because that's what Elizabeth told the police. She waited to hear him snore. Bless her heart, she was just trying to be honest. She was sure that once they heard her story, they'd understand. But in cases like this, police and prosecutors can be the least understanding group of folks you'd ever want to meet."

McLeish paused to make sure his words were sinking in. Jack, Sophie and Elizabeth all looked at their hands. Claire looked down, too, and saw "PD sucks dicks" scratched into the varnished surface.

"Problem two," McLeish said. "In 1979, it will still be hard to find a jury who will buy the notion that a man can rape his own wife."

"She has to hear this?" Jack asked, nodding toward Claire.

"Problem number three," McLeish continued. "No physical evidence to substantiate Elizabeth's version of events, other than the knife ending up just where she said it did, in her husband's chest, and that helps us not one little bit."

Sophie stole a glance at Claire, who had already heard the details on the radio news and had been dreaming of a knife sticking out of her father for three nights by then.

"There were no markings on her body, no bruises," McLeish continued. "We know why, and Elizabeth will explain it to the jury. But the way it stands now, those folks will just have to take her word for it. When you get right down to it, the only incontrovertible facts at this point are that Rory Calhoun was stabbed to death in his own bed while asleep, and his wife was the one who did it. Like I say, there are problems."

Claire's mother let go of her hand and began to weep.

"Let's not get ahead of ourselves," McLeish said, smiling bravely. "We know the truth. There are good reasons why Elizabeth did what she did that night. Solving problems is my business."

He seemed to be enjoying himself. He scribbled something on his legal pad, as if a great idea had just come to him.

"I think we can get a jury to bite on manslaughter, second degree," he said. "From there, with Elizabeth's good looks and gentle demeanor, with her clean record, with a little girl who dearly needs her, it's only a tiny leap to probation, especially if we can put on testimony that the deceased was a cheating lout on top of everything else."

The adults straightened.

"But we need to establish extreme duress, closely proximate to the event," McLeish said. "Elizabeth tells me that a few days before, the deceased comes home in the morning for the sole purpose of trashing the living room and destroying her most prized possessions, her piano books and some old magazines she'd been saving. Did I get that right?"

"Yes, sir," Claire's mother said.

"Claire came home from school to see the aftermath, the mess," McLeish said. "Is that right, honey?"

Her heart raced.

"All...All...All the furniture was tipped over, the television was broken, and pieces of paper were all over the floor," she said.

"Perfect," McLeish said.

He leaned forward, both elbows on the table. He pushed his glasses up, and focused on her. He was no longer smiling.

"Your mother says you're a real smart girl, smartest girl in her sixth-grade class," McLeish said.

Claire shrugged.

"She sure is," Sophie said. Claire's mother put an arm around her shoulder and squeezed.

"Great," McLeish said. "Claire, let's you and me play a little game. You ever seen a trial on a television show, where there's a judge and a jury, and lawyers, and witnesses?"

She nodded.

"That's the game you and I are going to play. Let's pretend you're the witness and I'm the lawyer asking you questions."

"Uh-huh."

"First thing, you have to answer yes or no to my questions, not uh-huh or uh-uh. Get it?"

"Uh-huh," she said. McLeish winked. "I mean, yes sir."

"Super," he said. "Let's go back to the night before your daddy died. You remember that night?"

"Yes."

"Watch a little TV, maybe?"

"No, sir," Claire said. "My dad wrecked our TV that day, too."

McLeish scribbled in his legal pad and underlined it twice.

"Put the leg of a chair through the picture tube if I recall correctly," he said.

Elizabeth nodded.

"So what did you do?" he asked.

"I read Sherlock Holmes," Claire said.

"Which story?"

"The Hound of the Baskervilles."

"Christ. A classic," McLeish said. "You're what, twelve?"

"Yes."

"OK," McLeish said. "You were reading about the curse of Baskerville Hall. Then what?"

"I think I fell asleep, because the next thing I heard was my father's car pulling up into our driveway."

"Perfect" McLeish said, scribbling. "And then?"

"I heard him come in the front door."

"And?"

"I heard my mother scream at him."

"What exactly?"

"She told him to get out."

"What did he say to that?"

"He said he didn't have to," Claire said. "He said he lived there or something like that. He started laughing."

McLeish scribbled furiously.

"Then what?"

"Mother said she would call the police if he didn't leave."

"And your father said?"

"I don't really remember exactly. But I know he started laughing again."

"Go on, Claire, you're doing great."

"Then I heard my mother say that she and I were going to live with Uncle Jack and Aunt Sophie."

"What did he say to that?"

"He said we wouldn't survive a week without him."

"And then?"

"He said he wasn't leaving until he got what he came for, what belonged to him," Claire said.

"What do you suppose that was?"

"I don't know," she said. "I thought maybe some tools or something."

"Tools," McLeish said as he scribbled, shaking his head. "Then what?"

"I heard steps in the living room. Our floor makes noises when you walk on it."

"What did your mother say?"

"She was worried that he would wake me up," Claire said. "Then I heard her start to cry."

"Of course she did," McLeish said. "So your father came to get what belonged to him."

"Yes, sir. Oh. I remember he told her to suck it."

McLeish paused, and began to scribble again.

"And you hear him take some steps and your mother starts to cry," McLeish said. "Now the police report says you were asleep when everything happened. Doesn't sound like it to me. Were you asleep?"

"No," Claire said.

"No?"

"I was awake the whole night."

McLeish scribbled.

"How could a little girl sleep through something like that?" he said. "You weren't asleep. What did you see and hear that night?"

Claire looked at the faces around the table.

"I don't think you'll believe me," Claire said.

"Of course we'll believe you, darling," her mother said, squeezing her hand again beneath the table.

"Trust me, we'll believe you," McLeish said. "So will a jury."

Claire stared down at the table.

"Please, honey," McLeish said.

She looked up at McLeish.

"When my mother started to cry, something happened. Something I never expected," Claire said.

"Go on."

"For a couple of days, I had been praying for Jesus to come to meet me, because he had met my teacher, Sister Rosalie," Claire said. "That night, just when my mother started to cry, he did."

"Who did?" McLeish said.

"Jesus," Claire said.

212

"Did what?" the lawyer asked.

"He came to meet me."

"Jesus came to meet you," McLeish said.

"Yes. Or I went off to meet him, would be a better way of putting it."

"You went to meet Jesus," McLeish said. He stopped writing and looked at her. "Tell me about that."

"When my mother started to cry, I went away to a beautiful garden and was sitting with Jesus by a rock in the dark. We talked."

"Jesus, you say," McLeish said again. He removed his glasses. "At his rock."

"Yes, sir."

Jack and Sophie had turned to stone. McLeish returned his glasses to his nose.

"Listen, Claire," he said. "I'm thinking. It was Holy Week, right? The nuns and priests at school probably talked about the sad things that were going on with Jesus."

"I guess," Claire said.

"Maybe that put some ideas into your head, some fantasies, even nightmares," McLeish said.

"Maybe."

"Try to put that aside, and tell us what you heard in your house that night," McLeish said.

"I didn't hear anything after my mom started to cry," Claire said. "Nothing but the wind in the garden, and the voice of Jesus, who knew my name."

"You were dreaming."

"I knew you wouldn't believe me," Claire said and she started to cry.

Claire's mother laid her head on the table.

McLeish fell back in his chair.

"When did you come home from the garden?" the lawyer asked. "When did this little audience with our Lord Jesus come to an end?"

"When the lady policeman touched my arm," Claire said between sniffles.

"Then what?"

"Then I saw all the police in my house, and all the cars outside."

"What happened to the stone, to Jesus?"

"I don't know."

"Our time is almost up," McLeish said. "Let me ask you straight away. Did you hear what happened between your father and your mother that night? Did you hear or see the terrible things your father did to your mother? Because if you did, I really need to know."

"No, sir," she said.

"All you saw was Jesus."

McLeish lifted his briefcase onto the table, opened it, and dumped the legal pad and pen inside. Sophie was white, watching her sister cry. Jack scowled at Claire and shook his head.

"Like I say," McLeish said. "We've got problems. Maybe some hypnosis might help. I'll look into it. But that will be more money."

Chapter 33

The next morning, Claire sat next to Karen on the bus, but Karen spent the ride looking out the window. Sister Rosalie met Claire when she stepped down, swept Claire into her arms and kissed the top of her head while all the other kids around them watched. Sister Rosalie took Claire's hand and led her up the steps.

"It's so nice to have you back," Sister Rosalie said. "I had heard you went to stay at your aunt's house."

"My mom got out on bail," Claire said. "We went home last night."

"Claire, I'm so sorry."

"Jesus came," Claire said. "I couldn't wait to tell you. He came the night my mom killed my dad. He brought me to him, just when it all was happening. We sat and talked by this big rock. "

"Oh, my word," Sister Rosalie said.

"I thought you'd be happy," Claire said.

"You sweet little girl," the nun said.

"You don't believe me either?" Claire asked.

"But of course I do, sweetheart," Sister Rosalie said.

"It doesn't sound like it."

"Run along to your room. I'll see you at recess."

Sister Rosalie walked Claire onto the playground a few hours later. A kickball game was already in progress. Tommy Briggs was standing next to Dan Delage, waiting for their turn to kick. When they saw Claire, Briggs stabbed Delage in the chest with an imaginary knife, and Delage flopped onto the ground. Several of the children laughed.

After school, Karen sat with other girls at the back of the bus. Claire had a seat to herself. Jack's Cadillac was parked in the driveway when she walked up. Jack, Sophie and her mother were waiting around the dining room table.

"I brought cake," Sophie said. "How about a big piece and some milk?"

"I'm not hungry," Claire said.

"Just a little piece, then," Sophie said. "Have a seat and I'll get it for you."

Claire sat down opposite her mother, who was smoking and staring at a full ashtray. Sophie came back with the cake and a glass of milk.

"How was school?" Sophie asked.

"The kids were weird," Claire said. "Teachers, too."

"Claire, honey, there's something we need to talk about," Sophie said.

"What's that?" Claire asked.

"We need to talk about what you saw the other night," Sophie said.

"You mean when mom killed dad?" Claire asked.

"That's what I mean," Sophie said.

"But I already told that lawyer," Claire said. "The only thing I saw was Jesus."

Elizabeth bolted from her chair.

"But you were there!" she screamed. "I saw you, standing right there in the door, holding that fucking bear of yours. You were looking right at us. What in the fuck is wrong with you?"

She ran from the room but came back and stood over Claire.

"I did it for both of us," she cried. "Why can't you see?"

Claire's mother ran out again and the front door slammed loudly behind her.

The trial took place a year later. Claire was brought to the courthouse on the morning the jury started to deliberate. She sat with her mother, aunt and uncle in a small room. Jack had just brought Claire a hamburger for lunch when McLeish came in.

"They're back," he said.

The courtroom was crowded, and Claire felt the stares and heard the whispers as she walked in. Claire sat between Sophie and Jack on the front row, just a few feet from the defense table where Elizabeth was in a chair next to McLeish. The jurors filed in. Women on the jury were crying.

"Oh, oh," McLeish whispered.

Everyone stood and listened to the verdict. Elizabeth's legs gave out and McLeish caught her. Sophie sobbed next to Claire, who had a spot of ketchup on her dress that looked like blood.

Claire, her aunt and uncle returned to the little room, but Claire's mother did not. Sophie testified during what McLeish called the punishment phase. Late that afternoon, the jury filed back in. Elizabeth and McLeish stood. This time the lawyer put his arm around her waist. A man on the jury said thirty years.

Elizabeth did not collapse. A female deputy came toward her with handcuffs. Before she could put them on, Claire's mother turned to look at her daughter in the front row.

"How could you?" she hissed.

She was shackled and led from the courtroom. Elizabeth looked back at Claire before she disappeared through a door.

Chapter 34

Nausea rose from her stomach into her throat when she turned onto the road through the trees. Wendell's pickup was in its place, William's red Miata beside it. Wendell's son opened the front door and smiled, smug as ever, though his eyes were puffy. He was wearing the same clothes as the night before but his hair was pulled into a ponytail.

She waited on the porch. When Wendell came through the door he was in stocking feet and wore a white undershirt. His hair was mussed and his eyes bloodshot. He kept his hands in his pockets.

"I hope you don't mind me dropping in," Claire said.

"I didn't figure to see you today," he said.

"Returning to the scene of the crime," she said.

"Last night was a crime," he said.

"Life goes on," Claire said.

"Why aren't you at work?"

"I called in sick," she said. "I need to talk to you."

"About what?"

"About what?" she replied. "You know perfectly well."

"About what happened to you, I guess," Wendell said. "Your story."

"That one," she said. "Remember? Crazy mother. Drunken father. Ring a bell?"

"I remember," he said.

"So now you're too busy to hear it, I guess."

"There are problems," he said.

"You can say that again," Claire said.

"Go home and talk to your husband," Wendell said. "That's where you belong. Not here."

"You promised to listen," she said.

Claire staggered a few steps to the porch swing and slumped down.

"I'm sorry," Wendell said, looking down at her. "That's how it needs to be."

"Is it your son? Are you going to listen to that guy?"

"No."

Wendell looked out into the trees.

"This has become a mess," he said. "Mostly of my making, but a mess just the same. It would serve nobody to make it worse."

"And just how would we do that? By listening to me? I guess I don't see the harm."

"You should go."

She fought back tears. Then panic. Then rage.

"Claire," Wendell said.

She stood.

"It's been nice knowing you," she said.

He turned toward the door. Claire staggered a few steps toward her car and stopped.

"On the first day I came out here I told you my mom was in prison, but I never said what happened to my dad," she said. "Aren't you the least bit curious?"

"It's none of my business," Wendell said.

"Christ," she said. "You sound just like my husband."

"All the same," Wendell said.

"He ended up with a knife in his chest, put there by his wife, my mother. Right there in his own bed. He used it to carve the turkey at Thanksgiving. Cops showed up and there he was, knife sticking out of him like a pig. That's what the newspapers said. I was in my bed, in the next room. I was twelve."

Wendell took a hand from a pocket, which shook violently as he ran his fingers through his uncombed hair. He massaged the back of his neck and shook his head.

"The world is a horrible place," Wendell said.

"The story gets better, but like you said, my place is at home."

She walked down the steps and turned.

"Wendell," she said.

He hadn't moved.

"Yes, Claire," he said.

"Go to hell."

Chapter 35

She didn't remember the drive back to Arlington, had totally spaced out until someone in a pickup truck honked and flipped her off as she turned into the day-care center. Miss Dawn held a wailing infant behind the front desk.

"I thought I'd take Mike home early," Claire said.

"But Mrs. Cavanaugh," she said. "Your husband called this morning. He said the little guy wouldn't be here today."

Claire brought her hands to her face and quickly returned them to her sides.

"Of course he did," she said. "How could I forget?"

Miss Dawn handed the baby to a co-worker and came out from behind the desk.

"Are you OK, Mrs. Cavanaugh?" she asked.

"Never better, thanks," Claire said.

Larry had left a note on the bed. He and Mike would be staying with his boss. There was a telephone number. Mike's empty breakfast plate and Larry's cold pancakes and bacon sat on the kitchen table. She drove to a convenience store and bought a carton of Kools. She went to a cupboard and got a small plate for an ashtray and stumbled into the bedroom. She lit a cigarette and lay on the bed, watching the ceiling fan twirl. She thought about driving to a liquor store for a bottle of vodka but didn't feel like facing the world even that much. The butts piled up in the plate by her bed. Around midnight, she looked in the medicine cabinet, but aspirin was all they had and that would just make her sick. She knew she didn't have the guts to use a knife. She fell asleep thinking about what a failure she had been as a mother.

Claire woke up at dawn and forced herself out of bed to pee, then climbed back beneath the covers and sank back into a depressive sleep. Judging by the sun through the windows, it was midday when she opened her eyes again. When she sat up, Larry was standing at the bedroom door.

"Mike needed some things," he said

"I suppose he would," Claire said.

"And I was worried about you."

"Nothing to worry about here, Larry," Claire said.

"My boss has grandkids Mike's age," Larry said. "Keeps him occupied."

"OK."

"Smoky in here," Larry said.

"I've taken up my habits from the good old days," Claire said.

"What would you call the last twelve years? The bad old days?"

"It was just a matter of time," Claire said.

"Before what?"

"Before this," Claire said. "Your sisters were right, but damaged goods doesn't begin to cover it. Wendell has figured that out, too, evidently."

"What do you mean?" Larry asked.

"Never mind," Claire said.

"You went to see him."

"We had a brief chat, yes," Claire said.

"What happened?" Larry asked.

"Nothing," Claire said.

"Did he do something to you? Say something?"

"Oh, please. You going to go beat him up?" Claire said. "Like high school? Don't waste your effort. And no. He didn't do anything, other than come to his senses. Told me to take a long walk off a short dock.

Can't blame him, can you? You said it. I can't even be trusted around my own son."

"That was wrong of me," Larry said. "You're a great mother."

"This your idea of a great mother?"

"Stop it, Claire."

"When I went back there yesterday, Wendell said my place was here, with you," she said. "Only you aren't here."

Larry crossed the room and sat on the bed.

"But I am," he said.

"Not for long," Claire said.

Neither spoke for several seconds.

"I've been thinking," Larry said. "You were right."

"About what?"

"I never wanted to know what happened to you in Minnesota. I was afraid. There is something I've never told you. After that first Thanksgiving, I went back to give my sisters a piece of my mind. Margaret said, 'Larry, what if it's in her blood?' 'What do you mean?' I said. 'Murder,' she said. I said that was crazy, that you wouldn't hurt a fly. But I knew there was darkness in your heart. How could there not be. That's where I wanted it to stay, hidden away. I figured if I treated you right, I could help keep it there. Like I said, I guess I was scared."

Claire's eyes burned.

"So tell me," he said.

"Tell you what?"

"Whatever needs telling," he said. "I want to know. Maybe I'm finally man enough to listen."

Chapter 36

Minnesota 1979

He reached across the piano bench, grabbed her by the hair, and pulled her across the bench, tipping it over. He dragged her by the hair across the living room. That's why there were no bruises.

"Please, Rory," her mother pleaded again. "You'll wake Claire! I'll do anything you want. Please don't do this."

"Shut up," he said.

He pulled her into their bedroom. Claire followed them, holding her bear. He threw Elizabeth down onto their bed. He picked her up by the hair and threw her down on the mattress again. He tore open her pajama top. He ripped her pajama bottoms to her knees.

"Can your piano lover do this?" her father said.

Claire's mother lay beneath him, crying and moaning. She kept saying, "Oh, God, no."

He grabbed a pillow and pressed it over her face with both hands. He kept pressing and pressing as he straddled her. His naked rear end began to thrust back and forth, ramming Claire's mother while her arms and legs flailed, her screams muffled by the pillow.

Her flailing weakened. He arched his back and groaned, and collapsed on top of her, releasing the pillow. Claire's mother pushed it from her face, coughing and gasping. He rolled off, his pants around his knees. He lay back, looking up toward the ceiling, and laughed.

"That's what I came for," he said.

Chapter 37

"She's getting out in a few months," Claire said. "Sophie called and told me. She said that mother should come live with us. I thought the piano would be part of my penance."

She and Larry sat side by side on the back step, looking at the moon that peeked in and out of the oak trees as it made its way across the Texas sky. Larry lit her cigarette with a book of matches. Her trembling began to subside. She stubbed out her third cigarette before smoking it halfway.

"I was there," Claire said. "I saw everything. That's what was going on when I was with Jesus. Only our good Lord was some sort of a hallucination."

Neither spoke.

"Please tell me what you're thinking," she said.

"What if it wasn't?"

"What if what wasn't?"

"What if it wasn't a hallucination? What if Jesus was really with you that night, protecting you from things that a little girl just isn't meant to see?"

"But I did see," Claire said.

"You did and you didn't," he said. "Jesus helped you close your eyes until you were old enough to handle it."

"It was my fault that she went to prison," Claire said.

"If that's the case, then Jesus is to blame, too," he said.

He put his arm around her and kissed her cheek.

"I'm so sorry, Claire," he said.

It was a cloudy day and cool for that time of the year. A beautiful white tiger paced behind glass, just a few feet from where Mike stood, transfixed.

"Pet the tiger," he said.

"Not this trip, buddy," Larry said.

The boy marveled at the elephants and giraffes, and he laughed at the monkeys. The three of them ate hamburgers at a zoo cafe. They left the zoo and rode a miniature train that clacked over a river and through a long, shady park. Mike sat between them in one of the first cars. They waved at people having picnics, and joggers. Frisbees flew through the air. Mike slept in the back seat on the way home.

"Why?" she asked that night, lying next to Larry.

"Why what?" Larry said.

"Why did you come to my door that first night?" she asked. "Why did you ask me to that stupid dance? Why did you love me then? Why do you love me now?"

"You already know why," he said.

"No, I don't."

"It was your handwriting," he said. "Now sleep."

Chapter 38

The bartender was a woman in her forties with shoulder-length, platinum-blonde hair, big chested and pretty once. She had been talking to an old man in coveralls. She put her cigarette in an ashtray when William came in.

"What will it be, honey?" she asked, wiping her hands on a towel tucked into her jeans.

"A Budweiser and something a little stronger for good luck," William said.

"Coming up," the bartender said. "Haven't seen you in here before."

"First time." he said.

"Welcome to paradise," the woman said. "Yell if you need me."

William was good and drunk by the time he ran through his cash. By then he was alone with the bartender, who had plugged several quarters into a jukebox in the corner. Lively country-western music, Randy Travis and Hank Williams Jr., filled the dark little place.

"Next thing is you'll want to dance," William said.

"I'm on duty," she said.

"Course you are," William said. "And I'm sober."

"I get off at eight," she said. "Let the dancing begin."

He laughed and slid from the stool, trying to keep from staggering as he made his way to the door. He squinted in the late-afternoon brightness. The heat felt good after two hours in the cool dark. He sped off down the road, his mother's notebook sitting next to him on the passenger seat. William turned on the radio and found a rock station. He blasted Pink Floyd at full volume. William turned back into the trees of the home place and his car was swallowed by shade and late-afternoon shadow.

His father's pickup was still gone, still off chasing that crazy young woman, William thought. Where else could the old guy disappear to? The pond? William parked by the house, stumbled up the stairs and fell into bed, planning to catch a nap before returning to the little tavern to take up with that horny broad. When he woke up it was almost dark, well after eight. He had a throbbing headache. He looked out and saw his father's pickup, but the house was dark and quiet so he figured Wendell must be in his room. William gulped two glasses of water in the kitchen downstairs and remembered the notebook.

The night was warm and breezy as William walked to his car and retrieved the memoir. He sat down on the porch swing and opened it to where he had left off the night before, reading in what was left of the natural light. After a few paragraphs, he hurled the notebook out onto the grass, pacing the length of the porch.

He grabbed a rocking chair and chucked it onto the grass, too, then leaned over the porch railing, and the beer and whiskey and what was left of his lunch and breakfast spewed out onto the rosebushes. The retching continued for several minutes, but after the first convulsions all that came up was green bile. His breath came in rapid gasps, like he had just finished a sprint. His breathing calmed and the retching subsided and William stumbled down the steps to retrieve the notebook, lying open on the grass. When he turned back toward the house, his father stood in the doorway. William passed him without speaking, went through the door and climbed the stairs to his room, where he sat at his desk and put his head in his hands. After a few minutes, he heard Wendell's bedroom door open and close. William finished his mother's story.

Chapter 39

April 17, 1991

So long since I picked up this old thing. I wonder why moments of despair are what drive me here, back to our unfinished story? Maybe because there is so much hurt in what I remember from my life with Wendell, and the newest hurts force me to recall the old ones. This is my new hurt.

It's spring break at Texas Tech, and William is home for a few days from his teaching job, but he didn't come alone. Her name is Heather, and she is lovely and sweet and seems bright enough, but she is oh so young. No more than twenty-five would be my guess.

This morning was warm and sunny, so William put me in my wheelchair, but it was Heather who pushed as we took a slow stroll on the road through the budding oaks. I refuse to get attached to this girl because I've made that mistake before. Soon she will be gone, and there will be another girl, sweet and pretty and young, and another after that.

Tonight, my heart aches more than my body. Will my son ever grow up? Why does he need the adoration of lovers who could be his daughters? My heartache tonight is for him, and for me. Am I somehow to blame?

In a few days William and Heather will be gone, and I will be back to the business of dying with Wendell. My son is ensnared in this mysterious adolescence. But a woman could ask no more of a husband. Wendell bathes me now, and lays out my medicines, and cooks nice meals whether I eat them or not, and he carries me from chair to bed and back, and reads me poetry. With my son, there is heartbreak and disappointment. With my husband, I have discovered the true meaning of love. That journey to love has been a long one.

∎

After that night in my apartment I tried to put Wendell out of my mind. But in the months that followed, there was never a day that I didn't think of him, didn't remember the feel of his lips or the way he looked in the candlelight, stretched across my sofa, his head on my lap. I looked for his long frame after school, hoping to see him walking toward me down the hall, but he never came. It was all I could do to keep from driving out to the Smith place, to find Wendell and coax him into my life, and I don't know what stopped me. Maybe it was the enormity of Wendell's hurt that I had witnessed in my apartment. Or maybe it was the fact that, for a few months more at least, I was still the teacher of his younger brother. Or maybe it was because I knew deep down that Wendell and I were somehow inevitable, that my chance with him would come.

It did on a sultry night in May 1946, and once again I had Tommy Smith to thank. Tommy had insisted I come to his graduation party. Mr. Harrison was my escort. Tommy, his parents, and friends of the family were standing on the front porch when we arrived.

"There seems to be someone missing," I said to Tommy.

"He made a brief appearance," he said.

"Where is he?"

"In our room."

"He's in for a surprise," I said.

"It'll be like surprising a bear," Tommy said.

"I'll take my chances," I said.

Tommy laughed.

"Go right at the top of the stairs," he said.

He opened the front door as if to dare me. I slipped inside and climbed the stairs. The door at the end of the hall was slightly ajar and a light was on inside. I raised my hand to knock but pushed the door open instead. Wendell was stretched out on the top bunk. He turned his head.

"Looking for the bathroom," I said.

"This ain't it," he said.

"Long as I'm here, mind if I come in?"

"You're already in, looks to me," Wendell said.

"Some people have no manners."

"Or respect for privacy," Wendell said.

A Bisbee High School banner hung on one wall. Yellowed newspaper clippings were taped here and there. Two pairs of work boots were neatly aligned along the wall beneath the school banner. A football lay next to a battered pair of cleats. There were two desks, two chairs, books, pencils, stacks of paper, a fishing pole.

"What do you want, Miss Sanchez?" Wendell asked.

"You're missing quite a party," I said.

"Don't start that again," Wendell said, swinging his legs over the side of the bed and jumping down.

"Start what again?"

"How I'm mean to Tommy."

"I won't. He says you've been feeling much better. We still talk, you know."

"So he says."

"But I never told him about my apartment," I said.

"What was there to tell?" Wendell asked.

"A day doesn't pass that I don't think about it," I said.

He blushed.

"How often have you?"

"How often have I what?"

"Thought about that night in my apartment?"

He grunted.

"Was it my cooking? Is that why you never called?"

"Jesus, Mary and Joseph," he said.

"Or maybe it was my kissing."

"Stop it, Miss Sanchez!"

"I wanted to get to know you better after that night, to know your other favorite poems, to hear more of your stories from overseas. You didn't answer my question. Was it the cooking?"

Wendell's face was in shadow, but I could make out the hurt in his eyes.

"I thought after that night you would understand," he said.

"Understand what?"

"The person you saw on your sofa that night, shaking like a leaf, that's who I am," Wendell said. "Why would you want to get mixed up with someone like me?"

"Maybe I have terrible taste in men," I said.

"Lord, you don't stop."

He was the first to look away.

"I'll ask you again: Was it the cooking or the way I kiss?"

He still wouldn't look at me.

"Answer me, goddamn you!" I said "Or maybe you need something to refresh your memory."

I took a step forward, grabbed his suspenders in each hand and pulled him toward me. His resistance was half-hearted and momentary, and by the time I found his lips they were as welcoming as they had been that night in my apartment. His arms curled around me. Then I heard Mr. Harrison's voice from the bottom of the stairs.

"Selma?"

I put my hand to Wendell's face.

"It must have been the cooking," I said.

Wendell was waiting in the high school parking lot. He opened my door and helped me from the car, wearing black trousers and a starched white shirt.

We drove from Bisbee in his pickup. A picnic basket jostled on the seat between us as we passed through rolling hills and thickets of live oaks. Blankets of wildflowers bloomed along the road. After several miles, Wendell turned off the blacktop onto a narrow dirt road. Black and white cattle grazed on either side.

Wendell pounded on the horn to chase a calf and her mother out of the way. We rumbled across a cattle guard and climbed a steep hill through bushy cedars. The trees parted at the top of the hill. That's when I finally saw it—dark green water shimmering in the late morning sun, a lovely little lake. Wendell shut off the engine.

"The pond," he said.

"Paradise," I said.

He took the basket and grabbed a blanket from the bed of the truck, throwing it over his shoulder. I took his hand as he led me down through deep grass. Our palms were both damp. He led me to a spot in the shade beneath an old cypress. Wendell set the basket beneath the tree. He walked to the edge of the water, bent to pick up a small rock and hurled it. The pond swallowed the rock with a plunk and little ripples spread out across the glass. Lily pads flowered to our left.

"An underground spring flows into the pond so it never dries up, even during drought," he said. "A hundred years ago, this place would have been surrounded by teepees. When we were boys, and my brother and I would get tired of fishing, we'd poke around for arrowheads. I must have fifty of those things back home in jars."

"If only this tree could talk," I said.

We ate with our fingers, sitting across from each other on the blanket. Wendell's mother had cooked fried chicken. Now he was the teacher, the guide, pointing out the places along the pond where deer came to drink, or where the cedar trees were gnawed down by a beaver. He chewed slowly on a piece of chicken and followed the path of a hawk that circled in the sky.

"I told my mother I was going on a picnic, but wouldn't say who with," Wendell said. "She decided to cook for me anyway. I told Tommy about that night at your apartment. Said I was going to get you out of my hair today."

"What did he think?" I asked.

"He was a little jealous."

I laughed.

"He said to tell you hello." Wendell said.

I bit into a piece of celery, smiling out onto the water, thinking of all the times Wendell and Tommy had been here before, catching fish, being brothers.

"Where's your fishing rod?" I asked.

"I left it at home," he said. "I didn't figure you could keep quiet long enough for me to cast the damn thing."

I rolled on the blanket, laughing.

"I think I've just been insulted," I said.

Wendell smiled.

"You have to admit," he said. "You do like to talk."

"That's not all I like to do."

I moved tin foil wrappers full of celery and boiled eggs, clearing a space on the blanket. I moved to him on my knees, ran my fingers through his hair, and then put my hands on his cheeks.

"If I had to choose between kissing you and talking, God could strike me mute," I said.

I kissed him and he kissed me back, pulling me down onto the blanket. Perhaps it was a good thing after all that the cypress could not talk.

Chapter 40

William was conceived that day at the pond or in one of the passionate nights in my apartment in the weeks that followed. A few months later, the two of us, plus Francis, Wendell's friend from the lumberyard, drove to Waco in my Packard and met Tommy and Fay, the girl who would become Tommy's wife. Wendell and I were married there in a park by a justice of the peace.

William was born. In those early years, Wendell was a doting husband and father who came home for lunch and read poetry to me at night. I loved him so much. The bad dreams had disappeared after we married, his demons were banished. Or so I thought.

Then, on a hot summer night in 1954, Jim Smith collapsed from a heart attack and died in Wendell's arms. On the night of his father's funeral, Wendell soiled our bed and woke up panting from his first bad dream in years. He wouldn't speak of it the next day. Another terror followed the next night, and the next. Each nightmare seemed more horrible. One night Wendell's screaming woke up William, who wandered into our room wondering what was wrong.

Wendell became terrified by even the thought of sleep. Many times he spent the whole night sitting on the front steps, willing himself to stay awake, refusing my pleas to come to bed. The old horrors had just been biding their time, gaining strength, waiting for the opening in Wendell's soul that the death of his father had provided. I pleaded with him to talk to me, but he claimed he didn't remember his dreams. Like that first night in my apartment, Wendell had withdrawn with his agony to a place where I couldn't follow.

On that November evening in 1956, I drove down our road with the windows wide open, the smell of roast beef and mashed potatoes and gravy drifting out from tin foil-covered plates that were in the back seat. I guess you never fully appreciate anything until you face the prospect of losing it, so I loved our little road more than ever that night, stopping halfway down to listen to the rustle of the branches above me, and to feel the cool of autumn on my face. How many more times would I drive on this beautiful little road?

Wendell was waiting out front.

"I fed William and asked Judy Springer to watch him. We needed to talk alone tonight."

"I guess so," Wendell said.

"Help me carry," I said.

I opened the Studebaker's back door and bent to retrieve the two plates, handing them to him. I took a grocery bag from the seat and shut the door with my hip. Wendell's desk was in a small office in the rear. I put the bag on a chair and moved his paperwork, making room for two wicker place mats that I took from the sack. Wendell set out the plates and removed the foil. Steam billowed.

I brushed strands of curly hair away from his eyes. His face was ghostly pale and felt feverish.

"Eat, Wendell, before the food gets cold," I said.

Each of us took a few half-hearted bites. I set my fork and knife on his desk.

"William told me that he talked to you this morning," I said. "He said that you told him he must have been dreaming when he heard me cry."

The trembling in Wendell's hands intensified. He set his fork down and stared at his plate.

"That's what I told him," Wendell said.

"The boy's nearly eight years old," I said. "Lying to him will only make it worse."

"I didn't know what else to say, just like now."

"How I wish it was just another one of your nightmares," I said.

"I'm sorry," he said.

"Let me see your arm," I said.

"No," he said.

"Show me your arm or I'll leave this minute," I said.

He rolled the sleeve up his left arm to his elbow. A fresh, angry wound ran from just below his elbow to almost his wrist, and was starting to scab over.

"I didn't mean to hurt you," I said. "I'm sorry."

"You're sorry? Jesus Christ, Selma."

He looked over at me.

"Show me your neck," he said.

I had worn a turtleneck sweater.

"There's no need," I said. "We both know what happened. And it's not my neck that's hurting."

"I'm hurting, too," Wendell said.

When I think of what happened next, it's as if I'm watching another woman, a stranger who came flying out of her chair, sweeping her full plate of food from the desk, sending it crashing onto the tile. Gobs of meat, mashed potatoes, gravy and cream corn were everywhere.

"Then why won't you talk to me?" I screamed.

Wendell rocked back, stunned. I slumped back down to my chair and covered my face with my hands. Sobbing consumed me for several frightening seconds. Wendell started from his chair, but I finally got a gasp of air and I waved him off.

Wendell walked to the bathroom and came back with a handful of tissue.

"Thank you," I said after blowing my nose. "I'm sorry. That was no way to act."

"You have every right," Wendell said.

"Well, maybe I do," I said. "Do you know what it's been like for me the last few years?"

I blew my nose again.

"But I couldn't erase the memories of what it used to be like," I said.

"I'm sorry, Selma," Wendell said. "You deserve better."

"I'm not sure you're entitled to feel sorry for yourself," I said. "I've tried every way I know to get you to talk to me. But you were always too busy or too tired. Well, to hell with that. In some ways, I think you enjoy your anguish. It gives you an excuse

241

to disappear into that dark little world of yours. But I've had it. Like I said, spare me the self-pity."

I had never seen Wendell look so sad, but that night I realized that he had controlled me with that mournful look, manipulated me.

"So last night I wake up with my husband's hands around my throat."

"I don't know what happened," Wendell said.

"Of course you don't, Wendell," I said. "It was a dream. Only this time the dream spilled over. Only this time it wasn't enough to swear and scream and sweat and thrash beneath the covers. Who was I supposed to be, some German?"

"I don't know," Wendell said.

"What if I hadn't been able to wake you up?" I asked.

He rolled his sleeve back down to his wrist.

"I've done a lot of thinking today, Wendell," I said, straightening in my chair, dabbing my eyes with the soggy tissue. "You know one of the scariest parts? I'm not even surprised. Whatever it was that you have been running from over here at the lumberyard was bound to catch you some day at home."

I swallowed hard against another sob.

"I probably would have been willing to wait until the day I died for you to come back to me," I said. "But I can't live wondering when you'll finish what you started last night. I can't let William live in a place where that might happen. Our son has to come first."

"He's always come first," he said.

"You'd never know from the last two years," I said.

He didn't reply.

"My mother will be here in an hour or so," I said. "I called this morning."

It was like he expected what I would say next.

"I'm leaving with William tomorrow, taking him out of school for a week and going back to San Antonio with my mother, at least until after Thanksgiving," I said. "I need some time away to think."

I wondered if he had heard me.

"Is there anything you'd like to say?" I asked.

"There's nothing to say," he whispered. "Other than I'm sorry."

"I know you are, Wendell," I said. "I'm sorry, too."

"Things just aren't that simple," Wendell said.

"I don't suppose they are. But what does that change?"

A few hours later, I felt Wendell's touch on my shoulder, then his weight settle onto the side of our bed. I turned to face him.

"Don't go," he said.

"I need to, Wendell," I said.

"Will you stay if I talk?" he asked. "I'll talk until my dying breath."

"It might be too late, Wendell," I said.

"I'll sleep at the lumberyard until things are better," he said.

"Let's talk in the morning," I said. "Lie down."

He swung his legs up. I rolled toward him and tucked my head onto his shoulder. We were both asleep in a few deep, exhausted breaths. My mother found us that way when she peeked in at first light.

Chapter 41

August 10, 1991

A few minutes after 11 p.m.

There are moments when it feels as if I've crossed over already, when the world seems bathed in lovely yellow light and the edges of everything are blurred. Even the sad, loving face of my husband, who stands on one side of my bed, and that of our dear friend, Francis, who positions himself on the other side, looking down at me. But pain eventually clarifies. The throbbing returns and the yellow light wanes and once more everything comes into sharp focus, at least until Wendell decides enough time has passed and he can give me another one of those wonderful pills that stop the pain.

One of them is nearly always with me now. If Wendell is downstairs cooking or out getting a prescription filled, Francis is sitting in the chair in the corner, thumbing through a fishing magazine he's probably looked at ten times already. When Francis goes off to work, Wendell takes the chair, getting up every few minutes to rub my feet, or fluff my pillows, or change the channels on the radio, or run downstairs to put ice cubes in my water. Many nights he sleeps in that chair, though I beg him to go to bed in the room that he and Tommy shared when they were boys. He would be so much more comfortable there, and near enough if there was anything I should need. That's where he is now, thankfully. I can hear his soft snoring, and I am so glad that he is finally getting some rest.

Wendell's slumber also gives me the chance that I need. I feel strong tonight, unusually so, and the throbbing in my head and bones is mercifully faint. I throw my skinny little legs over the side of the bed and have just enough strength to get to the closet and back, trying to move noiselessly so I won't wake my husband. The old box is toward the back. My notebook is underneath my grandmother's serape. A pen is still attached to the cover. I see it's been four months since I wrote here last, and I know I have only a fraction of that time left to live. The pen feels nice in my hands, and the aching in my fingers is manageable. This must be done now.

·

William and I did not go to San Antonio. A good night's sleep and autumn sunshine weakened my resolve. William trotted off to catch his bus. I told mother that Wendell and I needed to take a drive and talk things over. She promised to be waiting when William returned from school.

Wendell drove with both hands on the steering wheel, his habit when the trembling was particularly fierce. He turned onto the bumpy dirt road and parked at the crest of the hill. We sat in the truck without speaking, looking down at the water that shimmered in the late autumn sun. It was our first time to the pond since the death of Wendell's father.

I finally grabbed my purse and a blanket from the seat, setting off ahead of him down the hill. I heard his door open and close and looked back to see him making his way through the brush. The air was crisp and without a whisper of breeze. A large white heron exploded from the weeds near the water, its long wings slapping the surface as it struggled to gain altitude. The great bird reminded me why I had adored this place from that first glorious morning more than a decade before.

I spread the blanket beneath the cypress and sat down Indian style with my back to the water. Wendell sat against the trunk of the tree. I took a book from my purse.

"Please do me the honor, Wendell," I said. "Just the last stanza."

Wendell opened the book to where I had it marked and cleared his throat.

"Thanks to the human heart by which we live,
Thanks to its tenderness, its joys and its fears,
To me the meanest flower that blows can give
Thoughts that do often lie too deep for tears."

"That's from the 'Ode,'" I said.

"It's been a long time since I read to you," Wendell said.

"I want you to read to me again," I said. "I want my husband back."

"You'll have him back," he said.

"There's a name you keep saying in your sleep," I said.

246

Wendell reached for a small twig lying by his leg and drew a small circle with it in the dirt. He didn't bother trying to hide the trembling in his hand.

"You mean Newby," he said.

"I know about Sergeant Newby," I said. "That first night in my apartment, remember? The name you keep saying sounds like Vance, or Vince."

"Vinny."

"OK, Vinny," I said.

Wendell drew in a deep breath, exhaled, and tossed the twig onto the ground. In all the years since, I don't guess I've forgotten a word of what he told me next.

Wendell didn't notice him until the second day out to sea, when the soldiers were standing on deck, watching dolphins. What caught Wendell's eye at first was his size, and the fact that he stood away from the others, looking out into the ocean like he didn't want to be bothered.

"Who's that?" Wendell asked his sergeant, another Texan named Henderson.

"A kid who pissed the bed last night," Henderson said. "A bed-wetter and not a hundred pounds dripping wet. They expect me to go fight a war with guys like that."

Vinny was assigned the bunk over Wendell's when they got to England. Wendell could smell what had happened the minute he opened his eyes on that first morning. Vinny rolled off the top bunk, pulled down his soiled mattress and dragged it toward the end of the barracks, where he stuffed it into a garbage can.

"Someone get Vinny a diaper," said a soldier named Kraft.

There was laughter. Vinny dug around in his duffle. Wendell rolled out of his bunk and walked over to Kraft.

"Keep it up and you'll end up in the same place as that mattress," Wendell said.

"The gentle giant comes to save the little pee pants," Kraft said.

247

The laughter stopped when Wendell grabbed Kraft by the shirt and pulled him out of bed, yanking him into a standing position. Kraft was only a few inches shorter than Wendell, but skinny.

"Maybe I'm not so gentle after all," Wendell said.

"Jesus, Smith," Kraft said. "We were only having a little fun with the guy."

"Have your fun some other way," Wendell said.

Later that morning, Vinny fell in beside Wendell on the first of their long hikes across the English countryside.

"I can fight my own battles," he said.

"Suit yourself," Wendell said. "But tonight, if I pee in my straw, I would expect you to do the same."

"Right," Vinny said. "Fuck you."

But that night, Vinny sat down next to Wendell in the mess hall.

"My name's Vincent Vilandre," he said.

A week or so later, Wendell and Vinny hiked into a nearby village and found a quiet little pub. Vinny ordered a big glass of dark beer. Wendell drank ginger ale and a few hours later picked up Vinny from the floor of the bathroom, threw him over his shoulder and carried him back to the base. Vinny peed in the straw again that night, though this time the other guys were quiet about it.

On a weekend pass a month later, the two of them ended up on a bench in London. It was late at night. There was no moon or other light because of the blackout. Wendell could see the red ember of Vinny's cigarette but not really Vinny himself. He smoked one after another.

"You played some ball," Vinny said, the end of his Lucky smoldering brightly.

"Some," Wendell answered.

"All-state, is what I heard," Vinny said. "Not a surprise with your size."

"I guess not."

Vinny added to the pile of butts at his feet and lit up again. Wendell saw his freckles when the match flared.

"I played, too," Vinny said.

"You're not exactly built for football," Wendell said.

248

"That's what Coach Sullivan said. He wanted me to be the ball boy. I told him to find some girl to carry the balls. I wanted to play. I was a junior, weighed a hundred and six pounds, but what the hell.

"My dad laughed when I told him," Vinny continued. "He was an old man by then, a retired carpenter close to seventy, and he spent most of his days drinking cheap whiskey and playing pinochle with his buddies in a back room of an auto body shop. The night I joined the team, I watched for him to come stumbling up our sidewalk like he always did, leaning on his cane. I met him at the door and told him. He looked at me and said, 'A runt like you won't last a week.'"

Wendell studied the ember next to him on the bench, trying to make out the expression on Vinny's face.

"Your dad ever come watch you play?" Vinny asked.

"Every game," Wendell said.

Vinny waited.

"Your folks?"

"Nah," Vinny said. "My mom was too worried I'd get hurt. My dad didn't because he never gave a shit."

"That's rough,'" Wendell said.

"I must have been stupid, but I never stopped looking for my dad to show up," Vinny said. "I'd watch for this white-haired old guy with a white beard and the cane. He never did. I got in a few plays here and there, mostly on kickoffs when we were either way ahead or way behind, and I kept looking for him. Did that every game my junior and senior year. One morning my senior year, I told him that I might get to play more because we had a few guys hurt. But he never came. I got two tackles that day and nearly picked off a pass. Even old Sullivan was pretty damn impressed. My dad came stumbling home like he always did."

It seemed to Wendell that Vinny's words had turned the world colder. Wind started to blow and rain began to fall. Then Vinny's ember started to shake in the dark. Wendell tried to think of something nice to say.

"I have this cousin, Joe," Vinny said. "Joe's about six years older than me. Last spring, Joe and I rode on the back of a potato planter. One day on our lunch

break, Joe starts telling me these things, which I first thought were lies, but when I started to think about them, I knew they weren't. 'Did you know about your dad?' he asked. 'Know what about my dad?' I replied. 'He knocked up your mom when she was fifteen.'

"The rest of the story went something like this: My dad was a carpenter who traveled from town to town, making enough to buy a room and pay for his whiskey, until he would be run off for fighting with the wrong men, or trying to screw the wrong women. Then he gets to my hometown and meets my mother, who worked behind the counter of her dad's grocery store, and one thing leads to another. My mom ends up pregnant at age fifteen, and she had six brothers who more or less insisted that my old man stick around and do the right thing. He was close to fifty years old at the time. So the two of them got married and had a son, who turned out to be me.

"So that's why my father always hated me," Vinny said. "I put an end to his rambling days."

Vinny crushed out another cigarette but didn't light up right away.

"You're never gonna get your chance," Wendell said. "You know that, don't you Vinny?"

"What the hell are you talking about?" Vinny asked.

"It's already November," Wendell said. "Newby told me the other day that Ike is betting the war in Europe will be done by Christmas. You're not going to be a war hero, impress your dad, unless they ship us out to the Pacific."

"Don't worry, Wendell," Vinny said. "There's plenty of good fighting left over here. Just you wait. Those fucking Germans will get a taste of me yet."

Vinny was right, of course. His birthday was December 16, which he and Wendell celebrated eating fish and chips in the local pub. Wendell bought him a girlie magazine as a present. But Hitler had an even better gift. In the early morning hours of Vinny's birthday, the Germans began their last push of the war. They smashed through Allied lines in Belgium and for a while it didn't seem Hitler would stop until he had gotten all the way back to Paris.

That was the beginning of the Battle of the Bulge. Wendell and the others started hearing that American soldiers were in full retreat. There were casualties by the thousands. A whole division surrendered. So the day after his nineteenth birthday, Vinny and Wendell were back on a ship, heading across the English Channel. Two days after that they shared a foxhole on the front. It was really cold, and Wendell was about to lose several toes, but his little friend would have his chance to be a hero, after all.

Chapter 42

August 18, 1991

1:45 a.m.

What is it about this remembering that banishes the pain better than any drug? There is a great temptation to put down this pen and just enjoy the peace, drink in the physical comfort that I haven't felt in years. Have I been granted a midnight miracle? Has the cancer left me? I desperately want to stand up and march to the room next door and make love to my dear husband, then go straight to the gardens and feel the cool, moist soil in my fingers, even if it is the dead of night. But my gown is riding halfway up my legs, and just look at them. Birds have more substantial bones. Across the room, in the mirror above my dresser, I see this gaunt old face reflected back, and a few tufts of white hair on an otherwise bald head. Maybe the miracle isn't physical healing but this chance to set down the truth about Wendell, and what he has endured.

·

So now it's January in 1945, after they threw Wendell from the tent hospital and put him on a truck back to the front. He found Vinny the night he got back. They had double-timed it through the snow from their foxholes to company headquarters for their one hot meal of the week, a tin plate full of watery stew, and Wendell saw him standing ahead of him in line. When he got his food, Wendell followed Vinny to where he sat down on a big log. Vinny's face was blackened by soot from the candles the soldiers used for heat in the foxholes. He looked up at Wendell, didn't say anything, and attacked his food. When he'd emptied his plate, Vinny dropped it in the snow, stood and lit a cigarette.

"Shit you smell nice," he said.

"How you been?" Wendell asked.

"It's about time we take it to these German pricks," he said. "What the hell is Ike waiting for?"

"Henderson says the push is coming," Wendell said. "Then I guess you'll get what you came for."

"Fucking right," Vinny said.

It was on one of the last nights in January that their company commander, a captain named Richards, called the men together when they had gone to the rear for food.

"Tomorrow is the first day of the end of the war," Richards said. "At oh-two-thirty we move forward and we're not stopping until we get to Berlin. The Germans will be waiting in fortified positions. We will destroy them with superior numbers and superior will. But many of you who hear my voice now won't live to see another sunset. Any last letters need to be written tonight."

He paced to let his words sink in. Wendell stared at the snow, thinking of his brother, his parents and the pond.

"Remember your training," Richards said. "Spread out. Use marching fire. Keep moving forward and leave the wounded to the medics. The squad corporals have been instructed to shoot any soldier who tries to cut and run, but I know that won't be necessary. I have the best rifle company in this man's Army. Good luck, gentlemen. Happy hunting."

Wendell thought about writing home that night, but somehow that felt like tempting fate. He passed the time by cleaning his rifle and checking his ammunition. Guys in the quartermaster corps ran from hole to hole, handing out new wool socks, gloves, and Syrettes of morphine.

Sometime after midnight Sergeant Henderson climbed from his hole.

"Saddle up boys," he said as his squad gathered around him. "It's time. Glass, you're first scout. Smith, second. The rest fall in behind them."

They started marching, boots crunching in the hard snow. Vinny's squad flanked Wendell's a hundred yards to one side. The third squad of their platoon was the same distance in the other direction. Wendell walked behind Morty Glass, a goofy kid from

Southern California who was always bragging that he grew up wrestling with sharks. He had the deadliest job in the infantry. Wendell's was second.

Wendell followed Morty to his right, so he wouldn't be in his direct line of fire. It was clear and bitter-cold, and by the light of a quarter-moon the soldiers could make out a line of woods about a half-mile away. Glass stopped and dropped to one knee, huffing from having to plow through the deep snow.

"Think they're in those woods?" Morty asked.

"I'm betting they are, but there's only one way to find out," Henderson said. "Let's move."

They stumbled forward through snow to their knees, rifles at their hips, ready to open up on enemy machine guns that they knew were out there someplace. No one spoke. The only sounds were the crunching of feet and the rumble of artillery as other units moved up against the Germans.

They came within a couple hundred yards of the trees and there was still nothing from the Germans. They closed to a hundred yards. They entered the trees and felt that a first great victory had been won. Maybe the Germans heard they were coming and had retreated, knowing what was best for them with the Army's best rifle company bearing down.

But the celebration didn't last long because the men saw that the tree line was only thirty yards thick. On the other side was a broad field of snow, surrounded on three sides by dense woods. That was where the Germans most likely waited. The danger became clearer as the sun rose and Wendell's unit could see the drifted field in front of them, and the woods surrounding it.

Their squads joined up and huddled in the trees to try and keep warm. Some guys fell asleep standing up. Wendell saw a small figure off by himself in the shadows, and by the ember of his cigarette knew it was Vinny. But at that moment Wendell was more concerned with Lieutenant Orlando, who had gathered his sergeants. Then the officer moved off by himself to use the radio, trying to call in some artillery to soften up the German guns almost certainly waiting in the opposite woods. Orlando threw the radio to the ground. The next thing Wendell knew, the sergeants were collecting their squads.

"Saddle up, boys," Henderson said.

Glass stepped from the tree line into snow up to his thighs. Wendell followed. Every member of their platoon cleared the trees and was moving toward the opposite tree line. Wendell was maybe a hundred yards away when the Germans opened up, their machine guns chattering from the trees. Morty fell, his helmet tumbling off into the snow. Wendell hit the snow himself, trying to burrow away from the bullets, and when he looked up, he saw blood oozing from a wound in the back of Morty's head.

Henderson yelled, "Hang on, Glass, I'm coming," but when Wendell turned, Henderson was down, too, lying face up in the snow with his eyes open. Snowflakes started to land on the sergeant's face.

Wendell knew he would be dead in a few seconds, but he didn't pray. He never thought of heaven or hell, or of God, because he knew that what had started to happen in that snow was way beyond God's ability to do much about. Instead, Wendell remembered feeling amazed by how fast a soldier can die, how easy it could be. Lying there in the snow, he wished his parents and Tommy could know that it wasn't that hard, thinking maybe that would make them feel a little better when they were burying him.

Morty lay still. No more sharks for him. The cold had stopped the flow of blood so only a few drops stained the snow. Henderson was just as dead a few feet to Wendell's rear. He saw the rest of his squad lying to either side, burrowing in to escape the machine guns. The only firing was coming from the enemy. Wendell heard Orlando yell above the noise.

"Get up! Advance! Use marching fire!"

Somehow they did. They climbed out of the snow, leveling their guns and firing at an enemy they could not see, the German machine guns yapping back at them. With Glass out, Wendell was closest to the Germans now. He guessed that their gunners trained their fire to his rear, thinking that he could be taken out at any time. Wendell had advanced twenty yards when he heard Orlando's voice again, ordering them to pull back.

Wendell hit the snow, amazed that he was still alive. He started crawling and came upon a guy named Swede Swanson, who was lying on his back without his helmet, as if getting ready to make a snow angel. The snow was bright red around Swede's head. He was missing his nose and most of his forehead, but somehow was still alive, smiling even, singing something. Wendell screamed for a medic and waved toward the tree line. The medics were crouched next to wounded men across the snow, so he pulled a Syrette from his chest pocket and stuck it into Swede's thigh. Wendell grabbed him by one boot and started to tug him back toward the trees, working alone, hearing the whisper of bullets whizzing a few inches above his head. Medics finally saw what Wendell was trying to do. Two of them ran out to haul Swede the rest of the way to the trees. His singing had stopped.

Seven men in Wendell's squad had been killed. Two more were wounded, nine casualties in a squad of twelve. The other squads didn't fare much better. More than half of their platoon, eighteen of thirty-four men were wiped out. Most of the dead were still out in the snow.

Wendell went looking for Vinny, wandering around in the trees, stepping around dazed soldiers. Sergeant Bowers cradled a kid named Davis, who begged for water, but their canteens had all frozen and Davis died before he could get a drink. Several other guys were hauled toward the rear on stretchers.

Wendell found Vinny in the trees, off by himself, a dent in his helmet where a bullet had glanced off. The nub of an unlit cigarette dangled from his mouth as he sat against a tree.

"Those fuckers," he mumbled to himself, over and over. "Those motherfuckers."

They were waiting for new orders. It had started to snow, and the wind kicked up. Vinny looked like a little ghost, heading out alone across the field toward the Germans, a shadow against the snow as the day came to an end and the wind rose and the snow swirled.

"Lieutenant, look at this," Bowers said.

"Jesus," Orlando said. "Who the fuck is that?"

257

"I think it's Vilandre, sir," Bowers said.

"It's Vinny," Wendell said.

"Figures," Orlando said.

The survivors spread out along the tree line to watch him plodding steadily toward the opposite woods, disappearing in and out of the blizzard.

"Vilandre, get your crazy ass back here!" Orlando yelled above the wind.

"Vinny!" Wendell yelled. *"Cut this shit out!"*

Halfway across the field, Vinny leveled his weapon and started firing blindly into the woods. The Germans must have been as surprised as anyone. They let him walk within fifty yards before they opened up, and Vinny's little body jerked several times. He fell backward in the snow, still firing.

The rest of the guys drew back from the edge of the woods, shaking their heads, returning to their huddles to keep warm. Wendell leaned against a tree, looking into the storm, watching the place where Vinny had fallen as the snow began to cover the dark clump in the field.

Then Vinny moved. Wendell wasn't sure at first, because of the snow, but there was no mistaking it the second time. Vinny raised himself up on one arm, and twisted to wave back toward them. He was yelling something, too, but because of the wind Wendell couldn't tell what. He ran up to where Orlando and Bowers sat together on the other side of the trees.

"Vinny's alive out there, sir," Wendell said.

"You're shitting me," Orlando said.

"No, sir," Wendell said. *"He's moving."*

The two of them followed Wendell through the trees and looked out over the field littered with their dead. Every so often, the body farthest out began to move, raising himself up and waving.

"I'd like to crawl out to him, sir," Wendell said. *"He shouldn't be hard to drag back."*

"I'm not sending another man to chase after that crazy bastard," Orlando said. *"I'm sorry Smith. I know he's a friend of yours. But I've lost all the soldiers I plan to in one day."*

Bowers was standing there with them.

"Sir, I've got an idea," he said.

Bowers walked down through the trees and bent to work over the body of a dead medic, pulling off the Red Cross armband. He slipped it up the sleeve of his own field jacket. He took the medic's blood-splattered helmet with the red cross taped across the front and placed it on his head.

"What do you think, Lieutenant?" Bowers asked.

Orlando shrugged. Bowers adjusted his armband, making sure the cross was plainly visible. He leaned his rifle against a tree and stepped into the field with his hands in the air. He had walked five paces through the snow when the machine guns opened up on him. A bullet shattered his hip. Another lodged in his thigh. He crawled back to the trees, cursing at the top of his lungs. The medics hauled him off on a stretcher.

That was the last attempt to rescue Vinny. Wendell watched him as the sun went down. He moved less often. Wendell wondered if he thought of his dad as he lay there dying. Then it was completely dark, erasing Vinny and the rest of the bodies in the field. Wendell walked back through the trees and wrapped himself in a tarp. He fell asleep to the sound of the howling wind.

The thunder of artillery woke him just before daybreak. The earth shook as Allied guns battered the woods where the enemy gunners had hid. The thunder lasted an hour, and when it was over most of the trees were shredded, their branches smoldering in the snow.

Another company moved past them to take up the assault. Orlando gathered what was left of his men for mop-up duty. They approached where the Germans had enjoyed their slaughter the day before. Wendell saw a German gunner dead at his weapon, his arm draped almost lovingly around the barrel of his machine gun. Several other German soldiers were sprawled on the ground, or partway out of their foxholes. Wendell looked back across the field, seeing it as the enemy had seen it the day before. They had been ducks in a shooting gallery.

"We've seen enough," Orlando said to his depleted unit.

He led them toward the rear. Most of the guys stuck to the tree line, avoiding the field where their dead were partially buried in the snow. Wendell set off across the field alone, plowing through the drifts to Vinny. He was on his back, covered to his waist in snow, like it was a heavy white quilt someone had pulled up over him as he died. There was frost on his eyebrows and eyelashes, twinkling in the morning sun. Snow filled his nostrils, his ears and his eyes. Wendell brushed the snow from his eyes and saw that they were open. His face looked peaceful.

His skin was still black from foxhole smoke. Wendell had melted the ice in his canteen at a fire that morning. Bending over Vinny, he took the canteen from his belt and poured water on a handkerchief. He touched it to Vinny's cheek, frozen hard. Wendell dabbed at his cheek until the soot started to come off, and he saw the thick field of pale freckles that always made Vinny look even younger than he was.

Wendell stood up and took one last look at the freckles, and plodded off through the drifts to rejoin the survivors.

Chapter 43

A front had blown in from the north as Wendell told me his terrible story, and a light rain started to fall. He sat beneath the cypress as still as a statue, his brown hair tossing in the growing wind. His eyes looked to the horizon. As the weather worsened, I crawled across the blanket and straddled Wendell, placing my hands lightly on his cheeks. I kissed him on the forehead and held him.

"I love you," I whispered into his ear. "Life will be different now. The war is over. Do you hear me, Wendell? The war is over."

He didn't move, didn't blink, didn't respond in any way, which frightened me. The rain started to fall harder, a thickening mist that dampened our clothes and hair. Wendell did not resist when I tugged him to his feet.

I left the blanket and book of poems lying there beneath the cypress, because it seemed there could be no poetry in a world like the one he had just described. The two of us walked up the hill. I guided him into the passenger seat, got in behind the wheel and fired up the engine, turning on the windshield wipers and the heater full blast, shuddering from the cold and the horror of what I had just heard. It occurred to me then that maybe some things are so terrible they are best left unspoken.

I turned off the highway and drove slowly down the road through our trees. As I parked next to my mother's car, I saw a little head pop into the picture window, and I started to cry. William flew out the door and down the front steps, wearing only a T-shirt and pants despite the bad weather, but he didn't seem to notice the cold. William ran to my door and pulled it open.

Chapter 44

August 18, 1991

3:10 a.m.

The pain has returned. The doctor said stay ahead of it, keep up with the morphine, but this night I did not do that. It was more important for me to be clearheaded and to finish, and now I have. I truly wish I could die, because it all hurts so much. But I have done it, and I will put my story away until William comes home, because he needs to be the one to read it first. He needs to understand.

The Army Buddy

Chapter 45

His trailer was four miles north of Bisbee on five acres Francis had bought with his wages. On the night of Wendell's cookout, after what happened with that girl and her husband, it was nearly ten when he pulled up in his truck and picked up his old cat from the front steps. He unlocked the door and stepped inside. He poured milk into a bowl and set it down for the cat, and fell back into his recliner. He took off his glasses and rubbed his eyes.

"Dear God," he said out loud. "I've pretty much toed the line. I've never missed Mass on Sunday, and I've confessed my sins every so often, and I've tried to be a good son, brother and friend. But now I'm wondering, God, what was the point?"

He sat for two hours, the cat sleeping at his feet, but the only sound he heard was the gushing of the window air conditioner. There were no words of direction or comfort from God. Only memories of Selma and her suffering that made Francis wonder, and not for the first time lately, whether there was a God at all.

He slept in the recliner and called in sick to work for the third time in four decades. He spent a few hours on his riding lawn mower, mindlessly cutting around the distant edges of his property. He fed the cat in late afternoon and slept for twelve hours.

He spent most of Saturday in bed. On Sunday, he missed Mass. Late that afternoon, he loaded his fishing gear into his truck and set off for the pond, but Wendell's truck was already parked at the top of the hill and Wendell was sitting alone beneath the cypress. Francis sat in his truck, undecided about what to do next. Selma would have wanted him to go down to the water, just to sit with Wendell in companionable silence as the two of them had so often over the years. Francis stepped out of his truck. Wendell looked up the hill when he heard the pickup door slam, and then looked back toward the water. Francis got back into his vehicle and drove away.

He went in early on Monday, and took on the biggest delivery. Francis looked forward to the hard work, as he had all his life. He set the big truck in gear and was beginning to inch from the lot when the passenger door opened and William climbed inside. He wore jeans, a T-shirt and work boots, and his long hair was tucked beneath a baseball cap. The smirk was gone from his eyes.

"There's something you need to read," William said. "It's about my dad, what happened to him in the war."

Francis looked over at him.

"I'm sorry, Francis," William said.

"Sorry for what?" Francis asked.

"For everything," William said. "Absolutely everything."

Chapter 46

Lucille rushed out from behind the reference desk and hugged Claire when she came in.

"I've been such a fool," Claire said.

"Larry told me about what happened to you when you were young. Lord have mercy."

"Lord have mercy about covers it," Claire said. "I'm just glad I still have a job."

"Not going to bite anyone's head off today, are you?" Lucille asked.

"If that old biddy comes in, you might want to take care of her," Claire replied.

She spent most of the morning restacking books. Rachel came by and asked her to step out.

"Not today," Claire said.

Her limbs grew lighter with every passing hour, her head clearer. She remembered her son's face as he watched the tiger at the zoo. At 3:30, Lucille hugged her again and Claire headed out the door. She squinted in the afternoon sun, digging in her purse for her keys as she walked toward the Impala in a distant corner of the parking lot. She saw Wendell's pickup. He was behind the wheel with the engine running, looking in his rear-view mirror. He opened his door and stepped out.

"Oh, no, you don't," Claire said as he limped toward her. Then she got a good look at him. "Wendell. What's wrong?"

He looked as if he had lost fifteen pounds in the three days since she'd seen him. His blue work shirt was wrinkled and grease-stained. His face was ashen. His gray eyes were glazed over, looking out at her from deep within their sockets. He smelled as if he hadn't bathed in a week.

"I just came to say that..."

He pitched forward and collapsed at Claire's feet without reaching out to break his fall. His head hit the pavement with a sickening thud. Wendell lay motionless, his eyes open, blank and staring. Claire screamed. She raced back across the parking lot. Lucille jumped from her seat at the reference desk.

"It never ends," Claire cried.

"What's the matter child?" Lucille said.

"That old man," Claire cried. "Call an ambulance."

A crowd gathered. Emergency technicians rushed to get Wendell off the hot pavement. He seemed awake but incoherent when he was loaded into the ambulance. Claire followed in her car to the hospital.

The waiting room was full. Claire dug in her purse for a quarter and used a pay phone to dial Wendell's number, hoping to catch his son. She slammed the telephone down when there was no answer. She dialed directory assistance for the Bisbee listing of Smith and Sons Lumber.

"Francis is out on a delivery," a young woman's voice said. "He's been working with Wendell's boy today. They should be back within the hour. Is there something wrong? Oh, here they come now."

William was the first through the door of the emergency room. Francis lumbered along behind him. Claire stood to meet them in the crowded waiting room. William's face was flushed.

"What in the hell have you done to my dad?" he yelled.

Her palm caught William flush on the cheek, making a noise like the crack of a whip. Others in the waiting room began to murmur. A security guard hurried in their direction and pointed to the door.

"All of you," he said.

The four of them stood in the sun.

"Someone is going to have to leave," the guard said. "Or you all can sort this out at the police station."

"My father is a patient here," William said. "He was just brought in. This is his good friend, Francis."

The guard looked at Claire.

"And you?"

"I'm a..." Claire said.

What? Like Wendell said. Her place was at home.

"I hope Wendell is OK," she said to William. "I really do."

Larry had picked up Mike at day care. The two of them were waiting at the door when she came home. With Mike occupied with Mister Rogers, Larry sat next to Claire on the back step as she smoked.

"I should pay a visit to that asshole," Larry said.

"Let it be, Larry," Claire said. "It's over."

The pizza was delivered an hour later. Claire ate three pieces and drank one of Larry's beers. She sat on the sofa with her husband and son and watched the ballgame. The telephone rang in the bottom of the fifth.

"Buzz off," Larry said, and hung up.

It rang again.

"With all your education, you would think you could understand English," Larry said when he answered.

"I better talk to him," Claire said.

Larry's face was flaming but he surrendered the phone.

"What is it, William?"

"It looks like dad will be OK," William said.

"Glad to hear it."

"I'm also calling to apologize," William said. "I deserved to be slapped."

"Apology accepted," she said. "And yes, you did. Now if you don't mind, I'm watching a ballgame."

"The doctors say he has a concussion from the fall and is dehydrated," William said. "But he'll recover."

"Tell him I said hi."

"At least physically," William said.

"Don't start," Claire said.

"He's not making much sense," William said. "But one thing I could make out was this. He said, 'I didn't listen.' Somehow I think he's referring to you."

"That part is true. He promised to and he didn't."

"It seems awfully important to him now," William said.

"Like you say, he's not making much sense," she said. "I'm going back to my family. Goodnight, William."

"My dad's got one, too," he said.

"One what?"

"A story."

"Doesn't everybody?" Claire asked.

"I just learned it myself."

"Good for you," she said.

"How about you and I lay down our swords," William said. "I mean, what do we have to lose? Things can't get any more fucked up than they already are. Excuse my French."

"I nearly lost my family," Claire said. "So things could get a lot more fucked up, as you say."

"Please," William said.

They sat around the kitchen table. Mike was in bed. Cans of beer had grown warm in front of Larry and Francis. Claire and William ignored their coffee. Claire had told a short version of the horror of her childhood, and a long silence followed. Francis stared at the can of

Budweiser. William had his elbows on the table, his head in his hands. Larry held Claire's hand.

"Wow," William said finally. "I'm sorry."

Francis cleared his throat, but didn't speak.

"Wendell understood it, at least as much as I got to tell him. From the very first. I don't know why," Claire said.

"Probably because he has an acquaintance with horrible things himself," William said.

He took a sip of cold coffee.

"Excuse me for a second," William said.

He disappeared out the front door, returning with an old notebook that he put down in front of Claire.

"My mother's," William said. "She finished just before she died."

"Finished what?" Claire asked.

"Why don't you have a look?"

"What's it got to do with me?" Claire asked.

"Maybe nothing," William said. "Maybe everything."

Chapter 47

Wendell was asleep with his head elevated, his arms at his sides. One side of his face was bruised and blistered. IVs ran from each arm to hanging plastic sacks of clear liquid. His hair was clean and combed. William sat by the bed until his dad opened his eyes.

"Good morning," William said.

Wendell stared at the ceiling. His eyes watered.

"Do you know where you are?" William asked.

"In hell, if there is any justice," Wendell said, before trying to cough out phlegm.

William handed him a cup of water. Wendell sipped through a straw.

"Francis told me you'd been driving off to the pond almost every day, needing to be by yourself," William said. "I thought that's where you were headed when you left yesterday, there or to the cemetery. If I had any idea you would come all the way to Arlington I would have taken your keys."

"You're not my keeper," Wendell whispered.

"I should have made you eat," William said. "I should have made you take a bath."

"You're not my mother, either," Wendell said.

"I should have made you talk to me," William said.

"There's nothing to say," Wendell said. "And I wouldn't talk to you even if there was. You're the last person."

"I know."

The television was playing soundlessly above Wendell's bed, one of the morning talk shows. His father still stared at the ceiling.

"I know about the war," William said. "I know what happened to Vinny. It was in mom's story."

Wendell looked at him for the first time.

"You don't know shit," he said.

"When you're feeling better, I'd like you to educate me."

"I'm a liar and killer," Wendell said. "That's all you need to know."

"You were a soldier, dad," William said. "That's what soldiers do. They kill."

"Just let me die," Wendell said.

"You know I can't do that," William said. "You want to be with mom, but you're going to have to wait your turn."

"I'll never be with your mother," Wendell said.

Wendell opened his eyes. He saw Francis first, then Claire. His eyes clouded.

"Still as ugly as I remembered," Francis said.

"Don't listen to him, Wendell," Claire said. "No wonder Selma fell in love with that big old schoolboy."

Wendell looked away and raised his hands to his face and he began to whimper.

"Could you fellows excuse us?" Claire said.

William was dozing in the waiting room when Claire touched him on the shoulder thirty minutes later. Francis sat next to him, with a magazine he wasn't reading open on his lap.

"I've got to get back to work," she said. "I told Wendell I'd be back tonight."

"Care to share what he said?" William asked.

"He said he came to the library to apologize," Claire said.

"Apologize for what, if you don't mind me asking?" William said.

"For being what he called 'a horse shit excuse for a friend,'" Claire said.

"He say anything about my mother?" William asked.

"Only that he was a horrible husband, too," she said. "But there is something else he's not admitting. It wasn't in your mother's story. There's a secret he wants to take to the grave."

"He tell you that?"

"He didn't need to," Claire said. "I know something about them."

"You seem pretty certain," William said.

"I'd bet on it," Claire said. "I see the guilt in him, horrible guilt. Just like with me. Vinny was bad, but that wasn't Wendell's fault. Whatever it is he's not telling, he feels he is to blame."

"From the war," William said.

"That would be my guess," Claire said. "Something old anyway."

Francis cleared his throat.

"I think she's right," he said.

They looked at him and waited for Francis to continue.

"The night your mother died," Francis said. "Those last few minutes. There was something he wanted to tell her. Something he needed to get off his chest, but he didn't. Selma saw it, too, as sick as she was."

"I remember," William said.

"Whatever it is, we need to figure it out soon," Claire said. "Your dad is in a real big hurry to die."

"I wouldn't have the first clue," William said.

"Franny?"

He shrugged and shook his head.

"Maybe I can help," Claire said.

Claire returned to the hospital just after seven. She met William and Francis in the waiting area and walked ahead of them to Wendell's room, where she sat down on the side of his bed. Wendell looked at her, then back at the ceiling.

"Me again," Claire said.

William and Francis stood in the shadows.

"I told my story to Larry, just like you said I should," Claire said. "If I hadn't, I never would have known what a wonderful man I married. You were right all along. Francis and William have heard it now, too. It's like I can't keep my mouth shut. And guess what, Wendell? I'm still here. They didn't cart me away in a strait jacket. I might be able to avoid the loony bin after all. Maybe Selma was right. Anything mentionable is manageable, and I mean anything."

She raised Wendell's hand and kissed it. Wendell closed his eyes.

"Say something," Claire said.

"Please leave," Wendell said.

"OK. I'll leave," Claire said. "But first, I'm going to finish my story. You promised to listen, and now you're going to get the chance."

She told it again.

"Your turn, Wendell," Claire said. "And I already know about Vinny, Henderson, Swede and the rest."

Wendell opened his eyes and looked at her.

"I've read Selma's thing, too," Claire said.

"Vinny," Wendell said.

"I'm sorry about your friend," Claire said. "But there is something else. What didn't you tell your wife?"

"Nothing," Wendell said.

"I know that's not true," Claire said.

"I'm tired," Wendell said.

He began to whimper again.

"Please, Claire. Leave me alone."

Chapter 48

William stopped for coffee at a burger place and put the top down on his convertible. He had not slept in two days and his mind careened wildly. A psych ward would be the best place for his father. Wendell might be able to starve himself to death there, but killing himself would be more difficult. William found himself going through a funeral checklist. He'd call the place that handled his mother's arrangements. Gravestones. Obituary. Minister or not? How to arrange military honors?

"But he's not fucking dead yet," William screamed into the night, tossing his Styrofoam cup into the wind.

At home he picked up the notebook from the passenger seat and headed toward the front door.

"Damn near a bestseller now, mother," William said.

He ate a few bites of cold spaghetti and brought the notebook to his room. He sat down at the desk and paged through the story one more time. The beautiful young teacher. Selma and a young Uncle Tommy on the doorstep after Wendell's accident. Sex at the pond. Will my son ever grow up? Hands at her throat. Vinny. Death in the snow.

William closed it, stretched out on the bottom bunk and was asleep in seconds. It was after three in the morning when he sat up, panting. The light was still on at his desk. He threw his feet to the floor and began to riffle through his mother's story until he found what he was looking for. He carried the notebook down the stairs, taking them two at a time. He slammed his shin on the coffee table in the living room but scarcely noticed the pain.

He rummaged around in a drawer for a pen and a piece of paper and picked up the phone, dialing directory assistance for Shreveport. He called despite the hour. The man answered on the second ring. His voice was raspy and his breathing seemed labored, but evidently he had not been asleep.

"This is Kendall Crawford," he said. "And just who wants to know?"

The interstate bore straight east through flat country, then rolling hills. William called Francis from a truck stop in Tyler.

"I need you to take my place at the hospital," William said. "I should be back this afternoon."

"Where the hell are you?" Francis asked.

"On my way to Shreveport," William said. "Does the name Kendall Crawford ring a bell?"

"From the notebook," Francis said. "The guy in the wreck with your dad."

"I called him last night and he says he knows something. I'll be to his place in two hours."

William crossed the border into Louisiana, turning north on a freeway that looped around Shreveport, then exiting onto a two-lane road. The road curved through faceless subdivisions carved out of hardwood forests, then through trailer houses and tumble-down frame dwellings in an increasingly rural area. The old brick liquor store appeared on the left. William pulled in and purchased a fifth of cheap whiskey and a carton of Camels.

Three miles farther down was the clapboard country church. He turned onto a gravel road. After a quarter mile he saw the tin mailbox and the tan trailer sitting well back in the trees, surrounded by the rusting carcasses of two pickups and an ancient green stock car with the number ten barely distinguishable on the side. William parked in a dirt driveway overgrown with weeds, gathered up the whiskey and cigarettes, and set out toward the front door. An old German shepherd stuck his snout through curtains at a front window and growled.

"Duke, mind your manners," William heard through the screen door. "Is that you Mr. Smith? Be damned if you're not right on time. Let yourself in."

William heard raspy laughter from inside the house.

"Don't mind the dog," the voice inside said, before coughing violently. "Old Duke hasn't bitten anyone in years. Neither have I, come to think of it."

There was more laughter and coughing. The dog, woefully underfed, met William as he opened the screen door, barking and snarling as William side-stepped past him into a small, filthy living room piled over with old newspapers and an assortment of dirty dishes where flies clustered. A window air conditioning unit was silent. The room was rancid-smelling and sweltering. A blue haze of cigarette smoke filled the place, coming from the shriveled old man in the wheelchair at the far end of the room. A breathing tube dangled from Crawford's nose, attached to an oxygen machine that purred next to him. The glowing nub of a cigarette dangled from his lips. Strands of greasy white hair were combed over a mostly bald head. Crawford wore a sleeveless, ketchup-stained undershirt, dirty jeans and old white tennis shoes that dangled lifelessly, not quite reaching the footrests of his chair. His bare shoulders glistened with sweat. As William took a few tentative steps, the dog stopped barking and lay down at his owner's feet.

"You're his kid, all right," Crawford said, looking up at William, smiling as the cigarette dangled from his mouth. "Big as old Wendell. Look just like him in the face. The long hair throws me a bit, and the gray, but none of us are getting any younger, are we Mr. Smith?"

"No, sir, I don't suppose we are," William said.

"Kind of you to bring me some supplies," Crawford said. "I hated to ask, but I don't get out much these days myself. What do I owe you?"

279

"Just tell me what I need to know," William said.

"Put those things right here next to me," Crawford said. "Why don't you clear yourself a place to sit."

William placed the whiskey and cigarettes next to Crawford on a stool, and was overpowered by the old man's odor. William backed away, grabbed a stack of newspapers from the end of an old sofa and dropped them on the floor. As he sat down, he stole glances at black-and-white photographs taped on the wall above the sofa: Grinning young men holding stringers of catfish, and young families sitting around picnic tables near a river or a lake. Another life.

"You've heard of me, you say," Crawford said. "From your mother."

"You came to the lumberyard, just after the war," William said. "The day of the accident."

"That goddamn accident," Crawford said. "I'll rot in hell because of what happened to those two girls. I would say your dad, too, but the death of those two girls is the least of his problems with St. Peter. Somehow I suspect you know that already."

"We all make mistakes," William said.

"We do indeed," Crawford said, crushing out his cigarette on a plate overflowing with butts. "But some are worse than others. Why don't we pour ourselves glasses of this whiskey and have a toast to old times. You'll find glasses in the kitchen."

"If it's all the same, just tell me," William said.

Crawford was forced to pause by more coughing. For a few terrible moments, William worried the old man would keel over and die.

"Wendell's taken ill, you say?" Crawford said when the coughing subsided.

"Yes," William said.

"By ill, I gather you mean a little off his rocker," Crawford said. "And you figure it might have something to do with the war?"

"We think that's possible," William said.

"I'd say you're on the right trail, young man," Crawford said. "How a man can live all these years with that on his conscience?"

Crawford coughed until he gagged, then spit into a yellowed handkerchief.

"I never really cared for your dad much," Crawford said. "He and I rode the ship over, and fought all the way through the Bulge. There weren't too goddamn many of us who lived to be able to say that. You'd think I'd have a soft spot for a fellow survivor. But he was a self-righteous bastard, the way he kept to himself and looked after that crazy little shit. He ever told you about Vinny?"

"I'm aware of Vinny," William said.

"I thought about trying to blackmail Wendell," Crawford said, grinning. "In fact, that's why I came to Texas that day. But I changed my mind after we had a few beers. I didn't want to have that big old bastard hating me, because I've seen what Wendell can do when provoked. Are you sure you want to know? I mean, this is not pretty."

William leaned forward on the sofa, resting his elbows on his knees. Fat beads of sweat ran down his face and dropped to the floor.

"I'm sure," William said.

Chapter 49

They crossed into Germany on a day in mid-March that was warm and sunny for a change. Just a few weeks back, they were getting chopped up in the snow, so none of the American soldiers had expected to see Germany. When they got to the border, the men were in a mood to celebrate, but that didn't last long. Wendell had been promoted to sergeant by then and was in charge of the squad. There was a long bridge over the Rhine, and he managed to get his men a ride across on a tank. It was a good thing he did, because otherwise they would have had to slog through flesh, arms and legs, heads no longer attached to their owners. Some of those body parts belonged to Americans who had tried to cross the same bridge the day before.

Two kids rode with them, replacements named William Boucher and Frenchy Vaudrin. They joined the unit a day or two before, right out of high school, straight from the senior prom, fresh from their mamas' Cajun cooking in the Louisiana bayou. The moment they figured out what they were seeing on the bridge, both of them started puking over the side of the tank. Wendell hung onto each one of them by their belts to keep those boys from tumbling off.

Crawford and the others laughed at the two greenhorns. But at least they wouldn't have to worry about spilling their own guts. The Germans stood and fought in brief skirmishes, but more often they threw down their guns and surrendered by the hundreds. Crawford and the others saw them walking down the road with their hands in the air, miles and miles of sorry-ass fucking Krauts.

Wendell's unit kept moving east. Most of the towns had been reduced to smoking piles of stone and junk, with pathetic-looking people standing along the road, kids and women and old people mostly, living ghosts who just watched them pass. It was a picnic, compared to what they had been through before.

One night, when they put up in a barn, Wendell got to talking to these two kids. They whipped out pictures of these pretty Cajun girlfriends and handed them to Wendell, who looked them over, smiled, and handed them back.

It had been two weeks since anyone in the outfit had fired a shot. Rumors got thicker that Hitler was either dead or about to surrender. There was no reason to think that the next village would be any different than the last.

There was a bombed out cathedral on the edge of town, but most of the other buildings were surprisingly intact. Little kids zipped up and down the street on bicycles, and a few of the GI's gave them chocolate. The Americans walked through with their weapons on their shoulders. They scanned for snipers but mostly out of habit. Vaudrin and Boucher had wandered out in front of the squad. One of them was taking a picture.

Wendell and Crawford saw the blond head in the second-floor window about the same time, but by then it was too late. The boy had popped his head up and looked down to the spot in the road where Boucher and Vaudrin stood. The head disappeared into the shadows for a few seconds and popped back up again. The second time the boy raised an arm.

Wendell yelled for his men to get down, and most of them fell to the street by instinct, but Boucher and Vaudrin weren't as jumpy. They just looked at Wendell. Crawford heard a metallic clink when the grenade hit the street at Boucher's feet, then the explosion. Boucher's left leg sailed through the air and nearly hit Crawford on the fly with the boot still laced up.

The squad waited for another grenade. When it didn't come, they jumped up and ran over to the kids. Boucher was screaming for his mother and grabbing for his leg, which was lying in the street twenty yards away. Vaudrin's eyes were open and blood poured out of his chest and from both legs. Blood puddled around both of them.

"Am I going to die?" Boucher asked Wendell.

Wendell set his rifle on the street, bent down and took his hand. The kid's face was getting pale and his lips were turning blue, and his teeth started chattering.

"You'll be fine," Wendell said.

Then Boucher's eyes went blank and he let go of Wendell's hand. Wendell knelt there for a few minutes, staring down at the kid's face. He picked up his rifle, got to his feet, and looked up at the window. Crawford had never seen a human being look so hateful. Wendell headed toward the building. Crawford followed him inside.

Wendell sprinted up the narrow stairway of what was a schoolhouse and Crawford had to run to keep up. At the top of the stairs was a hallway with empty classrooms on either side, wooden desks neatly lined up. They heard a noise, a door closing, coming from a classroom to the left. The door was open, and Wendell went through. By the time Crawford got inside the room, Wendell had set his rifle down on a desk, pulled the bayonet from the sheath on his belt, and headed toward a second door that apparently led to a closet.

Wendell plowed into the closet and was back out again in seconds, only now he had a handful of shirt that belonged to the murderous German boy.

Chapter 50

He couldn't have been more than twelve years old, with curly blond hair and big blue eyes. He had a birthmark on one cheek that Crawford had seen more than once in his dreams in the years since. He wore a brown shirt buttoned to the neck, short pants, boots and brown socks pulled up to the knee, and red suspenders. When Wendell pulled him out of the closet, the boy had a smirk on his face, as if what had happened down below was just part of some sort of kid's game. Even then, the boy might have left that classroom alive if he had kept his little mouth shut.

"Heil, Hitler," the boy said.

Wendell stopped, the boy's shirt in one hand, the big knife in his other. Wendell slammed him into a chalkboard, lifting him a foot off the ground, holding him there with one big hand.

"Smith," Crawford said. "Let's get this little bastard out of here."

Wendell's face was turning purple. His whole body started to shake, and this kid started to cry, gagging from how Wendell had him by the throat.

"Smith," Crawford said.

Wendell grunted heavily when he thrust the knife through the kid's chest, all the way through to the blackboard. Wendell stood there, holding the knife, his face an inch or two away from the face of this boy, who gagged a few times at first, and coughed, and flopped his arms and legs, then stared back at Wendell with a surprised look on his face.

Wendell let go of the knife and the boy tumbled to the floor.

"Holy fuck," Crawford said.

Wendell didn't say a word, just picked up his rifle and walked out the door, and in a second Crawford could hear him going down the steps.

Then it was just him and that dead kid bleeding on the classroom floor. Crawford stood above him, reached down, grabbed one of his suspenders and snapped it.

"Fucking Hitler Youth," Crawford said. "Burn in hell."

Down in the street, the bodies of Boucher and Vaudrin were being loaded into ambulances. The rest of the squad stood together in the middle of the street, smoking, looking at the blood. Wendell sat alone on a bench, elbows on his knees. After a few minutes he stood and walked to his men.

"Saddle up," Wendell said. "Nothing more we can do here."

The Germans surrendered that very day. Wendell's squad was camped that night in a meadow when a jeep came speeding up, and a guy jumped out with the news and a crate full of confiscated German whiskey. Crawford was good and drunk when he went looking for Wendell, who was sitting under a tree in the dark.

"We made it, Wendell," he said.

Wendell just looked at him.

"That little bastard back there got what was coming to him," Crawford said.

Wendell had his hands on his knees, his head resting on the trunk, looking up into the branches.

"Your secret is safe with me," Crawford said.

He had told the story one or two tortured sentences at a time, and when he came to the end his birdlike shoulders sagged even more. He seemed to have difficulty supporting the weight of his head. He smiled at William, but then his head slumped toward his chest, and another spasm of coughing caught hold of him, waking the dog at his feet.

Crawford's coughing broke through William's terrible reverie. He stood, grabbed the bottle of whiskey, and stepped around Crawford's wheelchair into a kitchen where more dirty dishes and empty pizza boxes were stacked across the counters.

William grabbed a glass from the stack in the sink and rinsed it beneath a gush of rusty water from the faucet. He unscrewed the cap of the whiskey bottle, filling the glass to the top, and took it to Crawford, who continued to hack but smiled up at William. The whiskey, gone in two gulps, quieted the coughing and put some color back into Crawford's face. He handed the empty glass to William, who refilled it. Crawford sipped the second glass.

"What do you think of that?" Crawford asked.

"It's none of your business what I think," William said.

"That doesn't sound like gratitude," Crawford said.

"I think there was part of you that enjoyed telling that story," William said.

"I'll tell you what I think," Crawford said. "I think your father is a fucking hypocrite. I seen what he did to that boy. Shit, he isn't a hell of a lot better than a Nazi himself."

William closed his eyes, letting the wave of rage wash over him. He walked toward the door.

"What do you plan on doing with this information, if you don't mind me asking?" Crawford asked.

William took one look back at the old man in the wheelchair and walked past the dog. He was stopped twice for speeding on the drive home.

Chapter 51

Francis sat in the corner of Wendell's room, looking up at the Chicago Cubs on television. Wendell was exactly as William had left him the night before, arms at his sides, eyes closed.

"Go get something to eat," William said to Francis. "I'll take over."

"I'll bring you something," Francis said.

"I'm fine," William said.

William sat down in the chair Francis had been in.

"You awake?" William asked.

Wendell didn't reply, but some color came into his cheeks.

"You're not going to make it," William said. "You're not going to die with your secret."

Wendell opened his eyes. They were filled with terror.

"I drove to Shreveport today and looked up Kendall Crawford," William said. "What a piece of shit."

"How in the…" Wendell whispered.

"Mom's story," William said. "Uncle Tommy remembered him from the day he came to the lumberyard. The day of the accident."

For the first time in two days, Wendell sat up in bed. He threw his legs over the side. He ripped both IVs from his arms and stood up.

"You're not going anywhere," William said.

Wendell took a couple of faltering steps toward a closet, but William blocked his way.

"I know about what you did to the boy in Germany," William said.

Wendell put his hand on a wall to steady himself.

"Get back into bed," William said.

"I'm driving away from here," Wendell said.

"Pretty hard to do if you have nothing to drive."

"I'll walk then," Wendell said.

"You killed a boy," William said. "A murdering little bastard, but a boy just the same. There. It's been said. No longer a secret."

William put both hands around Wendell's upper arm. Wendell did not resist when William led him back to bed. William sat on the edge.

"It all makes sense now," William said. "No wonder you couldn't bear to tell her."

The last of Wendell's color drained from his face.

"You were dreaming about him on the night that mom died. You almost told her. You didn't want her to die without knowing the truth. But you couldn't. Am I right?"

Wendell nodded.

"In some ways you were relieved after mom died," William said. "She never knew the truth, and you were glad about that. But then, out of the blue, this girl shows up. She looks like mom. She has a secret, too. It was like she came to torture you, to punish you for past sins. This German boy starts to have his way with you again. Am I in the ballpark?"

Wendell nodded.

"What if you had told mom?" William said.

He took one of his father's hands.

"I'm entitled to a guess," William said. "She would have grieved for that boy. She would have grieved for the hate in that kid's heart. She would have grieved for the way he died. But mother would also have grieved for you. She knew you weren't that man, swept away by the horrors. You would always be the man who loved poetry, who read to her, who took care of her when she was sick and..."

William couldn't finish the sentence.

"She would have loved you forever and no matter what," William said, forcing the words out. "That's just the way she was."

William stood and walked to the foot of the bed.

"I don't want you to die," he said.

Wendell rode between Francis and William on the way home. Francis pulled in at the cemetery. William had cut roses from the garden and gave them to his father, who walked alone across the burnt grass toward his wife's grave. He laid the roses at the base of Selma's tombstone. He knelt there in the hot sun for almost an hour before limping back to the pickup where Francis and William waited. William opened the door for his dad.

Epilogue

Two years later, on the day of his first T-ball game in Arlington, Mike insisted on riding to the field with Francis and Wendell.

"I hope I get to bat first, gramps," Mike said to Wendell, his blue cap falling down over his eyes.

"I hope so, too," Wendell said.

As Mike joined his team, the rest of them took seats in the metal bleachers—Wendell and Francis; Larry and Claire; William; and Claire's mother, a thin woman with long gray hair who chain-smoked nervously while awaiting her grandson's debut. She was living with her sister and brother-in-law in Florida, but visited Claire and her family in Texas every year.

The little cheering section roared when Mike stepped up to the plate. His coach placed the ball on a rubber tee and told him to hit away. The boy first looked up at the stands, took a couple of fierce practice swings, swung at the ball and sent it trickling toward the pitcher's mound. Then Mike sprinted toward third base. It might have been the first time William had heard his father laugh out loud.

A few days later, after their last delivery of the morning, Francis and William drove next door to grab Wendell for lunch. Wendell was not on the porch. There was no answer when William called his name. He led Francis up the stairs. They found him on his back with the covers pulled up to his chest, a smile on his face. It was as if his last living notion had been of a boy, not the German boy from so long ago, but the one who had looked into the bleachers just a few days before, saw the big old man he loved so much, swung hard, then ran in the wrong direction.

About the author

As a writer for the *Fort Worth Star-Telegram*, Tim Madigan was among the most decorated Texas newspaper journalists of his generation. The author of five books, *Every Common Sight* is his first novel. He lives in Fort Worth, Texas with his wife, Catherine.

For more information visit www.timmadigan.net, follow Tim Madigan on Facebook, or on Twitter at @tsmadigan

Made in the USA
Lexington, KY
27 June 2015